ETERNAL MOORLANDS

MK AHEARN

AZALA PRESS

To the English teacher who tried to hold me back, and thought I would not get very far. This series made me a bestselling author!

TRIGGER WARNINGS

This book contains swearing, sexually explicit scenes, violence, assault, human trafficking, discussion of death of parents, addiction, and PTSD. Please keep this in mind when reading this story.

WHAT DID I MISS?

This book is a spin off from Broken Flames and Warring Tides. You are not required to read that duo if you do not wish to, but here are a few contextual bits of information that could be important to reading this book.

- Nyla is crowned princess of Abelon, the kingdom of fire. Her brother is the king, and was the male main character of the duo this spins off from.
- The events of this book follow the aftermath of a war between the elemental kingdoms. This war was between the fire kingdom and the other three elemental kingdoms.
- Because the balance of power was thrown off between the elements, the four goddesses who created the kingdoms stepped in and decided to reset the scales. This turned the war into large scale elemental catastrophes, which the main characters were able to put an end to and finally brought peace to the kingdoms.

- In Warring Tides, the main characters visit an underground market which is a hub for illegal goods. This market is run by The Warden and is the main setting of this novel. The main characters of this novel have met before, which is why they reference knowing each other briefly.

ZETRON
GRALAR
THE MARKET

MORYA
LUHEO

MORWEN

ALUA
WULO
SERPENT'S COVE
RADEN
THE WATERFALL
DRAGON TERRITORY

ABELON

PRONUNCIATION GUIDE

GODDESSES
Mavalu: Mah-vah-loo
Aeris: Air-us
Odaesia: Oh-day-juh
Isleen: Is-leen

KINGDOMS
Luheo: Loo-he-oh
Abelon: Ab-ah-lon
Morwen: More-win
Zetron: Zeh-tron

CITIES
Huile: Hwa-eye-l
Gralar: Grah-lar
Raden: Rah-den

DRAGONS AND PANTHERUS
Olia: Oh-lee-ah
Veros: Vah-roh-s

NAMES
Thalia: Thah-lee-ah

Nyla: N-eye-lah
Xora: Zo-rah
Gryo: Gree-oh

CHAPTER 1
NYLA

IT HAD BEEN months since the war ended. Abelon, the kingdom of fire, was rebuilding—from scratch. My father's terrible reign still scarred the city, but my brother made every effort to scrub it clean.

He pardoned me, told me I could go anywhere I wished. In the moment, I'd said Zetron, yet here I still was, in the city that held my tainted past.

I spent every waking moment helping where I could, trying to atone for every atrocity I helped commit. It would never be enough. My sins were far too extensive.

I helped use my fire to mold metal and build foundations for the new bakery. The plans had started with the lower city nearest to the dock. Bellamy prioritized rebuilding homes there to replace what became rubble during the war. Now, we'd moved on to bringing back the livelihood of Raden, the shops and other buildings that brought the citizens happiness.

"This one as well, Nyla," one of the other volunteers called out to me.

I used my single hand to manipulate fire into my palm and hovered over the metal to heat and mold it.

"Thank you, princess," the man said, moving on quickly to another task.

I almost flinched at the word. I no longer considered myself the princess of Abelon. I'd betrayed my people, a complicit pawn in my father's plan during the war.

It was only by the kindness of our new queen that I survived at all.

I wiped a bead of sweat from my forehead, the heat of my flames intense.

My head hurt, and I knew it was almost time, the medicine, Inum, I relied on wearing off. There hadn't been a day since I lost my hand I didn't rely on it.

I walked away and used my hand to rub at the spot where my other hand used to be, a painful and constant reminder of the war and my part in it.

I had to learn to redo most things using only a single hand. Ever since my father burned mine away, things became harder and more complicated.

It wasn't a far walk back to the palace, and I enjoyed the peace walking alone brought me. The city was full of Abelonians rebuilding, but most only gave me short waves or nods. None interrupted my stroll back.

I knew what most of them thought.

I was the princess who supported the overthrown king, the one who did his bidding and never stood up to him. Compared to Bellamy, I was nothing to these people but a traitor. I aided in their misery, complacent to my father's games.

I regretted every moment of it.

Never once did I force myself to be stronger, be better. Bellamy was the one who finally broke away, escaped from the madness, and saved our people—the same people my mother had loved.

She would be ashamed to know me now.

The little girl she raised with such high hopes.

By the time I made my way back to the palace, it was bustling with people grabbing food for lunch. Many had returned to their newly-built homes, but we still had a long way to go before the city was self-sufficient again. The palace had more than enough to go around, and my brother was loving every second of allowing people within the gates, something my father never did.

I felt eyes on me as I passed through and nodded to a few of the guards. Bellamy had formed a system to allow people in and out freely without scrutiny. I barely understood it, but I didn't ask any questions.

My only thought was to stay as far away from decisions like that. The city didn't need my touch to it. Bellamy and Koraine were rebuilding it stone by stone, and for that, I was grateful.

My feet moved quicker as the stares grew. The whispers carried through the courtyard. I wasn't welcomed any longer than necessary. My brother pardoned me, but he couldn't force an entire kingdom to forgive me.

The guard posted at the door to the palace opened it and let me slip through, leaving behind the intense stares.

My stomach turned, wishing I could've stopped for food that lined the tables. Bellamy ordered them set up in the courtyard, and Ervin had taken charge of feeding the entire city, using volunteers and his own staff to accomplish it.

Every day, I was in awe of how Raden came together to heal.

I rushed through the halls of the palace, knowing Bellamy would be expecting me. Whenever I went into the city, I brought back reports of where Raden was at in progress. It made me feel useful in my own way.

Months had passed, and although I told Bellamy I'd travel and finally follow my dreams, there was far too much to do before I could.

How could I walk away from the city now?

Before the throne room, I passed through a hall of art and portraits. I didn't recognize many, my brother having them almost entirely replaced.

A new portrait of my mother had been hung, and I smiled, realizing how much I looked like her. After her death, I hoped her family would come—we'd never known them. The only thing I knew was that she was estranged from her parents and sibling after marrying my father.

They never came.

I never knew whether I looked like my grandparents, whether she had a brother or sister. My father banned all talk of them, another thing he took from us.

I could feel my frown deepening and tried to shake the feeling, moving on through the palace.

I heard the echoes of voices carrying down the hall from the throne room. By the time I was only feet away, I could see people moving in and out of the room. Most, I didn't recognize.

I stepped inside, and guards parted to let me pass. The

room was lively, and I'd never seen it like this under my father's rule.

Koraine hurried around, pulled in every direction. The pair had turned the room into a central command post for every project to fix the city. Men and women stood in different areas, glancing over plans on tables and comparing different options. I passed by a group debating which stone to use to rebuild the temple for the priestesses of Raden.

Koraine stood with a woman I recognized, Miriam chatting away to her. My brother had tasked her and her husband, Alaric, with building a new orphanage.

It made my heart swell to see them bringing that dream to life. War brought the tragedy of more children left without families. It broke me to know I played a role in it.

I walked over to Miriam, who embraced me. She was one of the few who treated me like I had some hope of being redeemed.

"How's the building coming?" Koraine asked, her blue eyes bright and piercing as they settled on me.

"It's coming along. In no time, the city will be better than what it was," I said, trying to plaster a smile on my face.

Each day became harder.

Everything inside me wanted to commit to being part of the city, but my mind was tearing itself apart. There was a war still in my own mind. I felt like I was being ripped in every direction. I spotted Bellamy moving towards his throne to take a break—my chance.

"Excuse me," I said politely to the pair.

They returned to the plans for the orphanage, and I headed toward my brother.

His face lit with delight as he saw me. He took every effort to include me in the family he built after the war. No matter how hard I tried to push him away, he wouldn't accept it. It was a hopeless battle. He was far too stubborn.

"You come with news?" he asked, his smile barely fading.

"The foundations of the bakery are set," I answered. "It should be fully built over the next few days, I imagine."

He beamed with excitement. Every little step was a win in his eyes, a way to bring the community back together after tragedy. "I appreciate your help in the city. As you can see," he motioned to the throne room, "I'm trapped most of the day."

A slight laugh left my lips. King befitted him, but I knew he had a far way to go before he felt comfortable. He'd been thrust into it, and that left little time for him to find his way in it all.

As his gaze drifted around the room, I found him staring past me to the one thing that mattered most to him: his wife.

The moon to his sun.

The pair were complete opposites, but somehow, I knew they were made to be.

I swallowed hard, waiting for his attention to return.

"Another shipment is gone," a man interrupted, pulling both of our attention to the right.

"What do you mean another?" Bellamy asked with a frown.

I went to walk away, but he held up a hand, stopping me in my tracks.

"This is the second shipment of supplies to go missing

from Zetron," the man explained. "At first, I thought it was nothing, but—" His brows furrowed, searching for the words.

"The Market," Bellamy finished.

He shook his head.

My brothers eyes fell to me, and I was met with growing worry. The smile was wiped from his face, and I watched him easily transform into the king these people needed.

"Keep detailed inventory and continue to report to me if more goes missing," he answered, keeping his face neutral and calm.

"Of course, my prin—" The man paused and quickly corrected himself. "My king. I apologize." He gave Bellamy a quick bow, his face fraught with concern.

"No need for that," Bellamy answered. "It was a simple mistake."

My brother smiled, and the man looked to me for reassurance. I tried to give him my own smile, but it barely reached my eyes. He turned and walked off with only a small glimpse back before leaving the room.

"What did he mean, a shipment has gone missing?" I asked, looking at my brother.

"The Warden is rebuilding his market. Things have gone missing, resources and supplies. Some workers as well. It's not just Abelon. The other kingdoms reported the same."

His face clouded with worry. I clenched my teeth, and my fist curled into a ball. I should've ended the place when I had the chance, but my hunt for Bellamy had stopped me.

"You have to end this," I said, suddenly trapped in an endless loop of regret.

"I don't have the resources. Everything we have is being

put into rebuilding the city. I won't ask these people to go to battle once more so soon."

"It will never end. He will never stop taking and ruining lives."

"I know," Bellamy said, defeat coating every word.

"He's vulnerable if he's building up supplies again," I pushed.

"Nyla, I don't have the men to give to fight," Bellamy reiterated.

Before I could stop, the word tumbled out of my mouth. "I'll go," I said firmly.

My fist relaxed, and I finally met Bellamy's eyes again. His mouth fell open slightly, and for once, he was left speechless.

What was I thinking? Traveling by myself to Zetron to stop it all? It was laughable.

Bellamy's frown deepened and his brows pulled in. "I can't send you to do that," he said slowly.

In my gut, I knew it was right. This was my chance to make up for everything I had put the kingdom through. Other men and resources couldn't be spared, but I could.

"Send me," I said, knowing I needed his approval. "You said you'd give me the ship and supplies to get to Zetron when I asked before. This is me taking the offer."

He looked past me again to Koraine. "She'd never allow it," he said, and I knew he meant his wife.

"It's my choice," I said, even though we both knew it wasn't true.

"How do I explain I sent you off? I can't leave you behind again," he answered.

"You aren't. I'm asking you to let me go," I said.

His eyes fell back on me, and sadness started to replace the concern. "Whatever you need, it's yours," he said.

With that, it was confirmed. My dream of sailing to Zetron was no longer a fantasy, but rather a promise fulfilled not only to myself, but to my people.

NYLA

FOR THREE MONTHS, I'd been in Zetron, and I still found nothing.

I traveled north of the city, hoping to clear my mind, and continued down a beaten path on the outskirts. Dust kicked up against my thin sandals. It coated the hem of my burnt orange skirt, the compromise between my kingdom and Zetron's colors. I refused to wear the greens most chose.

The moorlands at the border of the city expanded endlessly. Eventually, I broke off the path to the right, through a lesser traveled one. I'd made it myself, and having traveled it so many times, it was becoming more apparent. Soon, I needed to make a new one further up the path to prevent others from following me.

I continued until I spotted a small patch of trees that marked my destination. I tried to visit every day, but some days were harder than others. If anyone was out in the moorlands, I refused to be.

I let out a short whistle.

The shadow appeared above me before the beast itself.

Veros moved above me, and I looked up, shading my eyes from the sun. She swiftly dove from the sky and landed gracefully feet away from me. She moved with impossible poise for a beast of her size.

I stepped closer until I was in front of the beast, and she bowed her head. I lifted my hand and let her nuzzle into it. It was my comfort from home.

Some days, I debated using her to send a message back to Bellamy, but it was too risky. I didn't trust not going with her. The Market was looking for any new commodity to sell, and capturing a beast like Veros would fetch them a decent price.

A lump formed in my throat just thinking about it.

Veros settled, and I moved beside her, leaning against her torso and sliding to the ground. The shade of the trees above us blocked out the brutal summer sun.

Every day, I spent time clearing my head away from the city, visiting her. I didn't know where she went after, but I instructed her to find safety when I was away.

Part of me felt guilty keeping her from the mountains in Abelon, her home. But I also knew she'd never let me leave without her either.

I reached into the satchel I carried and pulled out a vial. The liquid inside swirled before I uncorked the vial and downed the Inum.

"Soon," I whispered to her after I finished.

She let out small sound like she agreed.

"Soon, we will be home."

I walked down the street of the city market lined with vendors. Everything from fresh fruit to plants to textiles was being sold. Many used their own manipulation to create the goods. The earth kingdom was magnificent, and I'd barely scratched the surface. I was stuck in this same city, hoping for leads.

A vendor reached out to stop me, offering up a taste of berries he sold. I took one and smiled at the older man. Its juice filled my mouth, and I let out a small groan of pleasure. There was no way I could pass up on them now.

"I'll take a small basket," I said politely.

He nodded and handed me one of the baskets off his cart.

I passed back a small gold coin and walked away. Before I made it far, I was already digging into the fresh berries. I wouldn't be able to focus on the task at hand if I was hungry.

As much as I enjoyed it, shopping through the market was not by choice.

In my months in Zetron, I'd been following leads and tips, most of them dead ends. I started with the one place I knew to look, but they had up and left.

The Warden and the Market disappeared, like they'd never been in Zeron at all.

I knew that wasn't true. I'd spent a short time there, but I was a prisoner and remembered it all. The second I left, the place haunted me. I promised myself I'd come back, rid the kingdoms of such a vile place.

I'd built all the homes and shops I possibly could in Abelon, and still, I felt nothing. No relief from the pain, no break from the nightmares that still plagued me. The guilt still ate me alive.

I needed to do something useful, to do something good for the world.

I was ready to give up, to go back to the small apartment I rented in the capital. It wasn't until I saw brown curls and dark golden skin I recognized that I halted. She looked more worn down than the last time I saw her, blending in with the rest of the citizens wandering the streets, but I would recognize her anywhere. I watched as one of the vendors handed her a satchel. More goods for the Warden to sell off or use.

This was my chance, the goddesses luck on my side. I never in my life thought I'd be so relieved to see Thalia again.

Every tip I followed paid off.

She walked away, and I made a split second decision, following her, careful to keep my distance.

My stomach sunk, but I brushed it off as the nerves of finally being able to take a step forward in finding the Market. It was easy, far too easy, but I didn't care. I'd spent three months with nothing. This was something. Even if everything in me told me to turn back, I had to push forward. I wasn't letting my one lead slip away, even if that meant letting myself walk straight into a trap.

CHAPTER 3
THALIA

SHE TOOK the bait and followed. The second the princess arrived, the whispers made it back to the Market. Capturing the princess of Abelon would be a large prize. She escaped once, but not again.

I'd been the one to let her go, and I would be the one to bring her back.

The Warden punished me for it, and I was ready to finally bring that to an end. If I could bring her back, maybe he'd forget. Maybe he'd let me see her.

I shook my head. I couldn't think about that right now. If I got distracted, I'd get sloppy.

My tips worked, leaving little whispers throughout the city that the Market was operating again. They were using the city's market as a front.

It wasn't true.

The Warden would never be so careless, but the princess fell for it easily. The moment I pulled out the coins and handed them to the vendor, buying myself a few of the vegetables from a stand, I felt her eyes on me. I didn't have to look to know it, but she was there.

The princess had lost me more than she knew. It had taken months to build back the trust I held at the Market.

We'd moved operations, built in a new place for the Warden to run his business, but I couldn't escape my failure.

My feet moved quickly through the market, trying to appear rushed but also making sure the princess could still follow.

The stone street kicked up dust against my ankles, and the warm summer sun beat down against my already dark warm-toned shoulders.

It wasn't the only thing bearing down on me. The weight of the Warden's expectations sat heavy in my stomach. His livelihood and operations had been disrupted because of Abelon. If I didn't find a way to fix that, I would be no use to him. I shook my head, not willing to think what that meant.

He afforded me enough freedom to have my own small crew of earth manipulators waiting for me at the city outskirts. They knew the plan, and I knew the second I stepped foot outside of the market, they would proceed with my exact instructions. All there was left to do was get the princess into place.

I rounded a corner, and there were fewer and fewer citizens around. The stone morphed into a dirt pathway, and the shops and vendors melted away.

My hand brushed against my side where my knife always sat. It was a comfort more than anything. I didn't really need it. Earth manipulation was enough to keep me safe, but I'd never take the chance and leave the blade behind.

I sensed the second the princess rounded the corner and hurried my pace, eager to get her away from the city. I wasn't exactly sure what she thought she was going to accomplish by following me. She seriously couldn't think she could tail me all the way back to the Market?

I locked eyes on the garden that marked the outskirt of the city ahead of me. Birds chirped, delighted with the warmer weather. I spent my entire life in Zetron, unsure if the rest of the kingdoms had such creatures. Their blue and green feathers caught the light when they flew and fascinated me each year when they came back out. No one saw them during the colder parts of the year.

My eyes were wandering, searching for the birds, and I refocused onto my target. The garden ahead held beautiful flowers and other form of vegetation, cared for by many of the citizens who lived in the city and needed time away from the bustling environment.

No one was in the space as I approached. At least, no one who could be seen at a first glance. I knew better.

I let my footsteps slow as I walked into the garden and down the main path. The princess wasn't far behind, but as I turned to admire a rosebush, I caught the movement that hovered just outside of the area. She was watching, waiting to see where I'd go from here, remaining just out of sight.

Or so she thought.

It's what I expected.

I needed to lure her further in, give her a reason to step foot into the garden.

I pushed further in and saw the path I marked earlier in

the day. I let my vines trail down my body, small tendrils barely visible. They spread across the space, searching for the ones I knew laid in wait. I found all three very quickly, and I knew my vines would alert them that the plan was a go. In the blink of an eye, I called the vines back.

I turned down a path leading to the right, well out of sight of the princess, knowing it would force her to follow if she truly wanted to tail me. I also knew it was the path that lead out of the garden into the fields away from the city, and she would hopefully believe I was leaving.

It didn't take long before I heard the yell followed by the muffled sounds of struggle. I hurried back the way I came. My sandals licked up dust as I ran, and I was surprised to find a bit of excitement growing in my chest.

In the middle of the path, the princess laid on the ground, covered in vines. Already, she was trying to use her fire to burn through them.

I wouldn't allow that.

She burned through the top half, trying to race for her legs before I could send more her way. With a struggled effort, she stood, bending to burn the ones off her lower half. I raced toward her, not ready to give up my prey so easily.

She braced herself for my attack, throwing flames in my direction.

I ducked and continued to close the space between her.

My crew moved to step in, but I stopped them. "She's mine," I barked.

My hand grabbed her arm the second she raised it to send flames my way. With a small tug, I pulled her to the ground and instantly pinned her with my weight. I sat, holding her arms to her side. She writhed against me, but I slammed her back down.

"You," she hissed.

"Lovely to see you too, princess," I growled.

I spotted nearby a metal statue and manipulated a chunk of it off quickly towards her. It bent into the shape of a shackle wrapped around her arms and torso, holding them in place. Again, I pulled another chunk from the statue and forced them into orbs around her hand and where I noticed she no longer had another. I wasn't taking any chances on whether the residual limb functioned the same.

Her mouth became gagged by a vine, but I saw the pure anger and hatred in her eyes as they settled on me.

My crew slowly appeared out of the bushes in different parts of the garden. Two men and one woman walked toward me as I moved off the contained princess.

"Good work," Lee, praised.

I nodded.

"The Warden will be pleased with this one," he added.

"It was a solid plan," Gryo praised from next to him.

My eyes flashed to our final crew member. The woman in our group was quieter, newer to the Market. I knew what the Warden held over her and felt the same pain.

I was her once.

"He'll be pleased with how your first run out went," I assured her. "It might be enough to convince him to let you visit."

I was careful not to say more—not in front of the princess and especially not the rest of the crew. We all held our secrets, our own reasoning for whatever kept us at the Market. None of that belonged to anyone else.

She nodded without a word.

"Let's move before someone wanders this way," I said.

Lee picked up the princess, scooping her into his arms. His tall, larger frame contributed to his muscular build, and he easily carried her until we made it outside the garden.

I let out a low whistle and waited.

Within seconds, my Pantherus appeared, bounding toward us. She was nothing more than oversized cat, but her large, razor sharp teeth kept most away.

Lee loaded the princess onto the back of my Pantherus, and I climbed on behind her. I wasn't taking my eyes off her until we made it back to the market. It was only a few days' ride away.

"I'm heading straight back," I said.

"We'll finish business here," Gryo assured me. "We'll only be a day out behind you."

I nodded. The princess was the only reason I'd wanted to come to the city. When I heard the Warden had a few tasks and leads to follow, I volunteered.

We couldn't return empty-handed, and he had no idea about our separate plan.

I wasn't risking keeping the princess another day in the city. Now that I had her, it was time to return to the Market. I pulled the vine away from her mouth so she could speak as I wrestled through a small satchel I'd also kept at my side. I pulled out a few berries and held them towards her.

"Eat these," I insisted.

"I'm not taking anything from you," she spat.

"Trust me, we have a long way to go. Don't make yourself suffer more than you have to," I said, trying to help her.

She shook her head.

There was no time for arguing. I groaned and quickly moved my hand, pressing the berries into her mouth before she could protest. I held my hand over her lips, forcing her to keep them in. She decided rather quickly that fighting me was useless, especially without access to her arms, and swallowed reluctantly.

It was for her own good. The ride otherwise would be brutal.

"Did you poison me?" she asked when I finally pulled my hand away.

"No," I said. "But you will sleep for quite a while."

Already, her eyes grew heavy, and I could see her muscles begin to relax. The berries were fast acting, a trick I'd learned from the Market.

As she started to doze off, her eyes met mine once more, but I could see the little bits of gold mixed in the dark brown.

"I hate you," she said, and her words trailed off.

It was hours into the ride before the princess even began to stir, the peace and quiet of riding alone while she slept keeping me well into my own thoughts. My Pantherus, Olia, kept a good pace, and at the rate we were moving, we'd make it to the Market's new location in exactly a day.

I needed sleep, but I couldn't risk it. There was no one else to keep watch or make sure Nyla didn't try to escape. I'd have to push forward and let my Pantherus continue. We'd rest once we were back at the Market. The feline had far more stamina than people did.

Instead, I used my manipulations to grow vines closer to me whenever we passed any sort of berry plants. It was small, but the food was enough to give me the little bit of energy I needed to hold out until we were back.

Nyla kept turning her head side to side, and I feared she'd wake up sooner than I expected. I was hoping I gave her enough to keep her out until we were back.

She winced, and I watched her brows furrow in her sleep. I realized quickly she was having some form of a nightmare and watched as a feeling of invasiveness washed over me.

The last time I'd seen her, both of her hands had been intact. War did awful things to people and left them scars to remember. My stomach ached looking at where her hand had once been, imagining the pain that would've come with losing it.

Each time she winced in her rest, I felt intrusive watching her. There was no way to avoid it, but it felt personal and private. She may have cost me more than she realized, but I was still a person with ability to have sympathy. No one deserved to have their ghosts put on display.

I shuddered with the thought of having my own out for everyone to see.

Soon, she stopped and settled again. I thanked the goddesses for allowing her to sleep peacefully the rest of the way. It made my life easier, allowed me to let go of the guilt that had stared at me.

The scenery soon changed, and the forest became darker. Fields and tall grass transformed into a thick layer of trees. The canopy above me blocked out most of the sun, and I let out a sigh of relief not having it beating down on me any longer. I felt the sting on my shoulders from being out in it too long.

Night came faster than I expected, and my Pantherus still pushed on. It took everything in me to keep my eyes open. Luckily, the beast's eyes allowed her to see easily in the dark.

Just a few more hours, and we'd be there. Once morning light started to peek above the trees, we'd be at the Market.

I just had to last until then.

I swallowed hard, anticipating the Warden and what he'd think when he saw the princess dragged back into his compound.

It had to work—I needed it too. I was the second in command, his most trusted and loyal worker. If I couldn't gain his trust back, then I was useless. I couldn't allow that. There was far too much on the line for that.

My entire survival rode on maintaining his trust. It had gotten me this far, and I wouldn't allow a single princess to strip me of that.

It took every ounce of strength I had to keep myself awake for those last few hours. It was brutal without any company; all I had were my thoughts and Olia.

The sun started to shine once more from above, turning the sky a breathtaking pink and orange. As the sun rose, I regained my ability to see farther than an inch or two in front of my face. The forest opened, and I found myself filling with relief as the gates came into view. Their large metal presence marked the boundary. We finally made it back to the market.

Pushing into the clearing, we found the tall gates, waiting unmoving for us. I manipulated them to unlock and open, and we were greeted by multiple guards who instantly recognized me as I pushed Olia through. They backed away, allowing us to pass and gawking at the person draped over my beast.

One approached as I stopped in front of the entrance to the new, expansive building. It took months to build it to perfection.

"Where is he?" I asked, barely waiting for the guards to stop in front of me.

"Away," one answered. "He'll be back by tomorrow."

It wasn't often the Warden left; it must have been urgent. I'd have to wait. I had no choice.

"Take her down to the cells for now and assign someone to stay there with her. No one takes eyes off her until the Warden is back."

He nodded.

No one questioned me, not when I was the right hand to the Warden.

I jumped off the back of the beast and left Nyla in the care of the guards. I needed rest. I trusted the other men and woman enough to watch her for a few hours. If I didn't sleep soon, my body would force me to. I recognized my own weakness and hurried back to my room. Just a few hours, and then I would take over watch duty myself.

CHAPTER 4

NYLA

FIRE BURNED ALL AROUND ME, and I coward away from it. I could feel the heat at my back and turned to find it surrounded me, closing in slowly. I knelt on the floor, overwhelmed by the weight of my reality.

I would burn.

Every choice I made and atrocity I committed, I deserved to burn alongside my father. I never should've made it through the war. Koraine had saved me, given me the power she held and made new life from it. A new chance, and I was wasting it.

A cry escaped me, and my head fell into my hand and residual limb. They slid across my face, pushing my hair out of it and embracing the sides of my head.

Voices echoed through the space. I wasn't sure where I was; the only thing I could see was fire everywhere.

Monster. Traitor. Weak.

I tried to push the voices out, but they just grew louder. My entire body felt like it was being torn in multiple directions. Part of me craved the fire, and another piece of me, ever since the war, was afraid to embrace who I was.

I couldn't access the full power of my flames. It blamed my hand, but I knew it wasn't that.

Something happened when Koraine gave me life. My power had been stifled.

I closed my eyes, squeezing them shut, and found myself faced with Koraine. The moment she saved me, and I felt her power fill me. A moon flashed into my vision, bright and illuminating.

"You can't run from this," the voice whispered, and my eyes flew open.

The flames still surrounded me, and I let out a scream.

The power warred inside me. Every piece of me felt like it was being ripped to pieces. I burned from the inside out.

My medicine was wearing off, I knew it was. The nightmares only came when it did.

I pinched my arm, trying to wake myself.

"Please. Release me," I begged to the empty space.

One last scream, and I let myself fall forward, catching myself on my forearms and letting my head slowly touch the cold ground.

Flames closed in around me, and I felt the intense heat flick against my body.

I accepted my fate.

Flames consumed me, and all I could feel was pain before I faded into darkness.

———

I sat up from the cold floor suddenly.

Darkness surrounded me, and I tried to blink the sleep from my eyes. The moment my vision cane back, I found myself in a recognizable cell. I hadn't been in them before, but Cyrus had described the cells beneath the Market where those for auction were held.

It took me a moment for the memories to stop rushing back.

Thalia had dragged me back to the Market, drugged me so I could not memorize the route she took, and now, I must've been beneath the Market.

I looked around closely for other prisoners but was met with silence.

Metal clinking softly caught my attention after a moment, and I found a guard staring in between the metal bars. He cocked his head, watching me.

"You're the princess who almost destroyed the kingdoms?" he asked, as if more to himself than me.

I froze.

A slow chuckle left his lips and grew until he was laughing in my face. He spat through the bars in my direction, and I pushed myself away from him.

"Completely made up shit, if you ask me," he scoffed. "Pathetic."

He banged a hand against the bars, startling me. I pulled my knees close to my body and refused to answer. I knew what the rest of the world thought of me.

A traitor to her own people and all four kingdoms. The princess who tried to bring destruction upon the rest of the kingdoms. It was my father's plan, but I did nothing to stop it.

My heart raced at the memory, the nightmare. The mercy of the Queen of Abelon was the only thing that kept me alive. I owed it to her and my brother to at least try to do something useful with the rest of my life. If I couldn't help them in Abelon, at least I could try in Zetron.

There were still people trapped in the Market, forced to work for the Warden. He used fear and power to coerce others into doing this. I knew the Market was vulnerable after we had destroyed the integrity during the war. After the war, everyone was rebuilding, but now was the time to strike and finish what was started.

"Where is Thalia?" I demanded.

The guard looked at me with shock "You don't want her to come back," he said, regaining his composure.

"Where is Thalia?" I repeated, gaining more confidence.

He scowled and moved away from the cell without an answer. I let out a deep sigh, knowing I would get nowhere with him.

"Here," Talia said, moving out of the darkness and walking towards the cell. The guard seemed surprised—he had no idea she been there. She moved on her feet, her footsteps soft.

The guard gave her slight nod of respect and moved away from the cell. My heart raced in my chest, still on edge from the nightmare that woke me. I needed to find the medicine I relied on and soon. It was the only way I could sleep without the same nightmares consuming me.

Somehow, I knew that wouldn't happen.

"Let's go," Thalia demanded.

I moved, my adrenaline wearing off. "Where?" I asked.

"The warden is ready to see you," she answered.

Thalia opened my cell and waited expectantly for me to move. I hesitated, hating every moment I had to give in to her demands. I didn't see another option.

Stepping out of the cell, I realized I was being kept in a small room by myself. The only other person inside was the guard watching me.

A metal door sat at the other end of the room. Besides that, the room was empty, the stone walls bare.

The second Thalia opened the door, I heard them. The metal had blocked them out before, but now, prisoners cried out.

My stomach dropped hearing the dozens of voices crying out to us.

"Move," Thalia stated from behind me.

I took slow steps, glancing around in horror at everyone trapped beneath the Market. We moved through a hall lined with cells, and many prisoners moved to the edge to watch us.

Thalia led me up a set of stone steps. The cells of prisoners echoed behind us as we left.

The moment we reached the top, she manipulated another metal door. It led out to the entryway of the Market.

Commotion sounded outside as we walked through the entrance hall. Thalia shot a concerned glance toward outside but said nothing to give away her thoughts. Another shout rang out, and I paused, trying to catch a glimpse out the entry door that was left cracked slightly open.

"Keep moving," Thalia stated.

"Sounds like you're under attack," I pointed out to her.

"It's nothing," she said.

I took another step, but another shout from a guard outside had me curious enough to disobey. I walked to the door instead and opened it, horrified by the sight before me.

Veros struggled against metal chain as multiple guards tugged on them.

I ran before I could even think. Seeing my dragon in such pain and panic devastated me.

"Stop!" I called out, running toward them.

Before I could take another step, vines shot out from behind me, wrapping around my body and forcing me to the ground. Thalia walked up behind me and pulled me up enough to kneel and watch.

That dreaded thing tracked you here. Now, the Warden has another prize for his collection."

I could feel her smug satisfaction, watching my horror.

"No!" I screamed.

I could withstand any pain, but watching my dragon endure it would kill me.

I was forced to observe as they walked away, leading Veros toward the back of the building. Before the beast disappeared, I tried to catch its attention.

"I'll come for you," I yelled out, tears filling my eyes.

I never meant for this to happen.

She disappeared before I could even tell if she heard me, and my heart shattered.

What had I done?

Thalia urged me forward, back toward the giant estate that made up the Market. My head hung, and my feet dragged the closer I got to the door. A sickening feeling took hold of me, and I dreaded the meeting I knew was bound to happen.

The second she led me inside and toward a staircase, panic filled me. My body shook, and all I could think about was my dragon, the companion that kept me safe, the only being that ever seemed to understand me.

I was a fool to come to Zetron, but there was no turning back.

CHAPTER 5
THALIA

"What have you done?" the Warden barked in my direction.

His hand pushed back his black hair and revealed more of the wrinkles on his forehead. The past few months of stress and difficulties had aged him far more than I'd ever seen.

We'd only been inside his office for a few minutes, and already, I could sense the heat radiating from him. His anger rose every second his eyes remained on Nyla. I held her arm, keeping a firm grip on her.

I felt myself sinking inward. I tried to hold his gaze when his eyes snapped over to me, tried not to give away the fear I felt building, but he always knew.

I swallowed before speaking, urging my voice out.

"I brought her back," I said, trying not to let my words waiver.

"I never ordered this," he hissed.

His eyes shifted between the pair of us. Heat rose to my cheeks, and I knew Nyla was soaking in every second of it.

"I thought you'd be happy after she escaped," I answered.

This was supposed to be my ticket back to the top. The Warden continuously punished me for what happened. It was entirely my fault, a moment of weakness when I let Nyla slip from my grasp. Something about her had been all too familiar, a woman carrying so much anger and looking for her escape.

I shook myself from the downward spiral.

"We are rebuilding. We had to move the entire Market that had been established for years because of her. The Abelonian royal family was the first to ever escape. It created hope for those trapped. If they could do it, anyone could. I couldn't have that. We moved and built a better fortress with no way out," he said, and I could hear the fury in his words. "Bringing her here risks all of that. They'll come looking for her. If she is in Zetron, she already was looking for us. Did you even think before you took her?"

"I—" I stopped, knowing it was no use. He was right; I'd made a grave error, but I had also thought everything through.

"She's been here months, and no one has come looking for her. I took her because I knew it was just her. Abelon is still rebuilding after the war. She is likely all they could afford to send," I said. "If you do not want to auction her off, then you can just kill her."

"We can't kill her," he answered. "She's far too valuable to kill her off. It would be a waste. She stays," he said, something new filling his eyes.

The shift in his body and attitude was visible. A new

confidence filled him, and relief flooded me, knowing the anger was receding.

"No," Nyla argued and writhed in my grasp. I pulled her backward, trying to steady her. "Kill me and get it over with!"

The Warden barely paid her any attention, his mind set.

"She will work in the Market like the rest. You will personally be in charge of her. I don't need to tell you what happens if she escapes again," he warned.

I heard the hidden words and understood the threat. It wasn't just my life at stake. There was far worse than the Warden killing me.

"Understood," I said.

"Now, get her cleaned up and into a room," he ordered.

I walked her out of his study and down the hall. I couldn't put her in the cells—it was far too big of a risk to have her with the rest of the people there. We didn't need more prisoners feeling inspired to escape. Also, the chance of one of them letting it slip that the princess was here was not one I was willing to take.

The Warden had said find her room, and I knew what that meant.

I walked her through the twists and turns of the Market. The halls were a maze, and the place was ginormous. I kept going until I reached the end of a hall with a single door on the far side. Approaching, I manipulated the metal to unlock; there was no handle on the door. By my own ability, I opened it and moved it just enough for me to shove Nyla in and follow behind her.

She stumbled forward.

"This will be your home until I decide otherwise," I said.

I didn't envy her. This had been my own home once, or at least a version of it, one of the few commonalities between the old and new Markets.

Everyone stayed in similar accommodations when they arrived. My time had been short, but I could still recall the way the metal walls closed in around me. I wanted desperately to use my abilities to let myself out, but I knew it was against the Warden's rules.

His punishments were far worse than being trapped alone in the room.

"Just kill me," the princess said. "You're a coward."

I swallowed hard at that. Something about her seemed far more broken than the last time I'd seen her, like she'd given up on life.

Her face was slender, her eyes far more tired. I could still see the whispers of beauty that was once there, slowly fading, as she gave up further.

I tried to remember everything she had taken from me, remain focused on my goal. Revenge had to be my only focus, or she would slip past my defenses again.

"You'll receive meals, and during the day, you'll be with me, working the Market. Any other time, you will stay in this room until I say otherwise," I warned.

She nodded, standing in the middle of the metal room, glaring at me. Her arms crossed, and my eyes couldn't help but drift to the limb where her hand had once been. A bit of me felt sorrow for what she'd lost only a short time before.

I couldn't think that way. I had a job to do.

If I couldn't kill her for what she cost me, I would make her life miserable.

CHAPTER 6
NYLA

THE SECOND THE metal door slammed behind her, I knew trying to escape was useless. The metal clicked into place as she re-locked it, and I ran over, giving it a push just to confirm what I already knew.

This was what I expected. When I followed her, I knew it most likely ended with me being captured. Even my gut knew it was a trap.

Three months in Zetron, and there was almost no possibility that not a single person recognized who I was. The rumors were spread back to the Market. I shouldn't have been surprised she came looking for me.

Being captured lead me straight back to their new set up . It wasn't ideal, but it was the only way I saw being able to get close enough to dismantle the place once and for all.

The only issue now was, I really had no plan. I didn't know what the new market looked like or how it was run. I didn't even know where it was until now, and even then if I left, I wouldn't be able to find my way back. Thalia had made sure of that, drugging me on the way.

My heart sank, realizing she had taken all my posses-
sions—the small satchel I carried with the emergency dose
of the Inum that kept me sane and kept the pain away from
where my hand once sat. Without it, it wouldn't be long
before I was left in agony.

My fist banged against the door, but the metal didn't
budge. No one came when I called out, and I knew it'd be a
while before anyone let me out again.

I turned around and took in the metal room. The walls
felt close together, making me feel trapped. A cot sat in the
corner with a pillow and blanket thrown on top. A bucket
sat in the other corner, and I shuddered realizing it was the
only bathroom I would receive.

I walked the perimeter of the room, my hand dragging
against the metal wall. No noise carried from outside, and
each wall of the room felt just as thickly built as the others.
There was no weak point.

"Dragon shit," I muttered under my breath.

I called fire to my hand and hovered it over one of the
walls, trying to manipulate the metal with heat. It barely
made a scratch, and I realized there was no escape. My fire
was useless.

Dread washed over me, realizing I hadn't thought this
through.

If they kept me in here forever, there'd be almost no way
for me to stop the Market and what they were doing. Part of
me had hoped they'd drag me down to the same cells they had
last time. My fire would've easily melted through those bars.

Perhaps they planned for that.

This room could've been made to contain someone with

fire abilities. I was foolish to think they didn't learn from last time. They had built this place with clever ideas, and I had to be smarter.

I crawled into the cot, knowing I needed rest. Even though I'd slept for a while after eating the berries Thalia gave me, my head pounded, and I felt like it was a fitful sleep. Most nights were now.

I laid down in the cot, thinking over everything I'd noticed or seen in the Market.

The Warden planned to keep me, to use me for whatever he pleased. That thought was enough to make my stomach turn.

The second I laid eyes on him, dread had filled me. His face was like a familiar whisper of something I should know.

I pulled up the covers right below my chin and tried to close my eyes.

With Thalia as my keeper, there had to be a way I could escape from her again. I did it once, and I knew she'd be determined not to let it happen another time.

I let my eyes slowly shut and drifted off to sleep.

***

Morning came, and I could already sense the sickening feeling in my stomach of missing the medicine I used to treat my hand. The pain had not surfaced yet, but if I didn't get what I needed soon, withdrawal would hit. I'd become so reliant, I wasn't sure I'd survive without them.

The metal door clicked, and Thalia's figure appeared in

the doorway. She carried a tray of food and set it down at the end of the cot as I sat up.

"Eat," she demanded. "I'll be back soon." She stalked from the room and closed the door quickly, locking it behind her.

I didn't have time to say a single word. My stomach growled, and I knew without the Inum, I need something to give me strength. I pulled the tray of food toward me, starting with the slices of breakfast meat and then working toward the bowl of fruit.

An unsettling feeling grew in my chest, realizing I was being well kept. I expected them to let me wither away to nothing. A warm breakfast and a room to sleep in was more than I ever thought I would have being back.

Nothing came without a price, though; it just was a matter of when they'd come to collect.

The second I finished, Thalia reappeared, along with another, shorter, quiet woman. The woman took my tray and hurried off while Thalia stayed behind.

"Let's go," she said.

"No," I said. "Tell me first where we're going."

"You don't get demands here," Thalia said.

"Then you'll have to drag me out of here," I said, crossing my arms and remaining firmly on the cot. I heard the slight groan that slipped from Thalia's mouth.

"Don't make this difficult, princess," she said.

"Don't call me that," I snapped.

The word was vile coming from her lips. I hated this place and the people in it, but even more, I hated the title that haunted me, the one I no longer felt worthy enough to hold.

Her eyes narrowed on me. "Let's go," she repeated, seemingly deciding it wasn't worth her breath.

I stood reluctantly and followed, knowing I had no choice. It was either follow her or spend the day in the middle of the metal room. At least outside of it, I could start to further my plan.

I trailed behind her as she led me through the winding halls of the Market. This new building was larger than the last, harder to memorize the layout of.

Thalia led me downstairs into a kitchen. Already, there were dishes beside the large tub of a sink. I spotted the woman who had taken my tray working at it, scrubbing dishes.

"You'll help Lyn get through the breakfast chores," Thalia stated.

"Excuse me?" I asked.

"You will help her get through all of those dishes, and then I will decide what we do from there," Thalia said, nodding toward the sink.

I wanted to argue, but my eyes flickered back to the woman working at them alone. She looked broken, her shoulders sinking inward. I held my tongue and swallowed hard.

"Do you think yourself above this, princess?" Thalia sneered.

"I told you, don't call me that," I said through gritted teeth. Without another word, I walked toward the sink and picked up a bowl. I found everything I needed inside the sink and started to scrub. I worked in silence beside Lyn.

Every once in a while, I felt her eyes on me, deciding

what to make of the Princess of Abelon scrubbing dishes beside her.

Thalia could give me every task or chore; none of it would break me. I knew what she was doing. She'd give me every last task no one wanted. My life would be misery because of her, all to make her feel better in finding her revenge.

It wouldn't work. I'd happily scrub dishes and slap a smile on my face while I did it, just so she couldn't have that satisfaction.

Once we worked through the pile, Thalia stood, inspecting the drying dishes.

"Lyn, go find the Warden. He needs help with a project today." She nodded and hurried off. "You follow me," she ordered and turned, leaving the room.

I rolled my eyes and followed. The sun was barely high, and already, I knew the day would be exhausting.

Thalia led me outside, and I noticed a group of earth manipulators working in a large nearby garden.

"Enri," Thalia called out.

A man hurried over, his linen brown pants already covered in dirt, his hands similar. The day barely started, yet I could see he'd already been out here hours.

"This is Nyla," Thalia said. "She'll be here a while."

My stomach turned at the words. A while was not part of the plan.

The man nodded, his eyes flicking to me.

"She'll help in the garden the next few hours. Put her to work wherever you need her."

My eyes widened, glancing over to the large garden filled with life. Everything I touched, I destroyed. The last place I should be was a garden that had already had so much care and work poured into it.

"I don't think…" I started.

"I don't care what you think," Thalia snapped. "You'll listen to him, and you'll help where he needs you. You do as I say here."

He led me silently into the garden while Thalia stalked off. I risked a glance back and found her watching me with anger in her eyes.

Strategically, Enri placed me in a corner away from most, where I could tell the least amount of work had been done. At least the man was smart enough to recognize I should be nowhere near most of the crops and plants.

"You will work here, digging a hole."

"Couldn't you just manipulate a hole into the ground?" I asked.

"The Warden does not permit us to use manipulations at the Market. It is not worth the punishment he gives."

I noticed no one was using their gift. Everyone was caring for the plants by hand, tending to them. "Wouldn't it make more sense if he let you? This garden helps feed you all, right?" I asked.

"It does, but that's the rule. Only a few are allowed to use their manipulations here. It isn't worth the risk of allowing everyone such freedoms," Enri said. His face softened, noticing my disbelief. "Tending to the garden helps us keep in touch with the power we are blessed with. Knowing the Earth and how each part of it works and functions gives us a better understanding of how we can manipulate it. We're planting an apple tree here. We need a large, deep hole for it. Think you can manage?"

Not only was I not an earth manipulator, but I only had one hand. The metal tool he handed me was small, and I knew the hole was going to take hours.

I nodded and set to work digging at the spot he pointed to. Little by little, I moved the dirt, and the hole grew. I felt sweat dripping down my face the longer I went at it.

A woman nearby worked on a second hole at a much faster pace. I caught her glancing over every so often, watching the way I slowly worked at the hole with my single hand.

"Nyla," I said finally after another hour of silence.

"What?" the woman said, glancing up from her own hole.

"My name is Nyla," I said. I paused, placing the shovel aside and wiping my hand on my linen pants. I reached out my hand toward her, but she just stared hesitantly at it.

"Xora," she said back shyly.

"How long have you been here?" I asked, unable to help myself. I needed more information, and this was the only way I was going to get it.

"A while," she said in barely a whisper.

"I don't understand," I answered, accidentally letting the words slip from my mouth.

She tilted her head and scrunched her eyebrows.

"Why stay? Why not try to leave if the Warden forces you to work and strips you of your power?" I explained.

"It's not that simple," the woman said quietly, her eyes glued to the dirt in front of her.

I glanced around for any unwanted listeners. This was my best chance at learning something about the Market's inner workings.

Thalia sat a distance away, watching me. She stood from the large rock she had settled on and moved slowly toward the garden.

I was running out of time. "What do you mean? He can't possibly keep all of you hostage. There has to be a way for people to escape," I insisted.

"Talk like that will get you killed," Xora said, trying to hush me.

"This isn't a life."

"I don't want to escape," she said quickly.

"You don't have to say that to me," I assured her. "Anything he could possibly offer you, I promise you can find other places. Food, shelter, all of it. There has to be a different way."

"It's not that," she said. "The Warden has a way of getting you here and keeping you here."

A shiver ran down my spine at the words. She went back to digging, and I could tell by the way her body shifted, I was getting no more information from her.

"Nyla," Thalia snapped from behind me. I turned to find her frowning down at my hole. "It's been hours and you're not done," she said.

"You didn't give me much to work with," I said. "And I'm limited on what I can do," I snapped and held up my residual limb.

I saw the way her eyes shifted a little softer. She glanced to where my hand once was, and I saw the sympathy in her gaze. I didn't want it, not from her.

"Another hour, and I'll be done," I said sternly.

"You want to keep digging?" she asked.

"If I don't, you're just going to give me a different task, so let me finish this one," I said.

She stared between me and the hole for a moment and then shrugged. Her body turned away from me, and she walked away.

I kept digging, making no more conversation with those around me. Something was deeply wrong with this place, the way every last person worked diligently without question. To have that control over so many people, I had to figure out what the Warden was doing and how I could stop it.

After an hour, Thalia came back to assess my work. She brought Enri with her, and he gave me a nod of approval.

"Let's go," Thalia demanded. I didn't have time to brush the dirt from my pants or wipe it away from my hand. I followed her covered in it, still dripping sweat from the summer heat.

She led me inside to a room filled with stalls of showers. "Clean yourself up," she ordered.

I didn't argue, the sound of showering too tempting.

I found the nearest stall and turned on the water overhead. It came rushing out, and I stood underneath it after tossing my clothing I pulled off to the side. I was caked in dirt and dust. Water rinsed over me, the tangles in my hair a mess. I worked through them and found a small shelf to my side with soap, which I used to scrub myself clean.

"Hurry up, princess," Thalia called, standing right outside the shower.

I groaned. This was the only peace I had all day, and it was short-lived. I finished cleaning myself and turned off the water. Thalia's hand appeared, pushing aside the thin curtain that separated us and holding out a towel to me.

"Thanks," I muttered.

The towel felt rough on my skin as I patted myself dry. My hair remained wet and dripping down my back. I glanced over to where I left my clothes but couldn't fathom putting them back on, covered in dirt and sweat.

Instead, I wrapped the towel around myself like some form of a dress. I tucked it in so it stayed in place and pulled the curtain to find Thalia standing directly outside, her arms crossed.

"Where are your clothes?" she asked.

"I need new ones," I demanded.

"You don't give orders here," she answered flatly.

"I'll do whatever tasks you give me, sleep in that metal room, but I need basic decencies, clothing and food," I stated.

She stared at me, her eyes assessing me. I felt my cheeks heat a bit at the intensity of her stare.

"If you'd prefer, I could just wear nothing," I suggested, trying to will the red from my face.

My hand found where I tucked the towel, and slowly, I started to pull it out, like I was going to drop it from my body.

"No," Thalia said, her eyes snapping up to mine. "Not necessary."

I tried to keep a smirk from my face. She turned and stalked from the room without a word, and I followed, keeping the towel firmly in place.

The tile of the Market was cold against my bare feet. A trail of water followed as my hair dripped down my back.

She led me all the way back to the metal room. For a moment, I thought she really might not give me clothing.

She locked me in without a word, and I waited for a few minutes before I heard it again.

She moved inside and carried a handful of clothing she placed down on the cot. Immediately, I noticed the tan and green colors.

"I can't wear that," I said.

"You wanted clothing, and I brought you some," she said. "This is what you wear, or you will wear nothing." This time, I caught the satisfied smirk growing across her own lips. "I figured we're about the same size," she said, crossing her arms.

She brought me her clothes? I don't know why, for a moment, my chest warmed at the small kindness. I knew she didn't have to share, and I imagined she worked hard to have the liberty of owning enough to do so while working for the Market.

She turned to leave, and I tried to hold my tongue, but that feeling wouldn't go away, no matter how hard I tried to shake it.

The door opened to her will.

"Thank you," I said quietly.

She turned and glanced at me before she disappeared again, and the metal door trapped me in once more.

CHAPTER 7
THALIA

I walked back to my room after leaving the princess alone. The second I got back to the small space I was afforded by the Warden, I cleaned up the wardrobe that was now torn apart to find clothing for Nyla. Why did I it, I couldn't rationalize, but part of me knew if she was going to survive this place, she needed what little basics she could get. The Warden was brutal, and no one was safe, not even his most valuable bargaining chip.

I hated the princess for what she had brought on me, but a small part of me couldn't help but feel sympathy for what she was going through, just like every new person the Warden brought back. Every last one of us had been through the same, maybe worse, when we came.

I never expected him to keep her here. That wasn't the plan. I expected him to sell her off or use her to bargain with Abelon for more money to build back the Market.

Now, I was stuck with her.

I slammed the wardrobe shut in frustration. This was complicated when it was supposed to be simple. She deserved what was coming for her. She deserved to suffer the way I had. She made my life misery for months; why was I helping her at all?

I made my way into the washroom attached to my room. I found myself standing at the sink and splashed water on my face.

I'd seen the way she surveyed the entire grounds as I walked her through them, her focus on every last detail of the set up and all the people here. Each time I moved her somewhere, I could see her taking mental notes.

The plan she was building wouldn't work. It's the only reason I allowed it. There was no escaping from the Market this time.

I'd seen her talking to Xora as far as I allowed her to. Xora was new, afraid of the Warden, I didn't expect her to tell anything of use to Nyla. The moment I saw the conversation shift and Xora looked like she wanted to crawl into the hole she was digging, I moved in. I could tell Nyla pushed her too hard and was moving in to dangerous territory.

Everyone at the market had their secrets, and it was better it stayed that way.

The last thing I needed was the person I was tasked with watching digging those up.

Once I cleaned up, I made my way from the room to see the Warden. Most days, I met with him to report on whatever tasks he needed. It was my first day watching Nyla, and I knew he would want to know every detail. It would benefit him to know how his new asset was adjusting.

Nyla was strong, stubborn, and would take a bit to break, but if he managed it, he would be unstoppable.

I carried on down the hall, the Warden's office nearby. I passed a guard who nodded to me. I was the Warden's right hand; everyone respected me and feared me all at once.

The rumors that surfaced of what I'd done to get here were unthinkable. In reality, it was far less fascinating.

Self-preservation.

That was all.

I would not give in, I would not let him break me until I was useless. I let him hone me into a weapon instead to protect myself and the people I loved.

I knocked twice on the door in front of me before pushing it open. The Warden sat behind his desk and lifted his head briefly to greet me.

The room was set up like his last office with a few small changes. My eyes picked them out immediately, but most wouldn't see the difference. I noticed the desk no longer had the carvings of the old one and the way he replaced books in his shelf with new ones, ones I didn't recognize. It was the way this room felt colder, less personal, like every bit of the person who lived inside him died with the rest of the Market.

I imagined it did. That was his life work, everything he ever wanted and needed. It was gone in a matter of seconds because of the royal family. Now, he allowed Nyla to walk freely around the Market. I'd never understand.

"What did you come for?"

"She's taking in the new layout, speaking to people who work here, looking for any weakness we have," I stated.

I kept the report short and to the point. I knew the Warden had no time to waste, and I wasn't prepared to be the one to disrupt him in his work longer than needed.

My hands remained firmly by my side, but I nervously pulled at the material of my pants.

"She won't find any," the Warden said.

"You will still allow her to work freely then?" I asked.

"Keep putting her to work, make use of her. If she finds any weaknesses, it'll be on you," he stated. He paused, shuffling through the parchments on his desk, and looked up at me. "I tasked you with making this place unbreakable this time. You better find out if you managed to do it."

I swallowed hard. "Yes, sir.".

I rarely addressed him so formally. Over the years, it had become less necessary, and the Warden never noticed, but now, it slipped out without me even thinking.

It didn't register to him.

"That's all," he said, dismissing me with a wave of his hand. To him, I was nothing more than a weapon for him to use.

My feet remained firmly in place as I hesitated. "Warden," I said, catching his attention again. "When can I visit again?"

There was nothing more to say. He knew exactly what I was asking.

"Until you prove to me you can handle Nyla and guarantee the new security has no weakness, I will not take you there," he said.

My heart sank, a stab to my chest. Months passed, and I hadn't been back, the Warden holding it over me.

"Go feed our prisoner dinner," he ordered.

I nodded, turning from the room and holding back tears that threatened to escape. I couldn't let anyone see my weakness. Strength kept you alive.

I moved to find dinner for Nyla, unwilling to trust others to enter and exit her room.

If I was going to regain the Warden's respect and favor, I needed to make sure whatever Nyla was working on, I was five steps ahead.

The kitchen was packed with workers preparing dinner. Everyone had a job, and everyone chipped in to make the place work.

Most of the newer people brought to the Market took on small roles like the kitchen and garden maintenance. Those who had been there for years were trusted to become guards or join groups on runs outside of the Market. The Warden was meticulous.

My team was the exception. The people on it were handpicked, sometimes newer to the Market. I knew what I needed, and the Warden never once question my judgment —until recently. He trusted me enough to know I could handle it if things went wrong.

I found a tray nearby and filled it with random foods already prepared. By the time I finished, a sandwich, a plate of vegetables, and a fresh apple sat on it.

That was enough to keep the princess well fed and nourished.

I nodded my thanks to the workers as I made my way out of the kitchen. I could've had one bring it up to Nyla, but she was my personal issue, and I needed to keep as many people out of it as I could. The only person I trusted enough to deal with her was myself.

My feet were heavy as I walked up the stairs, and I realized how exhausted I was from the mental weight I carried. I pushed it off, knowing once I delivered the food, I could retire to my room for the remainder of the evening.

Already, the sun was starting to dip outside, and it wasn't unusual that I didn't join the rest of the market for dinner. Often, I was far too busy to do so. No one would blink twice at my absence.

I walked to the end of the hall where the metal door sat and placed a hand against it. The entire room was made of metal. I could sense the princess inside, close to the door.

Far too close.

There was no reason she should be waiting like this. Was she really dumb enough to try and attack?

I unlocked the metal door. Maybe I caught her at coincidental timing. I stepped inside, and the tray immediately knocked from my hands as the princess threw her full weight into me. My feet stumbled backward, but I regained my footing rather quickly. It was far too close quarters for Nyla to effectively use her flames, but as she rushed toward me again, I felt the heat of her as she grabbed my arm. I pulled away, my skin burning.

"You're more delusional than I thought if you think you're escaping again," I hissed.

I pushed the princess back and quickly manipulated metal to peel away from the wall. It flew toward her and wrapped around her, flattening her arms to her side. The heavy weight of it knocked her down to her knees. It was over before it even started.

"Do not ever try that again," I said. "I'm giving you this one chance."

She writhed against the metal. Anyone else at the Market would have been put to death for these actions. The princess was lucky the Warden still had use for her.

"Eat your dinner. I'll see you in the morning," I grumbled, not picking the meal up off the floor.

My hand flicked, and the metal fell away from her, placed back into the wall. I walked out the door, making sure it locked behind me. I turned and pressed my back against the door as I slipped down, letting myself slide to the floor. My head fell to my hands, frustrated.

Balancing upholding my duty and revenge was becoming impossible. The princess had been helpless before me on her knees. I could've killed her there and then and have been done with it, but the Warden gave me a task. I was in no position to disobey.

He held everything over me; there was no way I would let him take the one thing I cared about in the world.

After a moment, I pushed myself up. I couldn't let anyone find me like this. They would lose their trust in me. I was expected to be a leader to these people, to keep them safe.

I let myself retire to my room, locking myself in for the night. Morning would bring a new day, another chance to break the princess.

CHAPTER 8
NYLA

How far was Thalia willing to go?

That was my entire goal: figure out how far she would take things. I needed to push her limits, learn her style, her every move. She would be more careful this time, and it would be near impossible to escape from her again.

I knew I wouldn't escape, not this time at least. She was strong, and I still had far to go in learning how to wield my fire with only a single hand.

Thalia had years of experience and training, and her strength was far beyond my own.

I spent all night thinking over every detail of what happened, the way she easily brought me to my knees.

The room was fully metal. I confirmed one of my suspicions the second she was able to manipulate metal from the wall.

I walked over to where I'd seen it fly from and ran my fingers along it. There was just barely a hint of a small crack, indicating there was a panel. There would be more throughout the room. I just hadn't found them.

Thalia wouldn't leave herself without some form of protection from those they kept in the room, the captives they brought back to the Market like me.

Her capability to manipulate metal was beyond anyone I had encountered from Zetron. It was no wonder the Warden kept her.

My only question was, why did she stay?

It was early morning, I could tell by the way I kept seeing shadows under the crack of the metal door as people left their rooms and made their way to the kitchen for breakfast. I patiently waited for Talia to return, but almost two hours passed, and no one came yet.

I could feel myself growing tired and anxious, knowing what was coming. It had been far too long since my last dose of the medicine, and I still hadn't managed to get my bag back. The first thing I'd see to was asking Talia for it. I'd be no use to them if I went through withdrawal.

In the month following the war, I managed to force myself to only rely on the medicine once a day. That kept my body and mind relaxed and happy. It drove the nightmares that plagued me day and night away.

The longest I could go before I started to feel the effects was three days. I was surpassing that, and my body was starting to feel it. I felt it the day prior, but all the tasks Thalia had given me and my goal of learning everything I could kept me distracted enough not to notice. It wasn't until the nightmares returned, and I had trouble sleeping through the night, that I knew I couldn't last much longer.

The metal door clicked and slid open. Thalia appeared in the doorway with a bowl of food.

"Eat," she said after handing it to me. She watched me shovel it into my mouth.

"My satchel," I said after a few bites of food.

"What?" she asked.

She leaned against the wall, her arms crossed.

"The satchel I had when you took me. Where is it?"

"Why would I give that to you?" she asked.

I thought it over for a second. I couldn't be completely honest, or she'd never hand it over, but there was minimal inside that would be harmful for me to have.

"There's medicine inside," I admitted, deciding on half the truth. "I need it."

She stared at me for a moment, deciding if I was lying. "I'll speak to the Warden," was all she answered.

I didn't have that type of time. I wouldn't be able to focus or complete a single task during the day without it. Soon, my body would shut down, and the waves of sickness would hit.

"Now," I demanded, slightly more impatient.

"No," she stated. "Right now, you will help with other tasks around the Market, and when I see the Warden, I will ask."

"I can't—" I started.

"You don't get it, do you, princess?" Thalia asked. "I told you I would speak with him, which is far more than you deserve and all I can promise."

It was a useless fight. I knew Thalia would never change her mind. I tried to shove away the growing anxiety in my stomach, but all it did was creep up to my chest, laboring my breathing.

She motioned for me to head toward the door. I walked

past her, pausing before leaving the room. I turned and raised my hand as words were about to fall from my lips.

Thalia acted without thinking. Her hand grasped my arm, and she pulled me forward, using her body weight to swap our places and pin me against the wall.

"Do not try anything," she growled.

"I wasn't," I said quickly.

Her forearm pressed against my chest and held me against the cold metal wall. I could see the way her chest rose and fell with quick breaths. Her deep brown eyes met mine and searched for any hint of a lie. I swallowed hard but kept her gaze. Something had her on edge.

She was close enough that I could feel the warmth of her body. Part of me knew she wouldn't hurt me. I could read the anger and resentment on her face, but everything inside of me told me I was still safe. Her muscles relaxed, and she stepped away, letting me peel myself from the wall.

"Sorry," she muttered under her breath.

That word echoed in my mind. I made my way from the room into the hall, and Thalia shut the door and followed. She led me outside of the building within a few minutes. I almost expected to be back in the garden working for the day. Instead, she led me to the backside of the Market.

I hadn't been further than the land in front of the building. It was where the garden was, the gate to enter, and a smaller building off to the side that I assumed was a form of stables for the Pantherus.

Behind the building was an open field. It stretched for a while before I could see a metal wall indicating the border of the Market. It was nowhere near as expansive as the old

Market, but it was still a lot of land to put between myself and the Market.

I noted it in case it came down to running.

Thalia continued to lead me along the backside of the Market. I saw a group standing at the far side of the back. I recognized a few from the garden the day prior. Xora was amongst them, and I smiled to myself, knowing I might be able to get her to trust me a little further the longer I spent with her.

"This recently toppled after a storm," Thalia said, pointing beyond the group to a pile of stone rubble. It looked as though it had formed some smaller building behind the Market.

"What was it?" I asked.

"A holding cell," Thalia admitted.

I swallowed, unable to bring myself to ask more questions. The closer I got to the pile, I saw remnants of what had been inside the small building. My chest ached, knowing there had been people here before me who had been forced to endure the pain and torture carried out inside.

Would they have used this room on me?

There were broken torture devices, and I spotted shackles amongst the rubble. I knew it wasn't just a holding cell. This had been where they brought those who didn't bend to their will. A space for torture, to break those at the Market.

Bile rose in my throat. I pushed it back down. The horror combined with my withdrawal had me teetering on the edge.

"I won't rebuild this," I said to Thalia.

"You have no choice," she said.

I noticed the way she wouldn't meet my eyes. Her gaze remained on the ground, avoidant of the pile of rubble.

"Clear away all the stone. You'll help carry pieces to over there," she said and nodded to a pile I spotted that had already been started.

"And if I don't help?" I asked.

"Just because this place fell apart doesn't mean the Warden won't find a way to punish you," she stated, trying to keep her tone even.

Her words seemed distant, her mind picturing exactly what the Warden would do. Had she been through the same?

For one moment, my heart ached for her before reality slammed back into me.

Without a word, I made my way to the pile, joining the others. Everyone silently picked up pieces of stone and carried them the distance to the pile. It was grueling work, and the sun was high above us, beating down on our backs.

Xora kept her distance, and I barely had the stamina to strike up conversation while carrying the heavy pieces. I felt myself growing fainter as the day went by. Without my medicine, I was useless. Soon, my body would shut down, and I wouldn't be able to carry a single stone.

I felt weak, but I forced myself to continue with the task.

An hour later of carrying stone back-and-forth, and my hand found its way to my chest, clutching at it as I struggled to catch my breath. My body ached, and my throat burned for a sip of water. I struggled to pull air in and out of my lungs, a burning feeling spreading to my throat.

Part of it was exhaustion, the work grueling, and part of it I knew was the withdrawal. More beads of sweat pooled on my forehead and dripped down the side of my face.

I picked up another stone, ready to carry it across the space. Everyone kept to themselves, no one speaking. My gaze lifted as I hauled the stone up and found Thalia close by, watching me.

Little black dots filled my vision as I stood straight. I tried to ignore it, to push the feeling away. The pile was dwindling, and there wasn't much left to move. Less than another hour, and I could be done.

I tried to take another step and felt my knees wobble. Another step, and it felt like I was walking through mud. My feet would barely move.

My vision grew blurrier, and the black spread until I could barely see in front of me. My ears went next; I couldn't hear the movement of those around me.

The stone dropped before I knew what I was doing. I had no control over my body.

My eyes grew heavy, and I could barely hold myself up any longer. I let my knees buckle and anticipated the hard ground rushing up to meet me.

It never came.

Strong arms caught me, and I swore under my breath. One of the other workers must have been close enough to stop my fall.

I could barely cling to consciousness and let myself slowly give in.

"Dammit, princess," I heard Thalia say from right above me.

My heart stopped, realizing the strong arms holding me up were her. I managed to keep my eyes open one last second to catch a glimpse of her concerned face before I fully gave in.

CHAPTER 9
THALIA

THE PRINCESS STRUGGLED MORE with each stone she took. I brushed it off as the summer sun beating down on all the workers. Lunch would be soon, and they'd all get a reprieve.

The moment I watched her struggle to take a step, I knew it was more. The way her legs shook, how she froze in place, I started moving toward her without thinking. Instinct took over, and before I knew it, I was stopping her fall.

All eyes fell on me, watching as I scooped the princess into my arms.

I needed to move her inside. With everyone watching me, they were expecting me to make a decision—help the princess or let her suffer.

I knew which the Warden would want.

Damaged goods were of no use to him.

I wasn't in a position to ignore his wishes. If I kept pushing my luck, he would withhold them from me forever. I would die before he took me back. When Nyla didn't turn out to be the way to win him over, I knew I had to follow all his orders without question.

I carried Nyla inside, her body heavy in my arms. The only person with access to a healer was the one person I dreaded seeing most in this moment.

I walked up the stairs, carrying the princess with me. His office was close, and I knew I'd find him inside. He barely ever left.

My mind raced with whether this was a worthy issue to bother him with. His temper was volatile, and I didn't want to chance him taking it out on me. I couldn't risk something happening to the princess and being blamed for it. That was a fate far worse.

I knocked twice on his door and pushed it open.

"Why are you —" the Warden started, but he stopped the moment he saw Nyla in my hold.

"I need the healer," I said calmly.

The Warden stood slowly from his desk and walked out from behind it. He approached me and held out a hand to brush hair from Nyla's face, looking her over before he left the office.

My arm trembled, tired, the adrenaline washing away. I knew I couldn't hold her much longer but pushed myself to remain sturdy until he came back.

I studied Nyla's face, her features softer than usual. Her skin was a light golden beige, and the pink of her lips returned after turning pale when she collapsed.

I hate that I took notice.

Everything in me screamed at me to hate her.

I should hate her.

And yet—

The Warden returned within minutes, a small, frail woman following behind him. Her dark hair and golden brown skin gave he away was Morwenian.

"Let me look at her," she said. "Set her down here."

She motioned to an open space on the office floor. I knelt and gently laid the princess as she directed. The healer began looking over her body for any signs of injury.

When she found none, she let water form in the palm of her hands and ran it over every inch of Nyla's body. I watched in amazement as she left no part of Nyla unchecked.

The Warden stood against his desk, his beady gaze watching over us.

"She's in withdrawal," the healer said, finally glancing up and letting the water disappear from her hands.

"Withdrawal?" I asked.

She nodded firmly.

"How did you miss this?" the Warden demanded.

The healer stood and backed toward the door.

"You're dismissed," the Warden confirmed to her.

In no time, she was gone, slipping out of the study and letting the door close softly behind her.

"I—" I started. I didn't know.

"She's your responsibility. You should've noticed. Find out what she's been taking and give her more," he said.

"What?" I asked without thinking. "You're going to feed her addiction?"

"Everyone has something worth more to them than anything else. It's the key to holding power over so many. Without it, I would be nothing," he stated. "We just found the key to making the princess do as I say. No addict can resist the temptation."

I swallowed hard, glancing back at the princess, who still

lay unconscious on the floor. Bile rose in my throat. As much as I hated every bit of her, I shuddered at the idea of allowing this to continue. It went against everything I believed in, everything I ran away from.

"Thalia," the Warden barked, snapping my attention away from Nyla. "Get out of here and figure out what she's been taking."

His patience dwindled, and I didn't hesitate. I lifted the princess off the floor without argument. There was no point. The Warden held the key to my cooperation, and I refused to let the princess take that one thing away from me again.

I carried her back to her cell and placed her gently on the cot. She barely moved through it all. I locked the door as I left and made my way back to my own room.

I knew where I needed to look.

My mind raced, recalling the way she demanded her satchel. When I brought her back, the guards stripped her of everything she possessed, and I knew all those items still sat on the desk in my room. They'd turned them over to me. I hadn't touched them or looked through them, but if there was anything useful, it would be there.

I walked over to the satchel the moment I got to the room and opened it. Inside, I found coins, a key, and exactly what I was looking for.

The small vial of liquid was no bigger than my finger. I held it in my palm, inspecting it. There was nothing special about it, yet it still had my pulse racing.

A gut feeling told me I knew exactly what the liquid inside was. I just didn't want to believe it.

There was one person who could confirm my suspicions, but the Warden had just sent her away.

I moved quickly, leaving my room and slipping down the hall. As I walked, I passed the Warden's office, pausing outside. In the short moment I stood by the door, I could hear movement inside. It was unlikely he'd come out anytime soon.

It gave me the freedom I needed to make one stop before reporting back to him. He'd expect an answer before the end of the day.

Using the healer was against the rules. She belonged to the Warden and no one else. I was one of the few who knew how to access her. I made my way through the maze of halls until I found myself at a dead end. The last door in the hall was white, made of wood. I hurried, glancing around, making sure no one would see me.

Without knocking, I slipped inside.

The woman within startled, dropping a bowl of water she held. I rushed to help her, spotting a rag on a nearby shelf and grabbing it. My knees pressed against cold tile as I knelt and wiped up the water.

"What are you doing here?" she asked.

I didn't know her name. The Warden kept her locked away from the rest of the Market. She was entirely off limits.

"I need help," I said.

"I can't help you," she started quickly. Her eyes widened, and I knew her fear of the Warden outweighed any other feelings. There weren't many behind these walls who would cross him.

"I don't need healing," I stopped her.

She looked me over as I stood, her eyes narrowing until I held out my hand.

"I need to know what this is," I said to her.

Slowly, she reached out, taking the vial. She turned it over in her hand and removed the small cork, keeping it shut. The vial moved quickly under her nose as she moved it to inhale the contents. I watched as her nose crinkled and her eyes grew wider.

"That is not something you want to use," she said simply.

"What is it?" I asked, blood rushing in my ears.

"A very strong pain medicine," she said. "The kind used on those injured in war when there's nothing more to do for them. Highly addictive," she warned.

That much, I already knew.

"Inum," I guessed.

"You're familiar?" she asked.

"Unfortunately," I admitted, unwilling to say anything more.

My fists clenched. Why hadn't Nyla told me sooner? Did she think she could hide this from me?

"Wherever you found this, I suggest you get rid of it before the Warden finds you have it," she warned.

"The Warden is the one looking to find what it is," I said and sighed. "Thank you," I added before turning to leave.

Before I could open the door, her voice caught me.

"Whoever is taking it, I pray to the goddesses they stop," she started. I paused and turned back to her. "They need help."

My stomach sank, knowing she was right, knowing there was nothing I could do about it.

Nyla was on her own. It was not my responsibility to stop her if she wanted to throw her life away. I couldn't let myself become involved. It only ended in pain last time.

"I know," I said, my voice barely a whisper, before I left.

I couldn't spend longer than needed. The faster I made it back to the Warden, the better.

"It's Inum," I said after entering the Warden's office.

He sat behind his desk, hands folded on the top.

"Very good," he praised, which was rare. The calm look on his face was an even more unique sight. It set me on edge. "You will continue to give it to her. The healer will provide you with whatever amount you need."

"You can't give that to her," I said pointedly.

He shifted and stood, making his way toward me. His hand outstretched for the vial I clung to.

It was only an hour after I'd brought Nyla inside, but I found myself back in the Warden's office, my mind torn on following orders and ridding the entire compound of the substance.

"I can and I will," the Warden stated flatly. He moved behind his desk, carrying the vial I had pulled from Nyla's satchel. He examined it, looking it over. "I should've recognized the signs," he noted. "So common and yet so potent."

"I won't give that to her," I insisted.

"If you want to visit again, you will," he reminded me.

A lump formed in my throat, and I felt like I'd be sick. Everything I had avoided my entire life, everything I ran from, was coming back to haunt me.

"Take it to her," he said, and I heard the ultimatum behind it all.

Take it or lose privileges, ones I'd been fighting to get back after my mistakes. I couldn't allow that.

I held out my hand, waiting for him to place the vial in it, and the second he did, I turned, tears stinging my eyes.

NYLA

THALIA CAME BACK to the room soon after I woke in my cot. My body shook violently, craving the medicine I'd been deprived of. Nausea stirred in my stomach, and I knew it was more than just hunger.

She approached slowly, a scowl grew on her face, watching the pathetic sight before her. It had been months since the last time I let myself get this bad. Soon after the war, I tried my best to let go of the medicine.

If Bellamy knew, he'd never allow it.

When I did, all I'd experienced was pain, the inner turmoil that pulled me apart, the power that saved my life squandering my own flames, the haunting nightmares that plagued me every night.

It was enough to drive someone mad.

The Inum was the only way to calm it. Without it, I felt myself on the brink of insanity, wishing for swift death.

Thalia held out a vial, a small amount of liquid but enough for me to know.

I looked at her, unsure. It was the same as the vial I

carried and the medicine I took daily, but there was no way to be sure it wasn't just a new ruse.

"What is that?" I asked, unmoving.

"You know what it is," she said quickly.

She held it out further, like the thought of it repulsed her. Every second she held it was one too long.

I still didn't move. No part of me trusted Thalia, and I couldn't find a single reason it benefited her to give me this.

"Why?" I pushed. I'd asked her before for the satchel, and she'd ignored the request.

"The Warden needs you in healthy condition to work. You can thank him for this," she answered, not meeting my eyes.

Before I could respond, she tossed the vial at me. My hand moved without thinking, catching it before it could fall and break.

"Keep working and stay in line, and there will be more," she promised, her tone harsh.

Thalia left the room, and I turned the vial in my hand, looking it over. Another violent round of nausea had me opening the container and quickly downing the contents.

It was the only thing that kept my mind clear enough to plan a way out of the Market.

If I could make it through the withdrawal, I'd be stronger, more able to fight my way out. But without the medicine, I was also weak. My own mind would work against me, the nightmares exhausting me and my power still locked in its own battle.

I laid back down, knowing it was growing late. My eyes felt heavy, and I let them shut, hoping for at least one sleep free of the never-ending nightmares.

I woke up feeling refreshed and in better condition than when I'd fallen asleep. The shakes left my body, and I pushed myself up in my cot. No longer did nausea plague me just for movement.

Not a single nightmare filled my head as I slept. Never did I imagine I would feel a bit of gratitude toward the Warden. That was how he trapped people, found their weaknesses and made them reliant.

It worked.

As much as I wished to fight it, I knew I would do anything to never feel the pain of withdrawal again.

I waited patiently for Thalia to arrive. The look on her face was scarred into my memory when I took the vial from her. Judgment and disgust had been written all over it.

I didn't expect her to understand, but I never thought she'd care enough to feel any of those emotions. Why did it bother her?

The Inum kept me complacent, made me less likely to escape. That only made her life easier. So why did she care so much?

When I arrived, I swore she'd kill me. Revenge was the one thing she was owed. She gave me a second chance the last time I was at the Market, and I crossed her, left her there to deal with the aftermath of my escape.

I knew the Warden would never have forgiven her. It was a miracle she was even still his second in command.

The metal door creaked open, and I realized I'd become lost to my thoughts. Thalia slid inside, carrying a plate of eggs and meat.

Without a word, she placed them beside me and moved to the opposite wall to watch me eat. We stayed like that, silent, for a few minutes. I spooned bites of food into my mouth, feeling her gaze on me.

Everything in me hated the look of disgust she wore. I shouldn't care. She was the reason I was trapped here, yet everything inside of me turned at the thought.

"Thank you," I tried, desperate for anything to break the silence.

"The Warden wants you fed and strong enough to work," she stated.

I looked down at my now almost empty plate, realizing she thought I was talking about the food.

"I meant for yesterday," I added. I could feel my cheeks warm, and the intensity of her gaze on me only made it worse.

"I was only following orders," she answered without single bit of emotion in her voice.

"Still," I pushed. "You helped me when I collapsed. If you hadn't done that, he never would have known or agreed to give it to me."

"Like I said, he needs you able to work. He doesn't allow damaged goods at the Market," she said like she was reciting something drilled into her.

Her eyes narrowed on me. I couldn't take the heat of her stare any longer. I stood, holding out the tray to her. She took it without hesitation.

My stomach turned, sensing her disappointment. I couldn't place where her disgust grew from. The nagging feeling didn't recede as we left the room. It only grew worse. Thalia strode ahead of me, and I trailed behind her.

"It's for the pain," I explained, unable to bear her judgement.

I heard a small huff escape her. "I don't care," she answered plainly.

My arms crossed growing in frustration. It shouldn't bother me, but it did. No one hated what I became more than myself, but it was what I had to do to survive. Everyone found their ways to cope after the war.

I wasn't lying when I said it was for the pain. Not only the pain of the hand I lost, but all the memories of everything I'd done, the pain of my own power tearing itself apart.

"You should care," I blurted out before I could stop myself.

This was the most honest I'd been since arriving to the Market. She paused, turning to face me. She was taller than me, and her golden brown eyes stared down at me as we stood mere inches from each other.

"Says the princess willing to destroy our world without a single care," Thalia growled. I sank into myself, her words hitting me like a blow. Not a single one was false. I stared up into her eyes even as I felt myself retreating.

"Not a day passes when I don't live with that pain," I admitted. My body trembled, and I knew it wasn't the effects of withdrawal anymore.

Thalia held my stare for a moment, and her lips parted to say something, but she decided against it. She turned, leading me away again in silence.

I clenched my fist and told myself I'd take whatever she threw my way.

Weeks passed, and Thalia barely spoke to me.

Every morning, she came with food and my small vial of liquid. It was less than I normally took but enough to get me through the day. My body was growing used to the dose, and I felt relief knowing maybe it wouldn't be like this forever. If I could force my body to accept less, maybe someday, I could force it to accept nothing at all.

Today was not that day.

I swallowed the dose in front of me and moved on to the small bowl of fruit. Every day, Talia watched from the other side of the room, clinging to the metal wall with her arms crossed. I barely pulled more than a word out of her. Each time I took the dose, I could feel he resentment toward me growing.

It made her life easier, the Warden satisfied. No matter how hard I tried, I couldn't place her anger.

Thalia motioned for me to follow from the room, and I moved with no clue as to which task I'd be assigned to for the day. I alternated with kitchen duties, helping in the garden, and finishing clearing the collapsed structure behind the Market. There were other small odds and ends jobs I completed with no issues.

I saw Xora a few more times and was able to learn more about her. She told me about her family who lived back in the city. She hadn't seen them in a long time, but she was hopeful she would. My heart ached, knowing Koraine and Bellamy waited for me in Abelon.

I walked behind Thalia, leaving the room and carrying my own tray down to the kitchen. I thought I'd stay and help clean up breakfast, but Thalia waved for me to leave the tray.

We continued out of the kitchen down the hall to the front entrance. I tried hard to keep up, assuming it would be the garden instead.

Thalia walked straight out the door and toward the front gate. I continued after, glancing toward the garden and realizing there was no one around. One glance in the sky told me why. In the distance, I could see dark clouds heading in our direction.

"Keep up," Thalia called back to me.

I glanced back and realized she put distance between us. I jogged to catch up. Guards manipulated the metal gates, allowing her to pass. I followed hesitantly, expecting them to try and stop me. I was never allowed to leave the Market.

"Let's go, princess," Thalia called.

I hated when she called me that. The name filled my stomach with grief and rage. Yet, Thalia continued to use it. I knew she did it just to get under my skin.

I followed her into the forest, keeping a close distance. It wasn't until we came to an open field of grass that I paused.

My stomach sank, realizing no one could hear me this far out. I was sure Thalia thought of that already. If she killed me, all it would take was one excuse, and the Warden wouldn't question it.

The princess tried to escape, so I had to.

The Warden would have to accept that answer no matter how much he wanted to use me. He wouldn't allow disobedience. He couldn't afford to allow someone to escape again.

I slowly backed away to edge back into the forest.

"Don't even try it," Thalia warned without turning.

Her powers were strong; I knew she could sense me just through the Earth beneath her.

"Why are we here?" I asked quickly.

Thalia stared me down from the field. Her dark curls framed her face, and I watched her eyes narrow on me.

"Why are we here?" I repeated.

"This is your chance," Thalia said. "Leave."

I swallowed hard. She couldn't be serious. "No," I said.

I refused to fall prey to her games. I wouldn't give her a reason to kill me. I survived this long. My only purpose was to stop the Market.

"I'm ordering you to fight me," she said, her fists clenched.

Even if I gave in, there had to be a different reason she wanted me to use my power. Thalia would never let me leave the Market. There was far too much for her to lose. She made that clear.

"Why?" I asked, cocking my head.

"My usual sparring partner is gone for a bit. I need someone else," she stated and shrugged. "The Warden won't let me kill you, but that doesn't mean I can't have a bit of fun."

A wicked smile grew on her lips and made me shudder. She was powerful; I'd seen firsthand what her abilities could do.

"I won't fight you," I said.

I turned back toward the forest and took a single step before a vine wrapped around my ankle and wiped my feet from under me. I cried out as I slammed into the ground. The vine pulled me back toward Thalia, and I struggled to move. Panic washed over me, and I writhed against the vibe tightly wrapped around my leg.

"Show me what you can do, princess," Thalia coaxed.

The way the name rolled off her tongue made me heat with anger.

I called flames to my hand and used them to burn away the vine around my ankle. They retracted back to Thalia, and I stood quickly.

"What is wrong with you?" I asked.

Thalia threw a massive rock in my direction, and I rolled to the side to avoid it. It crashed into a tree deep behind me and shattered on the ground.

I didn't hesitate. I threw a flame her direction. I didn't want to take the bait, but she left me no choice. I wouldn't die out there.

I launched into battle with Thalia, trying to close in and using my proximity to my advantage.

My hand and residual limb manipulated the fire in Thalia's direction. It was nothing compared to the power I knew I had. My entire being was fighting against my own power to bring it out.

"Enough," I stated, getting closer to Talia.

"No," she answered, and another rock barreled in my direction.

We continued for what felt like hours, our attacks going back-and-forth. My fire scorched the Earth around me and left little flames burning. If I didn't stop them, they'd spread to the forest.

I hesitated, putting one out nearby and allowing Thalia to gain the upper hand

Thalia sent vines crawling around my body and pulling me down to my knees.

I struggled against them without any reprieve. She stepped in front of me, looking down, and for a moment, I thought her eyes softened. I blinked, and she was back to frowning.

"You've grown weaker," she noted.

I refused to answer. She was baiting me again.

"You're not the same princess here once before," she observed. "What happened?"

"War," I answered.

"Is that how that happened?" she asked, glancing to my residual limb.

"No," I answered. I saw no reason to lie. "That was the product of my father's disappointment."

I saw the pain that flashed through her eyes and dropped my gaze, unwilling to see sympathy.

"What was the point of this?" I asked.

"I needed to know for certain whether you would try to escape if you saw the chance."

I sucked in a sharp breath. Escape seemed like such a distant idea now. I wanted to destroy the Market from the inside, but at what cost?

"Now I see you aren't capable," Thalia stated.

I didn't know why her words stung. I didn't need her approval, but still, my stomach dropped as she said the words. Only months prior, I'd been stronger, escaped. That wasn't the case anymore.

The war did something to me, and now I was stuck in an endless loop of battling myself.

Thalia pulled the vibes away from me.

I let myself sink back onto my heels. My head remained hung.

"I could still try," I whispered.

"I don't think you will," she answered.

Thalia knelt in front of me. Defeat filled every inch of my body. I refused to look up and see the smug satisfaction I expected on her face.

Fingers touched my chin lightly and tilted it up. I wanted to resist, but everything inside of me gave up.

I was forced to meet Thalia's golden brown eyes. I was surprised to find sadness. She held my gaze, and I felt chills along my spine. She was breathtakingly fierce.

My heart raced, and I found myself forgetting why I felt such intense sadness.

"The princess I once knew is still in there. Fight to get her back," Thalia said softly.

I froze, stunned by her words and more confused than before. The same woman had kept me captive and brought me to the Market. Why did she care if I ever made it back to myself?

She moved to stand, but my hand shot out, holding on to her toned arm.

"Why do you care? You should hate me, kill me," I said.

"I wanted to hate you for everything you did. I thought revenge would make me feel better," she said. "But I found you remind me of someone."

She stood before I could ask more and walked toward the forest. She didn't motion for me to follow, but I did. My mind raced, and I felt on edge trying to work through everything she said.

CHAPTER 11
THALIA

My plan didn't work the way I wanted. I needed to draw out Nyla's power, give her something irresistible and force her to fight for it.

Freedom was the one thing she wanted.

I saw the way she eyed the door every time we passed it, how her eyes lingered far too long on the guards at the gate.

The second the Warden left, I knew it was my only opportunity.

I pushed her to use her abilities, but she held back. The way she fought last time she was at the Market proved this wasn't her full power. Maybe the loss of her hand had hindered her abilities, but I doubted it. Something else was holding her back.

The medicine could be dimming her abilities.

My fists clenched thinking about the next dose.

I should be thankful it made her power dormant, but all that vile liquid did was ruin lives.

It ruined my life.

Maybe that was why I pushed her to fight, to release the

building tension and anger I held for everything her accepting it stood for and reminded me of, only I couldn't follow through. I saw how desperate she was to hide from her pain.

I was doing the same, hiding the past somewhere deep down within me where I didn't have to confront it. Maybe that was why I saw so much of myself in Nyla when I pushed her to her limit.

I nudged the thought from my mind, the memory too painful to relive. I sacrificed everything to protect myself from the past. Everything I did for the Warden was to never have to face that again.

He knew exactly what he was doing asking me to continually give Nyla the drug—my never-ending punishment.

I was looking for a fight and took my frustration out on Nyla. There was a weak link in the Warden's Market, and he'd push it as far as he could to see at what point it would break. I had no intentions of letting him win.

I wasn't weak or broken. I played his games for years, worked my way up the chain to be his second in command. This would be no different. I'd climb my way back from this.

I stormed back the Market, knowing Nyla was following behind me, using my abilities to sense her there.

Her steps were slow and hesitant, keeping a healthy distance from me. I knew she could sense the way I was on edge.

Good.

Maybe it would keep her in line.

For once, she had no snarky comment or attitude to push back. Th silence was deafening but needed. I couldn't think clearly usually around her. She was relentless, fierce in a way I both hated and admired.

Bitter loathing took over, and I found it hard to even acknowledge her presence the more she caved to the drug. It wasn't fair that I placed all these assumptions onto the princess just because of my past, but I couldn't help it.

She had a choice, and she made it. She chose to throw her life away, to bring those around her down with her. The drug consumed everything and anything with it.

I wouldn't let myself be pulled back into that. The Warden wanted me to keep giving her the medicine, and I would, but that was all.

Each day, I gave her jobs and watched, but I kept my distance. It was better that way. I didn't need to know the princess. All I needed to know is that she hadn't found a way to escape.

The Warden returned within a day after I pushed Nyla to her limits. I knew it wasn't the full extent, but it was the best she had right now.

I found the Warden soon after his arrival to give a report and swallowed hard, knowing I'd have to tell him what I did. I'd prepared for the scolding I expected to receive.

His orders where to find our weakness, and that's exactly what I did.

"How was our prisoner?" he asked when I finally stood before him.

"Better since getting the Inum," I answered, keeping it short.

"Good. Keep taking her doses," he ordered. "I need her reliant."

My stomach turned, knowing that once addicted, there

was no turning back. I saw people do anything to get their hands on the medicine.

"It's made her dull. I don't think we need to be worried she'll find a way through our security."

Beady dark eyes met mine, and I watched the sneer grow on his face.

"And how do you know this?"

"She fought me," I answered.

"So she did try to escape?" he asked.

"Not exactly," I said softly. "I forced her to fight me. You tasked me with finding our weakness, and she is the only threat here. I needed to know what she was capable of."

I caught the way his fists clenched and his eyes narrowed. A mistake. I calculated, and I'd been wrong.

"How do you know she wasn't holding back, making you think she's weak?" he said slowly.

I swallowed. "I sensed it," I admitted. "It was like she couldn't access her full power. It's there, but she can't access it."

His hand raised his face, stroking at the dark stubble.

His dark hair and light tan skin made him stick out in Zetron. He wasn't from the kingdom. It was a guess I'd made soon after I arrived at the Market.

He fled the fire kingdom long ago, and I didn't know more than that one detail. It was all he was ever willing to admit. His hatred for the kingdom he came from was enough to know there was more to it.

He stepped closer. I held my breath, the closeness of him freezing me.

"If you ever go behind my back again," he threatened.

His hand reached up to my face, brushing one of my

short curls away. For a second, I let my guard down, thinking that was the end, until the pain came. It almost toppled me over, except the Warden caught me by my face and held me up.

His free hand held flames far too close to my face. Their heat burned at me. It wasn't close enough to leave burn marks but enough for me to feel the intensity.

I winced in pain.

"I will not hesitate to end her life and yours," he spoke, and I knew he didn't mean Nyla's. "Are we clear?"

I nodded as fast as I could, desperate to get away.

"Yes," I breathed, his nails digging in to my chin.

He tossed me back and strode back to his desk.

"Get out of my sight," he warned, and I knew not to anger him further. People were killed for less.

I sat in my room hours after visiting the Warden.

It was approaching dinner, and I knew I would have to visit Nyla soon. I'd been avoiding her the best I could. Her addiction brought back old memories I couldn't bear to face. The urge to help and follow orders was tearing me apart. My chest ached, and being in a room with her felt suffocating.

Without a thought, I crossed over to my dresser and pulled open one of the drawers. Tan and green clothing sat piled inside, but I brushed it to the side. I pulled out the small bag I kept tucked away under everything.

I moved to my bed and sat down, letting myself lose my composure for a moment. Behind closed doors, no one could see me. I didn't need to be the Warden's perfect solider. I could just be me, even if only for seconds.

I let out a deep sigh and opened the bag. It tipped over into my hand, and a small locket fell out.

My heart instantly stopped seeing it. I never pulled it out, keeping it safely hidden from prying eyes. Knowledge and secrets were one of the few ways to gain power within the Market. If someone knew the truth of why I fought so hard to be by the Warden's side, they would hold power over me.

I couldn't allow that.

Feelings and remorse would get her killed. That was the only thing pushing me forward. Every horrible ask and order the Warden gave, I completed without question—until the princess arrived and made me question everything.

Could I really forget the past I spent so long running from?

It was a test, and the Warden would continue to push me as far as I could go until he knew whether I would break or stand stronger. It was what he did to everyone. He had no use for the broken. They served no purpose to him besides creating weakness.

Each second I spent locked in the room left opportunity for someone to find my weakness. I needed to pull myself together.

The locket felt cold against the palm of my skin. The small metal heart turned as I picked it up. Inside, I knew what I would find: a past I tried so hard to shove away. At the Market, there was no use for who you were before you came.

This was the only reminder of that.

The temptation to open the locket pulled at me, almost magnetic. It took everything in me to shove it back in the bag and hurriedly hide it back in the drawer.

A small tear slipped down my cheek before I could stop it. I wiped it away before I made my way back to the door, ready to continue with my duties.

Behind the tough and unbreakable façade, there was only a woman who had faced a world of pain. All of this was to stop that, and somehow, no matter how far I ran, it kept finding its way back to me.

CHAPTER 12

NYLA

After finishing my dinner, Thalia led me to one of the large rooms where most of the others spent their time. There were still far too many rooms I hadn't seen. My routine had become firmly set.

Except this one night.

Thalia needed to find someone, and for some reason, she let me tag along before bringing me back to my cell. Maybe after our fight, she felt pity for me. I was becoming weak, and I knew it.

I saw the way she looked at me like I was broken. It made my stomach turn. I was once feared across all four kingdoms, and now, I was pathetic.

Shit.

This wouldn't get me any closer to stopping the Market or finding a way to release Veros from her captivity. The thought of my dragon spending any longer in the Warden's control was sickening.

I spotted Enri sitting with Xora on a small sofa and a

few others standing around them. They broke into laughter, and the urge to join them hurt my chest.

I couldn't.

Not now, not ever.

I was here for one thing, and I needed to keep everyone at arm's length. Even if I felt I'd found a twisted form of friendship at the Market, that didn't change my goal.

Thalia continued toward a group of men standing at the far side of the room.

"Wait here," she ordered when we were only steps away.

She walked up to the group, and I waited, tapping my foot and watching her. My arms crossed, and I tried to make out what she was saying, but I couldn't. The other conversations in the room were far too loud.

The man she seemed to direct her focus to furrowed his brow, his smile fading. The others backed away, like they could sense his growing frustration. He stepped forward, but Thalia held her ground.

His dark beard and brown eyes, along with his warm beige skin, told me he was from Zetron. His complexion was similar to Thalia's.

The man moved forward, getting in Thalia's face, and began to talk down to her.

"Back up," I heard her growl at him.

The anger on her face sent rage through my own body. I didn't like the way he tried to tower over her, not after she specifically asked him to back up. I was far too familiar with men looking down on woman with power. They were terrified of what we would do.

First my father, then Cyrus…

He pointed a finger at her, and it poked straight into her chest.

I really didn't like that.

My feet moved before I could stop them, solely because Thalia reminded me so much of myself in the moment. As much as her ever-looming presence was a nuisance to work around, I wouldn't continue to let men like this think they could do whatever they pleased.

Could Thalia handle him herself? Certainly. She'd taken me down easily. But something held her back.

The anger growing inside me grew tenfold when he shoved a finger into her chest. Something in me snapped, and I was moving before I could stop myself.

"I believe she said *back up*," I said, trying to lower my voice to almost a growl.

The man peered over his shoulder and scoffed. I was far smaller than both of them and immediately deemed not a threat.

Thalia remained firmly in place as he turned back to him. The disrespect had my body filling with fury. Heat poured off me, alerting me I was close to losing control.

My hand lit with fire, and I heard a few gasps, but I didn't care. The longer he remained towering over Thalia, the worse my anger grew.

I walked forward and grabbed the man's arm, letting the heat of my flames take him by surprise. The second they touched his skin, I doused them. I wasn't looking to maim him, just to scare him enough so he'd back off.

He hissed in pain and turned away from Thalia. The look of complete shock on his face was my chance. No one was foolish enough to use their abilities in the Market.

Or so he thought.

I called the flame back to my hand after letting go. He looked to the bright red handprint forming on his arm and then to me.

"Touch her again, and it will be far worse," I warned.

A slight pain lanced my head the second I reignited the flames, but I ignored it. The usual war inside me pushed me to limit my power.

"You bitch," he growled.

He took a step forward like he might attack. My flames pulsed and caught his attention, stopping him in his tracks.

"You aren't worth the trouble," he scoffed and turned to stalk off. "Tell the Warden this is the last time I do this for him, Thalia. He needs to find someone else to keep taking night shifts at the gate."

A satisfied grin grew on my face, and I let the fire die away.

"I had that handled," Thalia growled. "I didn't need your help."

I placed my hand on my hip. "Sure looked like it."

Thalia rolled her eyes.

"*Thank you* is what most people would say," I offered.

"You're insufferable," she groaned.

"And you're unreasonable," I countered.

She stepped closer and towered over me, but not in the way the man had. Her gaze had heat to it as she glanced me over. I blinked, knowing I'd imagined it.

After a brief second, she backed away and moved toward where she'd been heading in the first place.

I let out a deep sigh. The games were becoming harder and harder to detach myself from.

CHAPTER 13
NYLA

BACK IN THE same ring of fire, my heart raced. Usually, the Inum was enough to keep the nightmares at bay, but not tonight, not after what Thalia said.

I screamed for help, but my voice was caught in my throat. I choked and gagged on the smoke filling the room. This time was different. The fire felt more tangible, and the smoke was far too thick for me to see beyond the glow of flames behind it.

I coughed, trying to move, but I was stuck in place. The flames moved, closing in on me. I couldn't budge from the spot where I knelt on the ground. Beneath me, cold stone dug into my knees. The pain was enough to snap me out of the trance I was falling into, watching the fire move closer. It distracted me from finding a way to escape it.

This happened each time the nightmares claimed me.

I was always stuck surrounded by the flames. This time, it was the smoke; others, it was voices, or even flashing of images I did not want to remember.

I squeezed my eyes shut, hoping to protect them from

the smoke and block out the nightmare. If I could will myself awake, everything would end.

Instead, I found myself staring at a sea of bodies. I glanced out across the battlefield and recognized it. It was where I fought and lost in Abelon.

Bodies littered the ground, and I couldn't find a single survivor. I was utterly alone.

I let out a scream across the vast landscape. My body struggled to move, and I was stuck in place, staring down at all the casualties.

Blood seeped into the ground, turning the land red.

Glancing around, I hoped to see someone moving, any sign of life to give me hope. This wasn't how it ended. I knew that, and still, I felt the agony growing in my chest.

Within minutes, I spotted someone familiar. My feet resisted, but I forced them to move forward the few steps I needed. The long black hair was impossible to mistake.

I bent down and flipped her over.

My own face started back at me. It was pale, my lips a light blue.

The fate I deserved.

Koraine never should've saved me. She should've let me die that day with all the people who fell.

"Why" ? I cried.

"You can't keep running," a voice behind me answered.

I turned, tears streaming down my face, to see a woman walking toward me. Her feet didn't touch the ground as she moved with across cross the field of bodies.

A blue and white glow emanated from her body, and her long, white hair matched Koraine's.

I tried to close my eyes again, hoping to wake from the dream.

It didn't work.

"Why?" I asked again, this time to the woman.

"She gave you another chance at life," she spoke gently.

Her body stopped right before me, and she sank down to be at my eye level.

"I didn't ask for this," I said.

"I know, child. But this is the life you were given," she said. "You need to accept that."

"And if I can't?" I asked.

"Then it will consume until you no longer exist," she said.

The options weighed on me. Since the war, I spent every day wondering why I was given this chance. If I continue down this road, I would receive the death I thought I deserved.

Is that what I wanted?

"Accept who you've become, and only then will you be able to make the difference you crave," she said.

Without another word, she disappeared, and my stomach suck.

I'd been at odds with myself since the war ended. It never stopped for me. The battle continued to wage in my mind. I was no longer the woman I was before, but I couldn't accept the woman everyone wanted me to be.

My mind raced, and I closed my eyes again, trying to tame the thoughts.

Suddenly, I was falling backwards the second my eyes fluttered shut. Darkness consumed me and surrounded me. I continued to fall for what felt like hours until I woke with a jolt.

The room I entered was larger than I imagined when Thalia first told me where she was leading me. My heart hadn't stopped pounding since the nightmare, but this was close to a distraction.

I spotted Xora across the room with a man I learned was Bastian. He laughed, a deep belly chuckle, as Xora's cheeks turned a shade of pink. Without permission, I crossed the room to them. I was familiar enough with Xora not to care what Thalia thought.

"What do they have us doing today?" I asked when I stood only inches from them.

Bastian startled and politely excused himself. Xora gave me a nervous glance before watching him walk away.

"Am I that hated?" I asked, groaning.

"No," she answered far too fast.

"Xora, tell me," I pushed.

"It's just—" she started, glancing around the room to the other workers to see if any were within hearing distance. "Some of the others are concerned about why you're actually here. They heard the rumors during the war."

"The unhinged and murderous princess?" I guessed.

She nodded sheepishly.

"I can't blame them," I groaned.

Her lips pulled into a weak smile. A bucket sat on the ground nearby, and she grabbed it, passing it to me.

"You're with me," she offered.

"You never told me why we're here," I pointed out.

I glanced around, spotting others with buckets and rags standing around and chatting.

"The Warden wants the entire estate spotless," she groaned.

"You can't be serious?" I asked, looking back to her.

She didn't laugh or even crack a smile. We were deeply in trouble. Looking around just the room we stood in, I knew it'd take hours, if not days.

"Why has he chosen today to torture us?" I complained, with a side glance to Thalia to see if she'd noticed my displeasure.

To my surprise, she was locked into conversation with two men I didn't recognize, smiling and chatting.

"You don't know?" she asked.

I raised my brow, waiting for her to elaborate.

"Auction day is approaching," she said, sighing. "She tells you nothing."

I caught Xora's glance to Thalia. "Yeah, she doesn't," I muttered my agreement.

The last time I'd been at the Market was during an auction. The events were hectic and high profile. Every dubiously wealthy person across the four kingdoms would come. Criminals appeared from underground to purchase whatever they needed. The highest priced item was the labor the Warden sold.

My stomach rolled, bile threatening to come back up.

"You look like you might collapse again," Xora said worriedly.

"You saw that," I groaned.

"Everyone did," she answered. "We also all saw her rush to your side."

I didn't have to look again to know she meant Thalia. It bothered me that I couldn't read her. Nothing she did made sense. She hated me one day and the next saved me from my own vices.

"The Warden can't have damaged goods, can he?" I answered. It was it was only explanation. I also didn't need to make more enemies with others thinking I was somehow being favored or given preferential treatment. It would do me no favors.

"Very true," Xora agreed, nodding along.

If only everyone would see my side as easily as her.

We threw ourselves into the work assigned to us, barely having a chance to talk further. Only a few hours in, I heard other's discussing the logistics of the Market. The more I was able to listen, the faster I realized I had an opportunity.

The Market would be most vulnerable with outsiders visiting.

If I could find an opening, I could push the limits of their security, find each of their weaknesses and how I could exploit them. It was the first opportunity to present itself since I had arrived, and I would be a fool to waste it.

My hand stung as I continued to scrub at a section of the floor with a rag. The work was grueling, and others groaned their displeasure every few minutes. The Warden was not exaggerating when he said he wanted the place spotless. The tasks Thalia and others continued to pile on were endless.

Xora stood on the other side of the room, washing a stained glass window. I paused from my scrubbing to wipe a bead of sweat from my head.

"Giving up?" Thalia asked from behind me.

I turned to find her rich brown eyes staring down at me.

Goddesses, I wanted to pull her down with me and wipe the smug look off her face. The thought of pinning her beneath me made my heart race with something I couldn't recognize.

Perhaps exhilaration at the prospect of finally being the one to pin her down.

"Just taking a break," I muttered.

"Save me the trouble and keep working," she said. "There's still plenty to clean."

I stood, my temper coming fully to the surface. The more Thalia poked at me, the harder it became to contain it.

"Save you?" I asked and stepped closer to her. "The only people I will be saving are the rest of those here. When I burn this place to the ground, you will be on your knees, begging for mercy."

"You'd like that, wouldn't you?" she breathed and closed the distance between us. Our chests grazed each other, and she glared down at me. "The sight of me begging, on my knees in front of you."

The words sent a chill down my spine. "Careful," I warned. "I'm starting to think you might enjoy it."

That snapped her out of it. She took a step back, glancing around and realizing everyone was still occupied with the endless cleaning.

My cheeks reddened, knowing I'd spoken out of line. I

couldn't help it. The way she pushed me was the most alive I'd felt in months.

"Get back to work," she snapped and stalked off.

Whatever I had done worked. Thalia was flustered, and that meant she was doing sloppy work.

Another opportunity for me to exploit.

CHAPTER 14

NYLA

THE WARDEN ORDERED everyone in the Market to gather outside.

I had been helping Thalia in a small library, organizing the books, when someone found us to relay the order.

A crowd gathered outside, and I spotted a post raised in the middle of the open space. It was hard to see past everyone, but Thalia led me towards it all.

I followed, still unsure why we had been summoned. It was unlike the Warden to address everyone in the entire time I'd been captive.

"This is what happens when you are disobedient," he spoke.

Thalia and I pushed to the front of the crowd, and that's when I spotted a man tied to the pole.

"He used his abilities," Xora whispered, slipping next to me.

"For what?" I asked.

"To grow a tree close to the wall. No one knows if he

intended to use it to escape," Xora answered under her breath.

The Warden stepped forward, across from the man. All of us stood in silence, watching, waiting. I wanted to run and untie the man. His crime was nothing compared to the atrocities I committed.

Using the abilities the goddesses blessed us with was how it was supposed to be. They weren't meant to be suppressed.

The man writhed against the ties holding him to the post. His eyes grew wider as he watched the Warden stalk in a circle around him.

My gut wrenched, feeling the dread creep in.

The Warden's hands lit with fire. Quickly, he aimed them at the ground and let fire trail toward the helpless man.

"Someone needs to stop this," I whispered in horror to Thalia.

"No," she said sternly and grabbed my arm to stop me before I could rush forward.

"He'll burn if we don't help," I pleaded.

Everyone remained firmly in place. The urge to manipulate the flames to stop took hold of me. I raised my hand and the arm Thalia didn't hold, but she stepped in front of me before I could.

"Just watch," she said. "I promise, I will not let that man die."

For a second, I believed her. The desperation in her eyes was enough to stop my rash actions.

She stepped to the side, and I watched, still on edge, as

the fire crept closer. The man wiggled at the ropes that held him, panicked.

I held my breath, waiting for the moment the flames reached him. The Warden watched with a smile plastered to his face. The crowd that gathered kept quiet, every gaze watching the man.

The fire licked at his feet, and I saw him marching to avoid the burning flames. His feet picked up in pace, almost dancing.

"He is burning him," I insisted to Thalia.

She shook her head and pointed. "Watch," she said.

The flames grew, burning at his legs. He cried out in agony, the sound hurting my soul. I wanted to close my eyes, unable to bear the thought of watching, but I couldn't.

The man's gaze met mine, and I held it. I couldn't look away. He needed me. I'd be there for him, even if I couldn't end the madness.

Another cry of pain had me taking a step forward. His legs were red with burns I knew would turn to blisters.

Thalia grabbed my arm again and tugged me back, hard.

"He's—" I started.

"Look," she hissed.

The Warden waved his arms, and the fire disappeared completely. Two men rushed forward and untied the man.

"Get him inside, and the healer will find you," the Warden ordered to the two helping.

They nodded firmly and each took a side to help lift him.

My head spun, watching them drag him away helplessly.

Flashes of memories crossed my vision, of the flames that burned my own skin. The spot where my hand used to be served as a painful reminder.

The beating of my heart picked up, and my hand moved to my chest. I tried to breathe, but it came in panicked attempts. The adrenaline from watching everything unfold was fading, and the anxiety that it could've been me again reared up. That man could've lost both his legs, and not a single person would've helped him.

I was no better, letting Thalia control me.

"Nyla?" Thalia said from beside me.

I couldn't answer. The rapid beating in my chest sent my hand clutching at it. Everything around me became a blur.

"Move her inside," I heard Thalia's stern voice command someone.

Arms linked with my own on both sides of me. They forced me to walk, heading for the house. I knew one was Thalia, recognized the feel of her pressed beside me. The other was more delicate.

I risked a glance in my spiral to my side and found Xora helping. She gave me a weak smile before continuing to guide me toward the door.

By the time we made it inside, I felt a bit more stable.

"I'm fine," I rasped.

"You're not," Thalia said, as if it was a well-known fact.

The pair led me back to my cell. Without thinking, I threw myself toward my cot the second we moved inside. Xora remained by the door, but Thalia moved.

"Is it the Inum?" she asked softly, looking me over like she'd find a wound.

"No," I bit out.

I didn't want to admit to her what was going on. The shame washed over me, and I squeezed my fist shut, trying to will the memories away. Each time, they just came back stronger.

My breathing picked up again.

"What's wrong?" Thalia asked, her voice a bit more concerned.

It did her no good if I wasn't kept in perfect condition for the Warden. That fact also stung. She didn't care; she just wanted to protect herself.

I stared past her to Xora, knowing she was still watching. She eyed me cautiously but remained silently.

Thalia followed my line of sight. "Go," she ordered.

"But—" Xora started, but Thalia cut her off.

"Go," she repeated, shutting the metal door as Xora backed up.

She knelt beside the cot and met my gaze.

"What's wrong, princess?" she asked, far more gently.

I hated it. The back and forth. Always trying to guess what her intentions were. The constant war inside me to just say fuck it all and let Thalia see me for who I was.

I didn't understand the effect she had on me. All sane thoughts left my mind when it was just us. That's what the medicine did—it dulled my senses to make irrational choices.

The flirting insults and moments spent far too close to her were just me seeing how far I could push it. They meant nothing, no more than a game between us. I was her prey and she was the predator toying with me.

The only problem was, I continued to play along.

My hand moved up to my face to wipe at the beading sweat and cover the growing red from embarrassment at my thoughts.

"Watching him burn," I started hesitantly. "It reminded me of my father's cruelty."

She tilted her head, trying to find my gaze again. My hand stayed firmly in place, obscuring her view.

"It reminded you of how you lost that," she said, and I knew she nodded to where my hand had once been.

I nodded.

"Princess," she said, and I felt her hand grab mine.

She gently tugged it away from my face. Her touch was soft and warm, far from what I expected. I could feel the few rough spots from years of hard work. Her deep brown eyes searched my own.

"He can't hurt you anymore," she promised.

"But the Warden can," I countered.

She bit her lip nervously. "I won't let that happen," she answered.

I shook my head. She should want to see me suffer. The pain I caused her was enough that I couldn't even blame her. I saw the agony on her face the first day she brought me back to the Market.

"You can't promise that," I said.

She didn't argue; she just squeezed my hand once before letting go and standing.

"Someday, you'll realize I'm not the villain you think me to be," she said softly.

"That's hard to believe when I've traded one prison for

another," I spoke before I could stop myself. I watched the words hit, the pain blossoming in her eyes.

She gave a single nod and left, leaving me alone again in my cell. I curled my knees to my chest and let a single tear slide down my cheek.

CHAPTER 15

THALIA

THE NEXT AUCTION WAS APPROACHING, the first in a while for the Market. It would be the first held in the new establishment, which meant the Warden was more on edge than usual. Everyone needed to be perfect.

More punishments were being doled out, most keeping their heads down and working hard to make sure everything was up to his standard. I avoided him the best I could, continuing to give Nyla the Inum and having her work throughout the day to prepare the Market.

The auction attracted the worst of the world—criminals, wealthy, anyone who wanted to get their hands on illegal items or labor.

"You'll be staying in your cell the next few days," I explained to Nyla the day before guests began to arrive.

"No," Nyla argued. Her lips pursed and arms crossed. I hated forcing her to remain in the metal cage. I told myself it was because I knew what it was like. My first weeks with the Warden were spent similarly proving myself, but I also knew part of me would miss her presence throughout the day. It was part of my routine.

"This isn't up for discussion," I answered.

It was for her own safety—not only from the Warden, but the wealthy as well. If someone prominent and wealthy caught her at the Market, there was little the Warden could do to keep her from being put up for auction.

I didn't know when it happened, but over the weeks, my desire to see her suffer and meet her end disappeared almost completely. It didn't mean I'd forgive her for everything it had cost me for her to escape, but part of me knew I made the decisions to let her go that day.

If anyone was fully to blame, it was myself.

"If I allow you out during the auction, it'll be an even larger headache for the Warden," I said, trying to hide my thoughts and pin the reasoning on him.

"If you keep me locked in here, I'll burn the room down," Nyla promised.

"You can't do that. It's fully metal," I reminded her, rolling my eyes.

"Can't or won't?" she asked.

I stepped closer and saw a wild look forming in her eyes. She breathed slowly, and the promise behind her gaze was deadly. My breath caught in my throat before I coughed to clear it.

"You'd be insane to try," I answered, keeping my voice flat.

I crossed my arms.

"You would end up burning yourself with the room."

"That'd be unfortunate for the Warden," she shrugged.

The medicine didn't just dull senses—she'd grown reckless. There was no regard for her life or the others trapped just like her.

"Do you realize it's not just you here?" I demanded. "Everyone at this Market will die if you do that."

Her jaw flinched, and I thought I struck a chord, but instead, she shrugged again.

"Are you willing to take that chance?" she answered.

I gritted my teeth and tried not to let my frustration show on my face. Every day, she became a bigger nuisance. Maybe I was wrong in wanting to protect her?

She tested my patience and had me questioning every little decision and thought that crossed my mind.

Everything with her was push and pull. I gave an ounce of understanding or chance, and she instantly had me regretting it.

I could kill her right there, put an end to the nonsense and finally get my mind back on track. My vines would slowly trail up her to her neck and suffocate her. No one would hear or know what I'd done. Except it created the issue of explaining to the Warden how his precious new toy had suddenly met her end.

That was not a lie I was confident I could weave.

I wanted to go back to the way things were, the Warden sending me out on different tasks and helping protect the Market. I wanted to go back to when I still had a bit of freedom around the Market, before the princess stripped me of even that. Instead, my days solely focused on Nyla, the most infuriating person I'd ever met.

She stepped closer. I hated the way she stood too comfortably only inches from me, but I didn't push her away. Part of me felt more alive. I couldn't explain it, but there was a piece of me that craved it.

"You can't be seen," I told her.

"I know," she answered. "I won't be."

"Try a single thing—" I started.

"And what?" she questioned, raising a brow and daring me to answer.

"I will keep you in this room the entire time, even if I have to stay in here myself to watch you," I answered.

"Try and find out what happens," she breathed, so close to my face, I could almost feel the way she tensed so close to me.

My heart still pounded later in the day after visiting Nyla. It was lunch, and I had to go back to bring her food and let her out to help with a few tasks the Warden had piled on to our endless list of things to complete within the day.

The kitchen was filled with others from the Market cleaning and cooking. The large space was spacious enough to hold dozens of workers. It was one of the few places where there was almost always someone found inside.

Luckily, I spotted the exact person I had been hoping to see.

The smells of lunch wafted to my nose, my feet carrying me across the space. I tried to avoid busy workers as they carried plates around the room. Gracefully dodging a few, I finally made it to the other side.

"Xora!" I exclaimed.

There were only a handful of times I'd spoken to the young woman. Unfortunately for me, Nyla took a liking to her. If she insisted on continuing to pry, I needed to be confident there wasn't anything to be concerned about.

"Thalia?" Xora said cautiously.

"I was hoping I could ask for your assistance?" I asked.

She beamed at me. The nerves I'd seen before slipped away, and her shoulders relaxed.

"I'd be happy to grab you food for yourself and Nyla," she started.

"That would be lovely, but I was hoping for help with one other thing," I admitted.

My hands clasped in front of me, and I fidgeted with my fingers. I just needed to spit it out. The worst that would happen would be she couldn't help, and then I was back to the same situation I was in now.

She tilted her head in confusion. "How else can I help you?" she asked.

"I need a favor."

A few days later, I found myself in a small sitting room with two of the people I trusted most within the walls of the Market.

Both stared back at me, clearly displeased.

"We haven't left this estate since you brought her here," Lee complained. "The Warden is punishing us all for the choice you made."

"If I recall correctly, you both helped me capture the princess to bring her back here," I answered.

"But we didn't have all the information, did we?" Gryo chimed in.

Fine, he had me there, but I wouldn't let him know it.

"Do any of us ever?" I asked, raising a brow.

"With you?" Lee asked before chuckling. "Never."

"It's always something," Gryo agreed.

I laughed. The pair was the closest thing I had to friends.

"You've got me there," I said, raising my hands in defeat.

It'd been awhile since I checked in with the pair, but they were my responsibility. The Market was not as structured as the royal guards within each kingdom, but there was a loose idea of a structure. I may have been the Warden's second, but these two were my own.

"How is the prisoner?" Lee pushed.

His never-ending nosiness was like an annoying sibling. I loved it and hated it all at once. He kept me on my toes, but at times, he also knew exactly what questions to ask to get under my skin.

"The prisoner is doing well, pulling her weight," I answered, a way of deflecting.

It was true, but I knew there was more behind his question. The Warden assigned me solely to Nyla. It wasn't something he did often. This was the first recruit to be given such a treatment.

"And the Warden?" he pushed. "What does he want with her?"

"I don't understand why she was allowed to live," Gryo chimed in.

I shrugged. "He doesn't share that information with me," I stated plainly.

That also wasn't the full truth. He'd given me a glimpse at why he wanted the princess, but I didn't understand all his motives. It made more sense to kill her, to get rid of the threat, but he insisted he needed her alive.

"So you'll continue to watch her until what?" Lee asked.

"Until he orders me otherwise, " I said.

Gryo shook his head.

"Well, I suppose if we're stuck with her, you should introduce us," Lee suggested.

My eyes widened, and I almost fell out of my chair. That was a horrible plan. Nyla was unpredictable, and the last thing I needed was her filling their minds with her games. Already, I felt like I was slowly losing my sanity around her.

"Absolutely not," I said.

"I agree. We should meet her," Gryo added.

"Two against one," Lee pointed out.

I groaned and rolled my eyes. There wasn't much I could do if I was out-voted. I may have technically been their superior, but I never treated them as such. I was solely the middleman between them and the Warden. I never wanted to command them.

"Fine," I grumbled.

We stood outside her door, and I hesitated, already dreading what I'd agreed to.

If I could run and take back the promise, I would. It shouldn't bug me so much, having to introduce the pair to Nyla, but somehow, the entire idea didn't sit well with me. What was wrong with me?

Months before, I would have jumped at the opportunity, eager to show them just how pathetic our new prisoner was. When Nyla left the first time, I imagined this moment over and over again. On long nights or trips to nearby cities, I ranted to Gryo and Lee about the many ways I would find my revenge.

And now…

I shook my head, unwilling to acknowledge how entangled the situation became. Every day was a new challenge, and Nyla continued to push my limits. The Warden found new ways to test my loyalty. And somehow I managed to lose sight of my original goals.

"Are you going to open it?" Lee poked.

"Yes," I muttered.

I moved my hands, knowing neither could manipulate metal the way I could. In one sweeping motion, the door slid open, revealing the small room behind. Nyla sat on the cot across from us, her head tilted.

'Lee, Gryo, this is Nyla," I said, pushing them inside.

I shut the door behind us, not allowing the princess an ounce of space to push the limits.

"Princess," I started and watched her roll her eyes. No matter how many times she asked me to stop, I continued to use the name as a weapon, if only because I loved the way it riled her up. "This is Gryo and Lee."

"I hate that title," she complained. "And you both were there when she captured me."

The princess eyed the two men, sizing them up. She was right to be hesitant. The pair didn't look like much, but the Warden assigned them to me for a reason. When he wanted something done correctly, we were the ones he assigned. He could trust us all, and the pair were far stronger than they appeared at first glance.

Nyla seemed to sense that and shifted uncomfortably in her cot. "Why are you here?" she asked.

"Great question," I muttered pointedly to the pair next to me.

My stare remained on them until Lee finally spoke.

"We wished to meet the woman who almost ended the four kingdoms," Lee said with a shrug.

My mouth almost dropped open—as if Nyla needed a bigger ego. I resisted the urge to strangle the pair where they both stood. My abilities remained with manipulating earth, but I could feel heat emanating from my body like flames.

"I hate to disappoint, but I'm not the person you're looking for," Nyla muttered.

"You aren't the princess of Abelon?" Gryo asked.

She frowned deeply. "I am," she admitted.

My arms crossed as I watched the tree interact. My entire body was on alert. I trusted the two men, but Nyla was my prisoner, and I didn't need them to give her any ideas or information that would help her.

"Then how are you not the princess who almost brought destruction to our kingdoms?" Lee asked.

Her head shook, and I saw her glance down to the floor.

"I am, but I'm not that person any longer. So, if you

wished to find the cruel and careless women on a warpath, you won't."

"Disappointing," Gryo answered.

I glared daggers at him. The man didn't know when enough was enough.

Each day Nyla was at the Market was a risk until the Warden broke her enough to fall in line. If he still had her in this room, it meant he did not believe he had yet. No one received a room until he knew they wouldn't try to leave.

Those who never broke were sold at auction to become someone else's problem.

"Let's go," I grumbled. "You both have jobs to do."

The pair rolled their eyes but obeyed the order. Both followed as I opened the door, Nyla watching with a predatory stillness that sent a chill down my spine.

"I suppose we may see you around for the upcoming auction," Lee called back.

As the door shut, I didn't miss the way Nyla's eyes lit with delight at the prospect.

CHAPTER 16
NYLA

The auction day came, and as Thalia promised, she let me out of the room early in the morning. I wore a scarf wrapped on my head and covering a portion of my face to navigate through the halls. It tucked my hair away and hid it from prying eyes. I knew it wasn't enough to conceal my appearance completely, but it was a start.

Thalia brought me an oversized, long sleeve top in a light tan.

"What's this for?" I asked, the clothing she gave me before still sitting in my cell room.

"Your hand," she said, nodding to the arm missing an appendage. "Anyone from Abelon will recognize you instantly when they see that, I assume," she said. "This is to keep your arms concealed."

I pulled on the shirt and realized the sleeves were long enough that my hand barely poked out. I shook my head, hating that Thalia was right.

"It will do," she said.

I pushed back my sleeve and held my hand out, knowing

she had something else for me. Unwillingly, she pulled the vial out of her pocket and handed it over. I felt the shift in her mood as she watched me open it.

It was for my own good, I told myself.

Thalia would hate me no matter what I did, so why did I care so much each time she watched with such disapproval?

We walked down to the kitchen, and I helped clean up from breakfast, more plates than usual with all the Warden's guests.

No one was allowed in the kitchen, but I could hear the lively voices carrying through the halls. I wanted to get a better look, but Thalia's watchful eyes remained on me every second.

I knew she would never agree to allowing me any further leniency. If I wanted to gather more information, I would need a far more creative way to do so. Somehow, I doubted the auction was the answer to how I would destroy what the Warden created.

"Have you ever experienced one?" I asked, finding Xora also on kitchen duty.

"Yes, at the old Market. I was there for the one you were at," she admitted, more open than usual.

"I'm sorry," I said, knowing my actions had consequences for others.

Surprise lit up her eyes. "There's no need," she said. "I was one of the prisoners up for auction at that one. The Warden didn't see a use for me any longer; he was going to sell me to the highest bidder. When we moved here, I worked day and night to help build this place. It was enough to convince the Warden to let me stay."

I shuddered at her response. Any moment, the Warden

could decide someone was useless. All they were to him were resources and money; he didn't see them as humans.

"I'm glad that didn't happen," I told her. "Otherwise, I don't think a single person here would speak to me. You're the only one who doesn't seem to hate or fear me."

She let out a laugh. Over the weeks, I'd grown to enjoy our conversations. It was only short periods of time I was able to see her, but I felt like I was truly making a friend.

"They won't always hate you," she assured me. "Just give them time."

I nodded and noted Thalia approaching.

"Let's go," she said, her hands in the pockets of her loose brown pants.

They clung perfectly to her hips and flowed out, allowing her some reprieve from the hot summer. My eyes wandered to the tank she wore that showed off a small sliver of her midriff. My cheeks instantly heated, realizing my gaze lingered too long.

"Is there a problem?" she asked impatiently.

"No," I answered sheepishly.

She led me through the halls and outside after that incident. There were still people arriving but none I recognized. I spotted a couple wearing red and black, careful to keep my face out of view from them. I didn't trust Abelonians at the Market enough to consider them loyal to my brother. Keeping away from them was better.

We crossed the outside space, heading toward a smaller building I had not been inside of yet. It wasn't hard to deduce what it held. I'd seen the beasts moved in and out.

The smell of the stable hit me first. On the hot and

brutal day, the stench slammed into me. I had to hold my breath until I could bear it.

"You grow used to it," Thalia muttered under her breath.

Thalia led me over to an area with an assortment of tools. She handed me a long wooden pole with metal prongs at the end.

"What's this for?" I asked.

"To clean," she said.

I glanced around, unsure what she meant. Nothing stood out as obviously out of place. It was cleaner than I expected. I caught her eye and saw the slight look of satisfaction on her face.

"Follow me," she said.

She proceeded to the far end of the stable, many of the large felines watching as I passed their stalls.

At the far end, there were two people I hadn't noticed before. They worked quietly, organizing what looked to be breakfast for the beasts. Red meat sat in buckets, and they continued to add more.

"Dex," Thalia started, "will be with you until the auction is over."

The older of the two men turned around. His wrinkled skin was like leather, but his brown eyes were soft.

"Perfect. We can always use more hands here," he said in welcome.

"Will I be helping with that?" I asked, looking at the raw meat, my stomach turning.

Thalia let out a slight laugh before Dex answered. "No," he said. "You will be cleaning out the stalls."

My nose crinkled. This had to be Thalia's way of getting

back at me for making it impossible for her to keep me in my cell. For a second, I thought I'd won the battle, but she always found a way to get right back on top.

I turned to face her, my eyes like daggers. The grin on her face slowly slipped away, and she turned to Dex.

"I have to attend the Market. The Warden expects me to be there. I trust you can handle her," she said.

She was entrusting me to someone else? Thalia never allowed anyone else to watch me. Every day, I spent all hours I was out of my cell with her.

I looked over to Dex and the man beside him, deciding whether I thought they were as strong as me. My strength may have been dimmed, but I still had fight.

The second Thalia left, Dex showed me to one of the stalls. He gave a command to the Pantherus inside, and it backed up. My eyes widened, watching the way the beast gave in to him with such ease.

In Abelon, lessons of the beasts always taught it was untamable, a fierce creature that prowled the forests of Zetron. Only the earth manipulators were able to control it.

"You're from here?" I half-asked, half-already knew the answer.

He gave a firm nod. "I've been at the Market over fifteen years." My heart ached hearing the number. "I used to live in the capital, begged on the streets for whatever gold coin people could spare. One day, the Warden found me and offered me a new life, so I took it."

"Why?" I blurted out.

"Because no matter what you think, princess, there are punishments worse than this. A life with no food, no home, no money—it wasn't one I wanted to live. I was starving.

The Warden offered me a place to stay, warm food, and in return, all I had to do was work. I've fallen in love with this job, regardless of what goes on inside the Market."

I nodded along, a part of me able to understand.

"Whatever that makes me in the eyes of the goddesses, I have made peace with."

Even with the atrocities the Warden committed, many of these people knew nothing else. To them, this was the only option they had to live.

"There are other ways," I pointed out. "You could leave now, find another stable to work at."

I refused to believe they were stuck forever.

He pushed in to the stall and walked straight up to the Pantherus. I froze in place, afraid to follow. The large beast eyed me until Dex's hand distracted it. It nuzzled into him in an affectionate way.

"I could never leave them," he stated.

I was starting to understand. Every person had their own reasons for staying. It was how the Warden kept everyone complicit. I couldn't blame him when already, I knew there wasn't a single ounce of me that wanted to leave when the Inum was so easy to access.

The Warden found my weakness and used it. It was the same for Dex; the Pantherus needed someone to look after them. They didn't deserve to suffer, didn't deserve the treatment Veros received.

"Do you know where they keep her?" I asked.

"Beneath the Market. They have her chained down there," he answered, reading my expression and knowing.

I thought back to the isolated room they kept me in and realized that easily could fit the dragon inside, hidden away from everyone. The space would be enough to keep her immobile, and I knew without my command, she would never risk using her fire inside.

I had to make it back to her. A sinking feeling filled me, and guilt washed over me as I realized I'd let the Inum dull my sense of urgency. My first priority needed to be getting her out and burning the place to the ground.

I knew the second I started to feel such dread, the dragon would sense the anxiety that grew inside me.

I tried to push it away, to ignore it, refusing to add to her pain and helplessness. She needed me focused. If I didn't gather myself, I would never make it out of the market alive.

Each time I took the Inum, it was a risk. It allowed me to forget and feel less and less. It drove away the nightmares and the dreaded memories of war, but more importantly, it blurred my sense of purpose, and I couldn't allow that.

I had to sort through it. The urgent feeling of needing to bring down the Market was fading, a distant memory.

"Where do I start?" I asked, trying to get a hold of everything warring inside me.

I felt an all-too-familiar sense of the battle being waged between my abilities and that feeling of holding back. I assumed the Inum was to be credited for it. It came after the war, as soon as I became reliant on it, and never went away.

"Clean out each of these stalls. Rake all the waste from the floor into a pile, and then you'll use one of those buckets," he said, nodding to buckets hanging on the wall behind us. "Carry the waste you rake out to where you'll see a larger pile."

"Couldn't we just burn it?" I asked.

"Fire is too unpredictable," he said

"Not when you can control it," I said and called a small flame to my palm.

"Are you trying to get us killed?" he asked, his eyes widening. "If the Warden sees that, we will all be dead."

I closed my hand, extinguishing the fire and trying to calm his growing nerves.

"Alright, let me start," I said and rushed by him with the makeshift tool Thalia had given me.

The second he walked away, I entered the first stall. The beast inside barely acknowledged me, letting me do the job I was assigned. The smell of the waste gagged me, but I continued to push through the work.

After finishing the first stall, I realized Dex was completely distracted with other tasks. It was the perfect opportunity. I needed to gain information and more insight to the Market's weaknesses without Thalia breathing down my neck.

I moved down the hall of stalls to the far end, away from Dex.

He was out of sight, and I knew it would be a while before he realized I was missing. I slipped out the door and glanced around. The outside was mostly empty. The stables provided me cover as I peered around the side toward the gates.

My heart raced, watching the two guards that remained to protect the entrance, far fewer than the usual five or six. Most had been moved inside, as I expected. Moving the prisoners and items required labor, and the Warden would trust very few with the task.

A weakness.

One I could use.

I tried to push my luck and see how much more I could gather. Out in the open, I was exposed. Dex could spot me or any of the guards, but it was the only chance I'd get for a while.

My palm turned clammy, and my body tensed, waiting for the right moment. One of the guards moved down the wall, pacing away from me. The other remained at the gate.

That left one side open.

I moved around the backside of the stable and walked the length of it, careful to keep out of sight. By the time I reached the far end and poked my head around, I let out a sigh of relief, seeing the guards were still in the same positions.

The one walking the border of the wall moved further away. The other kept his focus on the front gate.

I moved out into the open and toward the wall, heading in the opposite direction. There were no guards in sight; all I found was the tall length of the metal wall.

It was too high for me to climb and too dense for me to burn through. I didn't have that kind of time, not when I intended to completely burn the place to the ground. The second I did, I'd become an enemy to most.

Something told me Thalia wouldn't let me go that easily.

That eliminated the wall as an escape.

I could take one of the guards hostage for them to open the gate, but if they were willing to die for their cause, the entire plan would backfire and trap me.

The auction created the perfect opportunity to escape, I knew that—there just had to be a better way.

There was distraction-less security outside. I needed to

find a way to ruin the Market once and for all but also still be able to escape.

I swallowed hard, realizing part of that may mean I had to allow many of the despicable people who came to the auction to escape as well. It was the only way I saw to end the predicament.

If I used them as cover, I could burn the place to the ground and kill the Warden and still escape. It would create enough chaos for me to slip out unnoticed and itch everyone.

It had to be perfectly timed.

I had plenty of time before the next auction to think it through.

Noise behind me told me I overstayed my time, and I bolted back to the stable. The door creaked as I slipped in at the far end. Thankfully, Dex was still distracted with his tasks. The other man had disappeared entirely.

I found my tools and the stable I left off at, throwing myself back into work.

It felt like hours before I was on my last stall. The final one was much larger, and the beast inside, I recognized. It was by far the most muscular and tall kept at the Market, the same one Thalia brought me on.

The stall had far more waste and took me double the time. The pile grew larger, and I dreaded having to shovel it into buckets. It would all be far simpler if I could use my flames.

I couldn't shake the anxiety that still had a grip on me from hours before. My heart was pounding and my hand remained jittery.

Neither of the men were watching over me, having

moved on to other tasks. If I could just burn through the one pile, I'd be done. I wouldn't need to shovel the waste.

I called fire to my hand, and for a moment, it sparked and sputtered. A few stray sparks jumped, a vibrant white, almost blue color.

I imagined it.

I blinked quickly and spotted the last red spark trailing down.

I shook my head and grew the flames in my palm. A bit of it bounced to the top of my residual limb. My head spun a bit but I ignored the warning. Regardless of the goddess' warning, I was determined to force my flames to bend to my will.

The pile sat feet away from me, and I took aim. Before I could send fire toward the pile, I lost control.

A blue explosion projected away from me and slammed into the side of the stable. The pile went up in flames, but so did the wall I'd hit accidentally.

I'd imagined it.

The flames that left my body weren't blue. Was withdrawal coming sooner, making me hallucinate?

It was the medicine—it made me unpredictable. Inum continued to have unknown consequences.

The explosion was a miscalculation caused by my dulled senses.

I knew I'd become weak, but now, my power was reverting to that of a child with no control.

Slowly, the flames crept up the side of the wall. The pile I gathered was gone, and I felt a slight relief that I wouldn't have to continue to rid the stable of it.

Smoke filled the stable, funneling out of the growing hole in the wall.

"What did you do?" Dex asked.

"Nothing," I started. "I was trying to burn this pile."

"You're going to burn us all. You can't use your abilities here!"

With a wave of my hand, I tamed the flames burning the side.

I glanced up through the hole left behind to find, on the other side, Thalia stared right back at me. Her eyes promised death.

CHAPTER 17
THALIA

PEOPLE GATHERED outside of the Market after spotting the smoke. The windows in the auction hall were almost floor-to-ceiling and provided a view of the flames the moment they appeared.

The Warden stormed closely behind me, but I soon lost him in the crowd. I knew exactly what caused the display.

The moment I stepped outside, I went straight for the stable, spotting the smoke coming from it.

Directly behind the hole, now made in the side of the stable, Nyla stared right at me. The wild look in her eyes was one of both fear and confusion. She couldn't be dumb enough to try something with this many powerful, influential people around, could she?

I heard the Warden's voice calming people behind me, and I hurried into the stable. He was unaware Nyla was out for the day, and I intended to keep it that way.

I found her quickly and grabbed her hand, leading her away from the eyes outside the hole in the wall.

"What did you do?" I demanded.

"Nothing", she said.

"There's a burning hole in the stables. I saw the smoke and the flames. Do not tell me it was nothing," I said. My patience was running thin.

"I couldn't control it," she answered.

Lack of control was never something I expected from her.

There wasn't time to argue or hear more—the Warden wouldn't be far behind me.

I found Dex at the other end of the stable, watching.

"I will have this fixed by tomorrow," I promised him, knowing the stable was his entire life's work at this point.

"She's not welcome back," he stated, his tone furious.

"No, she is not," I said, glancing down at her and watching her shrink into herself.

"What of the Warden?" he asked.

"Tell him one of the Pantherus knocked over a lantern, the hay and waste going up in flames and spreading."

His arms crossed as he watched me skeptically.

"I promise, this will be fixed by tomorrow," I said. "You owe me this."

I hated using favors, but many of those at the Market owed me a debt, ones I hoped not to collect on.

"If I had known when I asked you for more supplies out here that it would cost me this…" he started.

"I'll make sure next month, you get even more," I promised. "And then our debt will be even."

He stroked the grey stubble on his chin and seemed to think about it. Soon, he nodded slowly.

"Fine. Go," he said.

I exited the stables at the far end, where no one else

would enter. I led Nyla back inside and up to her cell. She kept quiet the entire way there, far from her usual chatty self.

By the time I'd unlocked and manipulated the metal door open, she walked in, defeated. Her shoulders hung limp, and she barely looked at me as she passed.

For a moment, I thought I should just shut her in without a word, but curiosity won over.

"What happened?" I asked again, this time less demanding.

"I don't know," she said softly.

She shuffled over and sat down on her cot, head hanging. Her eyes settled on her hand and residual limb.

"What do you mean, you don't know? I assume those flames came from you," I pushed.

"They did," she admitted. I could see she was holding back. "It was like I had no control for a second."

If Nyla's control over her flames was slipping, it put everyone at the Market at risk.

I could tell she could see the thought forming in my mind.

"It was nothing," she assured me. "It won't happen again. It must have been from the Inum."

I flinched at the mention of the medicine I provided her. Memories surfaced, ones too painful to acknowledge.

Nyla watched, her eyes searching for answers.

"I was trying to burn the pile of waste so I didn't have to move it all. It would've been faster. The second I tried, it was like something inside me wanted me to stop. I pushed on anyway. That's how the flames lashed out."

I nodded along, watching her panicked scramble for an

explanation. She never should've used her abilities in the first place. If the Warden knew, I wasn't sure I could protect her from his punishment. It was the one rule at the Market.

"Will you tell him?" she asked.

As much as I wanted to, it wasn't worth her blood on my hands. I made the choice to let her out of her cell, to take her to the stables. The fire was my fault.

"No," I said. Surprise flashed in her eyes, and she nodded.

When she first arrived to the Market, I wanted her dead. I would've given anything for this moment before. Somehow, I'd grown accustomed to her presence. I no longer minded watching her every day, being in charge of her. The snarky comments and the way she pushed me to my limits were part of my routine. I'd grown comfortable in it.

That wasn't something I was ready to face yet.

"Get rest," I told her. "I'll be back with food."

I walked out and shut the metal door, locking away all the feelings that were surfacing with her.

***

"Thalia," the Warden's grating voice caught me walking outside near the stables.

I was making good on my promise and beginning repairs for Dex immediately. First, though, I needed to evaluate how bad the damage was.

I should've known the Warden wouldn't leave it alone. My body shifted to find him staring at me only paces away. He snuck up on me without a single sound.

The inhuman, predatory silence he moved with set me

on edge. Everything in me went on alert. It was rare to see him in the open like this.

"Can I assist?" he asked.

A simple question, one that shouldn't have had my hairs raising and body tensing, but it did. What was he gaining?

"I'm assessing the damage," I spoke, even toned.

"I see that," he said.

I moved without another word, continuing my task and allowing him to observe. His eyes remained glued to me. One mistake, and I knew he'd swoop in.

"Perhaps we should move inside," he suggested. "I imagine that's where we will see the most damage."

The way he spoke, I already knew why he'd come. He didn't believe the story we gave.

My stomach sank, grasping for any other explanation or way to strengthen our story.

Dex hurried around inside the stables, and I had no opportunity to grab his attention without alerting the Warden. I needed us to be on the same page.

He remained only steps behind me, silently watching. I made my way down the center, looking for the stall I needed. In the direct middle, I found the one, no longer with a Pantherus inside. Instead, there was a large hole in the wall, looking out to the Market.

"Warden," Dex said in surprise, finally realizing we were there.

It was a shock he even remembered to take care of himself, his focus always wrapped up in the stable. It was no wonder Nyla was able to use her abilities unnoticed until she lost control.

My eyes flashed to Dex, hoping he'd look to me, but he didn't.

"Dex," the Warden answered, far warmer than when he'd grabbed my attention.

Shit.

I could already feel myself losing control over the situation. He couldn't speak with Dex; he'd realize everything.

"It looks like a few new boards is all we need to fix this," I interrupted, knowing it was the one thing Dex cared more about.

"How long will that take?" he asked.

"Only a day or two," I answered. "I can have a few people start working on it today." I tried to give him a warm and reassuring smile, but he crossed his arms and looked me over skeptically.

"Good. I have the Pantherus from this stall staying in the large one," he said and waved his hand in the direction of the stall. "But they aren't meant to stay contained together very long. They are independent creatures."

I nodded, knowing what he meant. Even my own beast was temperamental with others. No matter if I gave the command for her to cooperate, it wouldn't be long before she became anxious and unsteady. I knew she was the beast in the larger stall.

I swallowed hard, wishing I could rectify the situation faster. I never should've allowed Nyla out that day. The way she'd begged and threatened, I'd been backed into a corner with little-to-no options. I thought the stables would be enough of a distraction to keep her busy and away from the auction, but I was wrong. All it did was give her a new way to cause problems.

"They will have it done by tomorrow," the Warden promised.

My eyes widened, and my jaw dropped. Before I could argue, the Warden turned to me.

"He takes care of one of our most valuable assets, he should be treated as no less, correct?"

"I—" I started, ready to point how impossible the timing he gave was. I thought better of it and stopped myself. "Of course."

My shoulders dropped in defeat, and I knew the Warden had won whatever game he'd started.

"It will take quite a bit of work. You should go deliver the orders and get them started," he suggested.

"But—" I tried, not willing to leave him alone with Dex.

"That was an order, Thalia," he interrupted. "I made a promise to this man, and you will not make me a liar, will you?"

Dex's gaze shot to me, questioning. I'd lost him. The second the Warden promised him everything he wanted, I no longer had the power. It didn't matter what lie I spun— the Warden knew. Deep down, I knew it.

He held the key to controlling Dex, and I stood no chance against that.

"Yes, sir," I muttered and spun on my heels to leave.

As I did, I could hear their voices locked in conversation.

"So this was all caused by a lantern?" the Warden asked.

I didn't stay to hear the answer. Dex looked at Nyla that day with pure hatred. There was no motivation to protect her, not from the man who just promised him everything.

CHAPTER 18
NYLA

"Nyla."

The cold voice calling my name stopped me in my tracks. It was early in the day, and I was on my way to help clean up the auction room with everyone else.

My heart stopped, and I shuddered before turning to meet his eyes.

Everyone in the room froze to glance up the staircase, same as I had.

The Warden slowly descended, his eyes never once leaving me. Thalia moved instinctively in front of me, almost like she was compelled to.

I shut down the idea quickly. If the Warden had his sights set on me, it impacted her as well. That was all.

He approached, his feet moving at a slow place and setting me on edge. With each step, I felt my mask falling.

My body trembled, and I tugged nervously with my hand at the material of my skirt.

"Using abilities is not tolerated," he spoke to the entire room.

We'd gathered a crowd.

"I haven't—" I started, but he held up his hand.

"I don't have time for lies," he said.

Before I could comprehend, he moved with impossible speed. He grabbed me and yanked me from behind Thalia.

She glanced at me in panic, but I quickly looked away. I couldn't bear looking at her. No one else could have told the Warden.

Without wasting any time, he led me past all the gathered peopled toward a door I was far too familiar with.

He dragged me by the arm across the room. Everyone watched, pretending to mind their business, but I felt their curious eyes on me.

"Let go," I pleaded, my arm burning from his nails digging into my flesh.

"Disobedience is not tolerated," he hissed, loud enough for everyone else to hear.

Why had Thalia told him about the fire?

My heart ached knowing it had to be why he was now dragging me toward the door I knew led down to the cells beneath.

Maybe the Warden changed his mind. Maybe he would sell me to the highest bidder without regard for what they would do to me.

I imagined every twisted way they would make me pay for my crimes during the war. A punishment worse than death.

He led me down the steps, and I heard echoing behind us that said someone followed. I assumed it would be Thalia.

My heart pounded in my chest, and I brought my hand up, hoping to settle it. My head rushed, cdizzy.

Each step down, I knew Iwas one closer to whatever twisted punishment he had in store for me. My foot hit the bottom of the stairs, and I froze.

A gentle hand on my shoulder gave me a reassuring squeeze. I tried to imagine it was Bellamy. My brother, here with me, comforting me through whatever torture I would endure.

I squeezed my eyes shut, trying to picture him, but when I opened them, I knew it was only Thalia.

Without a word, I stepped forward, brushing off her touch.

Every inch of me wanted to accept her comfort, but I knew better than to trust her. She was the entire reason I was in this position.

The Warden led me through the maze of cells filled with other prisoners being kept beneath the Market.

Voices called out, echoing through the space. Moans of pain hit my ears, and I winced, wishing I could help each of them.

This was why I was there, I reminded myself.

If not me, then who?

I tried to keep my eyes forward, but they wandered. They landed on a cell with a family inside, and my gut filled with dread. The little girl with them had to be no more than ten. My feet stopped moving before I realized what I was even doing.

The father and mother locked eyes with me, but the little girl was the only one to move. She approached the cell bars with curiosity. I walked slowly toward them, the Warden not realizing I stopped following. Thalia waited patiently behind me without a word.

The girl stuck her hand through the bar and reached out to me. My one hand extended, barely touching her finger tips. She smiled at me.

"What's your name?" I asked quietly.

"Willow," she answered.

My heart shattered into pieces at the answer. She was no longer some random girl now, she had a name, one that would imprint on my memory until I finally did something.

"You're Nyla," she said cleverly.

"I am," I whispered.

"Enough! Keep moving," the Warden barked, finally noticing my absence.

"Will you come back?" she asked, pulling her hand back in and clasping it to her chest.

I paused, my time limited, knowing any moment, the Warden would lose his patience. I couldn't help it; I was no different than these people. All they wanted was a better life, a purpose beyond the misfortune they found themselves in.

"I promise, I will," I whispered.

The look on Thalia's face behind me had me looking twice to be sure I did not imagine it. She looked pleasantly surprised. I continued to follow the Warden, but I looked back again to see her paused outside the same cell, staring in.

When I turned back, I realized where the Warden was leading me: another door I recognized. My original place in the Market.

He commanded Thalia to open the door and pushed me inside, leaving her outside.

My heart sank the moment I stepped in. Veros laid broken and defeated on the cold stone floor. Each of her four legs were shackled with metal. There was barely enough room for her to move or stretch her wing.

"No," I cried out, trying to step forward, but the Warden held out his arm and stopped me.

"What do you want?" I growled. "I'll do anything. Just let her go."

He chuckled, a menacing grin spreading across his lips. "I want you to command the beast to listen to me."

An impossible ask.

Dragons took to only one rider. The bond between Veros and I was unbreakable. She wouldn't listen to anyone else.

"Impossible," I stated.

"You forget, I too started where you did," the Warden said and opened his palm, creating a flame in it. "I know this dragon will not listen to me without you. But I also know whatever you command it to do, it will listen– including instructing it to listen to me."

"No," I said firmly.

I couldn't let him use Veros. He had far too much power, and I knew this would tip the scales further. With a dragon in his arsenal, he'd be practically unstoppable. No one would dare touch him.

It was the perfect solution to his problem.

He was weak and vulnerable. I couldn't be the only one who knew this was the perfect time to strike. Others who wanted to take over his business, or even the earth kingdom, wanting to stop him, could launch and attack.

"You'll have to kill me if that's what you want," I stated.

He chuckled again. "If you won't help me, that's fine."

I swallowed hard at his words; the Warden was not one to let things go. My entire body tensed, preparing for the pain I was confident he would inflict until I agreed.

Instead, I watched, horrified, as he sent his flames barreling toward one of the metal chains holding down Veros. The second the metal heated and touched the dragon's flesh, she let out a heartbreaking roar.

"Stop," I begged.

"This beast is of no use to me now," he answered.

He sent his flames toward another one of the shackles. Veros cried out in agony, and I rushed forward, reaching out to the beast. Her head tipped down, and I tried to comfort her, rubbing along her cheek.

"Move away," the Warden warned.

I backed up, unwilling to allow him another reason to hurt her. His flames were gone, and the metal was cooling just as fast as it heated.

"You will command this beast to listen to me, or I will do it again," he said.

My eyes met hers, and I knew what she would want but couldn't bring myself to do it.

"You will listen to his command," I said as firmly as I could manage. I bit back tears that stung my eyes.

"Please don't hurt her," I begged.

"For now, I won't," he answered.

A sigh of relief escaped me before it was taken away again.

The pain slammed into me from behind. The Warden held his hand on the back of my neck, and memories flashed through my mind of my father burning my hand off, the way the flames felt against my skin. I could feel it now on the back of my neck.

As fast as it came, it left. I fell forward, my single hand catching me on the floor.

My neck ached, and I caught my breath, forcing myself to inhale and exhale deeply. The pain lingered, but without his flames against my skin, it was bearable.

"Stand," he said. "Do not ever disobey me again."

His words echoed through the room as I forced myself up.

I said nothing; instead, I followed him from the room, a shell of the person I was only moments before.

Thalia waited outside, her rich brown eyes searching for an answer. I had nothing to say to her. My heart ached at her for giving the Warden this piece of information.

"Nyla–" she started.

"Don't," I warned, barely able to keep my voice even.

"Take her back to her cell," the Warden ordered. "And clean up her wound."

Thalia flinched at the last command. She nodded silently, and I followed her, praying to the goddesses this agony would end soon.

Later in the evening, Thalia still had not come to visit.

I sat on the cot, growing worried the Warden would punish me further and withhold my meals, a luxury I had come to enjoy. I knew it was all a matter of time. This was never meant to be a long-term stay. Weeks had passed, and eventually, I needed to make my move, but I still had not found a way.

The Warden ran far too tight of security, and most under the Market were petrified of the man. He was no more than a man with far too much power, but I knew there was more to it. There was a way he kept them all in line.

Each time I left the room was an opportunity to learn more. I tried to make friendly conversation and observe my surroundings. The times I became close to learning more, most pulled away. My conversations with Xora were proof. She talked to me frequently, but anytime I questioned why she stayed and remained loyal to the Warden, even though her displeasure was clear, she would pull back and change the subject.

"Shit," I muttered under my breath, realizing I was no closer than when I arrived.

The door cracked open, driving away the thought.

Thalia walked inside, one hand carrying a small tray of food, the other a glass of water. The second I caught sight of it, my stomach grumbled, and my hand moved to it. I didn't want to move. I barely wanted to acknowledge the woman walking toward me.

My heart still stung with the pain of what the Warden did to Veros. The memory was burned into my mind, a fresh wound.

"I brought dinner. I thought you might be hungry," Thalia said softly, holding out the offering.

"You can leave it there," I said, staring back.

I couldn't bear to move closer.

"Nyla—" she tried.

"I don't wish to hear it," I answered, repeating the same warning as before.

Thalia stood, watching me, studying me.

"It wasn't me," she answered. "Whether you want to believe me or not, you will hear what I have to say."

I pulled my knees up to my chest and hugged them, wishing she would just leave. I was trapped and she knew it. No matter how desperately I didn't want to listen to her words, I was forced to.

My heart pounded.

"I never once spoke a word to the Warden about what happened," Thalia spoke.

"Dragon shit," I spat at her.

She raised a brow at my choice of words. Her mouth opened to speak, but it shut quickly to reconsider before she did actually continue.

"Nyla," she said my name, and it stung.

I'd been a fool to think there was any loyalty between us. Days on end spent together, and everything I thought had formed was only a figment of my imagination.

Never once would I have called it friendship, but I'd allowed myself to grow comfortable around her. Far too comfortable, since she immediately stabbed me in the back.

"Just leave the tray," I snapped.

"You and I are stuck together, whether you care to acknowledge it or not, princess," Thalia started. "I never asked for this, but here we are. I wouldn't have done this."

My heart ached at the words. I didn't want to be stuck with someone so heartless. The endless push and pull from her was exhausting.

I was tired.

So damn tired.

I missed Abelon and my brother. All I wanted was to make it back to them. Thalia had her fun tormenting me. Maybe that's what she craved—the power of pulling me in, making me believe there was something buried beneath everything, worth finding, and then breaking me.

Every witty comment, every lingering moment, I wanted to see something that was never there. The Inum made me desperate enough for someone to care about me after everything I'd been through. My mind fabricated this all.

"Please, just leave the tray," I said, my voice breaking.

I couldn't face her.

Everything inside me shattered, and I knew that small tether of hope was gone. She placed the tray on the floor and left without another word, leaving me to plunge into darkness.

The goddess told me to make a choice, to accept who I'd become, and maybe this was it finally consuming me.

CHAPTER 19

THALIA

The Warden sent Lee to find me late the next day. Nyla had already returned to her cell after helping with the same chores she did daily.

I was starting to work on a few of my own tasks I'd put off when he found me.

"He's requesting you in his room," Lee said.

"His office?" I questioned.

Almost all day, the Warden spent time in his office.

"No, he specifically ordered you to the top floor," Lee answered.

My heart raced, and my palms turned slick with sweat. There was not an instance I could recall when he'd ordered me to visit his personal quarters for something.

I made my way through the maze of halls until I found myself at a red door. Behind it sat a set of stairs, one most in the Market would never go up. I'd only been to the third floor once or twice in the years I'd been at the Market.

I took one careful step, the board beneath me creaking.

Another step, and I forced myself up the flight of stairs. My heart raced faster and faster the higher I climbed.

By the time I reached the top, where a small short hallway led to another door, I felt like my heart was beating out of my chest.

I walked the hall lined with portraits of the Warden himself, some dating back before I arrived. The man in the pictures was perfectly groomed, his black hair lacking little gray strands. He looked like a younger version of himself, full of life and hope, something I never saw in him now.

I walked to the end of the hall and tapped on the door, waiting to hear his voice call me in. When I did, I slowly opened it and stepped inside.

The third floor was massive. It was one giant room for the Warden himself, a hidden sanctuary inside the Market.

Inside, there was a full library, bathing chambers, a bed large enough to fit at least ten people, and other luxuries we would never be afforded.

I spotted the Warden across the room, staring at something on the wall. I walked over, and he barely moved to acknowledge me. The silence in the room was far too loud, and I shifted uncomfortably only steps away from him.

"You've done good work, keeping her reliant on the Inum," he finally spoke, not tearing his eyes from what I saw was a tapestry hanging on the wall.

"Thanks," I muttered under my breath.

I knew he didn't call me up just for that one compliment.

"Do you know what this depicts?" he asked, waving to the piece in front of him.

I glanced it over. The two woman in the piece looked

familiar, but I couldn't quite place it. One wore a long green dress, tending to the earth, and the other a blue skirt and top, staring out at the sea to the west. An odd choice for the man before me.

I shook my head.

"It's a depiction of Aeris and Odaesia when the kingdoms were created. It represents the control each had, the balance and division that resulted in our kingdoms. Without control, you have nothing. What do you notice about them?" he asked.

I studied the woman in the picture. They looked no more than normal people. There was nothing that set them apart from the rest of us.

"They're like us," I noted.

"Wrong," he said. "To assume so would be futile. On the outside, they appear the same as us, but they hold the control. Therefore, they hold the power. The same power that nearly destroyed us all."

I was starting to follow his line of thought. Without control over something, one lacked power.

"It's what you do here," I pointed out.

"Exactly," he said, finally turning toward me. "I hold the control over what many covet. It gives me the power to keep this place alive. Without it, I would have nothing."

I nodded my understanding.

"That is why I'm ordering you to stop taking Nyla the Inum," he added.

My eyes widened. Withdrawal would be a brutal process, one I thought the Warden was avoiding.

"She will not get that far," he promised, reading my face. "Just enough to remind her who holds the control here."

The key to it all. Control.

Gratitude should've coursed through my body. I despised the medicine he ordered me to give Nyla. After I'd run from my past, this should be happier news.

Yet, somehow, dread filled me instead.

I had to be the one to deliver the news. I had to watch her suffer to the brink of withdrawal. I had to listen to every plea and cry until my heart went numb.

It was as much my punishment as hers.

That was the part the Warden left unspoken.

I wouldn't let him see the dread grabbing hold of me. Instead, I nodded politely, accepting the orders. A tight smile formed on my lips, forced but enough to do the job.

"Perfect. You are dismissed and can let our prisoner know," he ordered.

I moved across the space and quickly hurried back down the steps, knowing I had to head straight for the princess.

"The Warden sent me," I stated.

Nyla watched me with hesitance.

"Where's my Inum?" she asked, a hint of frustration and disgust in her voice.

So that was how it'd be now. Transactional.

"There won't be any for a bit," I admitted, watching her reaction.

She flinched, and her brows pulled together.

"The Warden said—" she started.

"You crossed the Warden," I interrupted. "I warned you, but you didn't listen."

"And you turned me in," she accused. "What did that get you? Amusement? Revenge? Perhaps your place back by his side?"

If she wouldn't listen, I wouldn't beg her to believe me. My fists clenched at my sides.

"For the last time, I did not tell the Warden, nor was I the only one there when it happened."

Nyla glanced away and stared at the wall to my right, no longer meeting my eyes. She barely acknowledged my words.

"You will go without until the Warden changes his mind," I said, about to leave the cell.

"How long will that be?" she muttered.

"Could be days. He didn't say," I answered.

"I can't last days," she retorted.

It wasn't a lie. I'd seen firsthand how fast the absence of Inum turned to withdrawal.

"You'll have to try," I stated evenly.

Even if I wanted to, giving her Inum and disobeying the Warden would have grave consequences. I wouldn't give it to her, not when everything in me protested it in the first place.

This could be her chance to break free of the medicine she relied far too heavily on.

CHAPTER 20
NYLA

ANGER SEEPED THROUGH ME. The lack of Inum fueled it, and I couldn't wrap my head around anything.

Certainly not forgiving Thalia.

She forced me out of my cell during the day to continue with my chores. A few times throughout the day, Xora would try to speak with me, but I found myself nodding along, lost to my own thoughts.

My mind reeled with pain, both physical and mental. The withdrawal took a toll on my body. I moved slower, and every inch of me ached. My muscles grew tired faster, and I trembled each time I tried to move.

"You don't look very well," Xora pointed out one morning soon after. Was it the second or third day? I lost track; all I knew was withdrawal was going to hit me hard soon, and I couldn't stop that. "Are you growing ill?"

"No," I managed to get out, shaking my head. "Just didn't sleep well."

She dropped it, moving on to another task.

It wasn't a lie. The second I stopped with the Inum, the

nightmares came back. I barely managed to sleep a few hours through the night. Each time I closed my eyes, the horrors of the war plagued me.

Painful memories of my father and those I hurt rushed through my mind. I was helpless to stop them.

My feet dragged on the tile floor, pushing me toward the sink, where dishes piled up that morning. I usually handled rinsing each of the plates from breakfast.

The pile looked particularly endless as I sized it up. My hand gripped the counter to stabilize myself, and Xora clung to my side, watching me.

"I'm alright," I assured her.

"Then you won't mind if I take on scraps this morning?" she asked.

It placed her right next to me. I cringed at the thought of having someone so close while I was so vulnerable. The lack of Inum had my body trembling.

"Not at all," I answered, furrowing my brows.

My hand lifted a dish, shaking as I tried to maneuver it to the stream of water flowing from the sink.

It slipped from my grasp and dropped into the sink. The shattering as it broke into pieces pulled Xora's attention.

"Nyla," she exclaimed. "Are you alright?"

She grabbed my hand and checked it for cuts, and I let her. I don't know why I did, but I barely had the strength to argue.

"I'm good. Again, just tired," I said, staring down at the broken plate.

A strong set of hands shifted me out of the way before I could even register what happened. Thalia moved me to the side and began grabbing the pieces out of the sink quickly. A sharp piece caught her hand, and I heard her breathe a curse under her breath. Blood dripped into the sink, but she ignored it and finished picking up the pieces.

I reached out to help, but she cut me a look that stopped me. Her eyes were filled with worry and frustration.

Did she blame me for the inconvenience?

Of course she did.

She took away the one thing that kept me sane and expected me to continue to be her perfect prisoner. The reality was far different from that. It took everything in me to remain upright and functioning. Yet, they thought no one would notice?

What did the Warden expect from me when others noticed the new behavior? My inability to work like the rest?

Without the Inum, withdrawal would hit me hard, and that would be far worse than the beginnings I was experiencing now.

Thalia got rid of the pieces of shattered plate and moved back to the sink.

"I've got this," I muttered to her, trying to keep Xora from hearing.

Her side glance told me I was failing. I didn't want to speak to Thalia at all, but her blocking my path made that impossible.

"You don't,' she said firmly. "Go sit and get water."

The order grated against me, and I wanted to speak back but decided against it with Xora's eyes now fully on us. I may have been angry, but I wasn't foolish. Taking my anger out on Thalia in front of the rest of the group in the kitchen did no one any good.

Thalia took over washing the plates. I'd never seen her

join in on the chores, but everyone around her easily adapted to her presence, like it was common. The cold water slipped down my dry throat from the glass I filled before sitting. I watched my eyes narrowing on the way Xora and Thalia chatted, but I couldn't hear what they said, their voices low and shrouded by the other sounds around the kitchen.

"You alright?" a deep voice asked, startling me.

Enri took a seat next to me and eyed me cautiously.

"Why does everyone keep asking that?" I groaned.

"Possibly because you look ill and you're staring daggers into Thalia's back," he said and shrugged.

My head whipped toward him and away from her. A small smile grew on his lips, knowing he hit a nerve.

"Seriously, you didn't think we would all notice?" he asked.

"Notice what?" I asked.

He shoveled a bit of breakfast into his mouth from the tray he brought with him. He nodded to a spare biscuit and offered it to me. I shook my head.

"The pair of you are inseparable," Enri said. "And suddenly, for days, you haven't been speaking. Not since the Warden came for you."

"The Warden is the entire reason I am forced to spend every day with her," I grumbled.

"Trust me," Enri laughed. "That woman does not do anything she doesn't wish to. If she's put up with you this long, its for good reason. Which is impressive, because you're—"

I glared at him, and he threw his hands up.

"Different. A pain at times, yes," he admitted. "But also

a good change in this place. I've never seen anyone work as hard as you have. Besides, what other entertainment would I have without your sassy remarks?"

"I didn't know you paid that much attention," I admitted.

"We all do," he said. "Whether you realize it or not. Most here are hesitant, but give them time. You were a big change. The Warden doesn't often bring unknowns into our ranks, and you are the biggest unknown I have ever known."

I swallowed hard at his words.

Glancing around, I noticed the way others kept peering over at us. They watched quietly, but as I met their stares, each gave me a gentle smile.

"Just try to go easy on her," Enri said, surprising me.

His gaze was set on Thalia, who had her back to us. I followed it and watched as she made her way through the pile of plates without effort. She moved quickly and efficiently, and I knew her forcing me to take a break was not the insult I assumed. I would've slowed the entire process down and forced everyone to my slower pace. It would've impacted the tasks for the entire day. She was protecting them.

"She does a lot for us all, things not even you see," Enri continued. "Give her grace."

I turned back to him.

"I don't know if that's possible," I admitted, my heart still aching with betrayal.

"Give it time," the older man said. "With time comes clarity."

A little of the tension and anger I had been holding in my body released, and I realized all I felt was exhausted.

The weight of everything I had been carrying crashed down on me, and I knew without the Inum, I would have to face it all.

The war that persisted in my mind came to the forefront. Everything I used to be fought with who I was becoming. Was I ready to let go of all of that? Embrace where I had ended up after the war?

Thalia turned toward me, done with her dish pile, and let her eyes search over me. Her head tilted, trying to read the expression on my face.

I didn't have the energy to plaster the scowl I had been wearing for days back on. Instead, I just nodded a small thank you.

A truce.

Even if I couldn't find it in me to believe or forgive her, I recognized all she did for those around her at the Market. She looked after them, cared for them. The smallest gift I could give her was a bit of reprieve from all of the pressures the Warden put on her.

CHAPTER 21

THALIA

After a long day of work, I needed sleep. Nyla was still barely talking to me. Her ability to keep up with the tasks she normally handled was diminishing. I picked up the slack.

Xora barely had luck getting through to her either. She fed me bits of information, but Nyla barely opened up to her about anything. It wasn't helpful in finding a way to get back through to her.

She'd almost sliced herself shattering a plate in the kitchen, and I couldn't help but step in and keep her from causing more damage. The rest of the day went similarly, but she seemed less angry after the morning.

I'd seen her with Enri and wondered what he said, but I was too distracted with my own conversations to find out. Xora had provided me with an update on Nyla, the same as she had since I asked for a favor. Nothing huge or helpful, but enough to have a glimpse into her head. I couldn't let my guard down. Her escape would cost more than she knew to everyone else, and I would protect those around me with everything I had.

My muscles ached, my eyes heavy as I walked through the halls toward my room. My hand reached out for the doorknob as I approached my room, but I was stopped.

A hand on my shoulder made me jump. I turned to find the Warden only a step behind me.

"Sir," I acknowledged, my voice laced with exhaustion.

He held out his other hand, opening it to reveal a small vial I recognized. My eyes widened at the sight.

"Give it to her," he ordered.

The single thing Nyla craved. The one that might convince her to speak to me again. My hand trembled grabbing it.

It felt toxic to even hold. I hated the sight of it. All I could do was nod, too exhausted to argue and lacking the words for how I felt.

The war in my mind was rearing up again. All my feelings about the medicine rushed to the surface. Part of me had been relieved not having to poison the princess with it for a few days.

Could I really bring myself to go back to that?

The Warden left without another word, trusting I'd deliver the vial.

Tears stung the brim of my eyes, and I wiped at them. I hated this, forced to choose.

The choice had always been easy. Do what the Warden asked so he wouldn't keep me from the one thing I cared about. Be a loyal servant to him, and be awarded with safety.

Was I truly safe from the past if I chose to do this?

Fury rose in my chest. I knew the game he was playing, and it was working.

I was the weak link, the one he needed to push to see when it would break. If I did this for him, perhaps the pain would end. He'd leave me alone, and things would return to normal. It was a test of my loyalty. But I was done letting the Warden force my hand, making me choose to betray who I was. I'd gone to lengths to protect myself and the single person I cared about. This had to end.

I would be his loyal servant, but not with this.

I stalked to Nyla's room, my steps echoing in the hall.

I'd deliver the Inum, but it was her choice whether to take it. The one way around his game. The order would be completed, and I had won this round.

I opened the metal door and stepped inside to find the princess pulling on one of the tan shirts I had given her. The sight of her in my clothing distracted me from why I'd even gone to her cell in the first place.

"Can I help you?" she muttered, in a far worse mood than when I left her before.

That's when I saw it: how pale her skin had turned and the way her eyes were almost hollow. The life had been sucked from her, the will to continue draining away.

"The Warden has ordered me to bring this to you," I said and held out the satchel with the vial inside.

She stepped forward, a small spark of hope in her eyes. I hated it. The Inum had her on the same hook I recognized from all those years ago. My stomach sanke. I could turn back now and hand it over to her.

No.

This was her only chance. If no one broke the cycle for

her, she never would. That's how the Inum worked. Once someone was sucked in to its addictive properties, it was near impossible to break free.

I pulled the satchel back to my chest, and she froze.

"Not just yet," I said.

"Seriously? What do I have to do, beg?" she asked, the words labored and desperate.

She clutched at her chest, and guilt washed through me. I could see the strain even just standing put on her body.

"No," I said. "But I don't think you should take this."

Her eyes widened, brows raising.

"That's it?" she said with a weak laugh. "You don't think I should accept? Rich, coming from you! That would be very convenient for you. If I don't take that, I will die."

Her eyes averted to the floor at the last part. Her demeanor from earlier in the day was gone. The approaching withdrawal had to be terrifying. Fear made people lash out. Hurt people hurt others.

"You won't," I pushed. "You can break free of this, live a life free of this burden."

"Just give me the Inum," she snapped, her mood far more volatile than I expected. Even on her worst days, she still pushed back at me playfully. The game we played always toed the line of what our relationship was exactly. Captor and prisoner didn't seem accurate anymore.

"I am going to leave this here. You get to decide your fate. Take it or don't," I said and knelt to place the vial on the floor. "I will come back for it later, and I hope it is still here."

"You'd be killing me," the princess accused.

My heart ached at the words, only trying to help.

"Only you can decide that," I said.

"Without it, I'll be nothing. The withdrawal is too much. I can't face the pain without it," she begged.

I left the small bag on the floor, the Inum she craved inside.

"I can't decide for you. You get to choose, but I hope you choose to live," I said and turned before she could see my face.

I was too close.

This was far too much, too similar to the past I'd run from that led me to the Market. Why should I care if the princess chose to die? She had been no more than a prisoner.

But that was far from true. I just refused to let myself see the truth.

Still, that pain ached in my chest, and I prayed to the goddesses that somehow, she found the strength to stop.

CHAPTER 22
NYLA

THE CELL DOOR CLOSED, and I stared at it with heavy eyes. Withdrawal already dragged me down. I had to take more. If I didn't, I'd be dead by the next day.

Maybe that's what I wanted. I'd finally be free from the pain and take away one sliver of the Warden's power. If he wouldn't kill me, I'd let the withdrawal do it.

But I couldn't.

Too many were relying on me to put a stop to him. He couldn't win.

Thalia's face had been twisted in so much pain. She tried to hide it as she left, but I caught it just before she turned away: the agony in her eyes when she set down the bag, I knew what she wanted me to chose.

Yet, I didn't understand why.

She should want me dead. I caused so many problems for her by escaping, she should be the first to want to see me suffer and die.

Still, she was giving me a chance to live. The choice was entirely mine, and I appreciated that she gave me that one thing. Maybe that was the torture. Maybe letting me decide and watching me tear myself apart at the decision, or suffering through the withdrawal, was the revenge she needed desperately.

I pulled my knee in toward me, sitting on the floor of the metal room. Every piece of me wanted to crawl over and rip open the bag to take what was inside. I'd given myself permission to do so.

Yet, I sat entirely unmoved, still staring at it.

My eyes remained on the bag until they grew so heavy, I could barely hold my head up. Exhaustion was what came first, the warning sign before the excruciating pain. I could try to sleep through it, but I knew I wouldn't last long. I tried so many times before and failed. Every single time, I caved and took the medicine.

This time could be different.

If I made it to morning through the worst of it, maybe I could survive it.

I didn't think I was worth saving, but these people stuck in the Warden's control still were. I made a promise to myself, to make up for my sins, I would make sure this place never operated again. I couldn't do that if I was relying on the Inum, and I certainly couldn't if I died.

My mind raced back to the people I'd seen throughout the Market, working under the Warden's watchful gaze. They were stuck, just like me. I knew there were cells beneath the Market with even more trapped inside—those who would be sold off as slaves.

Again, my eyes lingered on the bag.

I could just take it.

The next time, I would be stronger. This time, I needed

the medicine. My mind wasn't ready to face the plaguing conflict inside it. Without doing so, I would never be strong enough to save anyone, let alone myself.

I crawled over to the bag and pulled out the vial. The liquid inside the glass bottle moved around as I lifted it. It was tempting to pull off the cap and quickly drink it before I could have any regrets. My eyes continued to watch it slosh around.

I just had to pull the cork out.

Then, I could rest and start the next day over.

Before I could even think, I smashed the bottle on the ground. All the liquid spilled out onto the floor, spreading far too thin to be saved.

I had no choice now.

I screamed, the resulting echo off the metal walls haunting me in the small room. The pain burned, and my skin felt like it was on fire, every inch of me tortured by flames.

I knew it wasn't true, but still, I trembled hard enough for my teeth to chatter.

I curled up in the cot to prepare myself, but still, it wasn't enough. I knew what was coming, and I still was hardly ready to face it.

The blanket fell off me as I pushed it back, sweat starting to form on every surface of my skin. My stomach turned, and I wanted to be sick, but I didn't have the strength to even try.

Another wave of pain rushed over me, and I let out an agonizing scream.

For a while, I tried to contain them, afraid the Warden would hear and force me to take the medicine. It grew unbearable, to the point where I could no longer hide it.

Another ripple of pain hit me in my chest, knocking the breath out of me. I gasped for air, tears stinging my eyes.

It never let up.

Another hour's worth of pain, and I was choking back sobs as I let out another piercing yell.

I heard a click, metal shifting, but I couldn't bring myself to open my eyes. If I did, the room would spin, and I wouldn't be able to hold back the sickness any longer.

The cot shifted as someone climbed into it. I felt my head move. Strong hands lifted it and placed it into their lap.

I had to be hallucinating. It had to be part of the withdrawal. No one was in the room.

I squeezed my eyes shut tighter, trying to will it all away.

Fingers ran through my hair, and I felt something cool press against my forehead. A wet cloth brushed the sweat from my skin. The dampness was the relief I sought. The cold water running over my skin sent a shiver down my spine.

I imagined my mother taking care of me when I was younger, the way she would play with my long, dark hair and braid it while telling me everything would be alright. The fingers running through my hair reminded me of those happy memories, the kind that would pull me through this all. I tried to cling to that.

"You just have to get through this part," Thalia's soft voice said, pulling me back into reality.

How was she here?

She couldn't be.

Another wave of pain washed over me, and I winced.

"I can't," I choked out, the little fires dancing across my skin again. If I opened my eyes, there would be nothing there, but my imagination ran with the idea.

It was the first time I'd realized how scared I truly was. There was far more I wanted to do with my life. This wasn't how I wanted everything to end.

The burning sent me spiraling back to the day I lost my hand.

The day that started everything.

The medicine was a shield I hid behind, but the longer I relied on it, the further it dragged me into the darkness I tried to run from.

"You can," she said quietly.

I risked opening my eyes to see how far my mind would take this. Her presence had to be a dream.

I found her piercing eyes watching me as I blinked my own open just enough to see her face above me.

I had hallucinated before trying to give up the Inum, but never this vividly. Never anything tangible that I could feel or touch or that looked so real. Most times, it was just whispers of ghosts from my past, haunting memories of my father.

My head spun in the small amount of time I opened my eyes. Glancing up at her was enough to send my stomach lurching.

I tried to move, but I was far too weak to even push my body up.

Thalia moved my hair away from my face and help me turn enough to lean over the cot. I coughed and gagged, but nothing came up. I sank back down, my head falling into her lap, giving up.

"Just breathe," she said. "You're almost through the worst of it."

How could she know? How could she promise that?

"You're not real," I said.

I thought I heard something similar to a very light chuckle.

"Tell yourself whatever gets you through this, princess. Just don't die on me."

It was the last thing I heard before my body gave up, too tired to remain awake.

On and off, I dozed in and out of sleep, only waking to throw up the contents of my stomach or from my body feeling like it was on fire.

Each time, I willed myself back to some form of sleep, but not before checking if she was still there. Through the long hours of the night, Thalia stayed.

"Just breathe," she'd say each time I gagged and heaved.

Her hands ran gently through my hair, coaxing me back to sleep.

"You can fight through this, princess," I heard her say before I finally settled into a deeper sleep.

The next morning, I woke violently ill.

The second I sat up, I grabbed the bucket beside the bed. I'd made it through the worst, but my body wasn't fully done yet. It would be days before the drug cleared from my system and I regained my bearings.

Until then, I would suffer.

I groaned, realizing Thalia would be coming soon to collect me for morning chores.

Thalia.

My mind reeled, recalling her voice pulling me back from the brink of darkness in the night. I had to have imagined it. The hallucinations during withdrawal were worse than I expected.

The door clicked, and Thalia stepped in. My cheeks warmed with embarrassment of the memory and idea that she could've seen me at my worst. It had to be a dream.

She walked over, carrying a plate with bread and butter.

"Is that all I get?" I asked, realizing there wasn't more than a cup of water also on the tray.

She furrowed her brows.

"Do you feel up to more?" she asked, eyeing me carefully.

I thought about the large breakfast she brought each day, and my stomach did a flip. The nausea returned full force, and I did everything I could to shove it away.

I shook my head, knowing my paling face was answer enough.

"That's what I thought," she answered.

She placed the tray beside me and backed away to watch me eat. It was the same as every other day, but somehow, her gaze felt lighter today. No longer did I feel the disgust emanating from her or the shame each time she brought my dose of Inum.

I finished the bread and was able to keep it fully down. After a sip of water, I realized how dehydrated the withdrawal had made me. My mouth felt as dry as a desert.

"You'll need to keep this between us," Thalia said softly, pulling my attention. "If the Warden knew—"

"No one will know," I promised.

It did me no favors to alert the Warden to my new awareness. The Inum was the one thing he held over me. It was how he thought he kept me obedient.

The only thing I didn't understand was how it served Thalia.

"Why?" I asked, tilting my head in question.

"That's doesn't matter," she said hurriedly. "We should go," she added.

I grabbed the tray and stood, but immediately, my knees buckled. The world spun, and my vision went blurry. Before I could hit the ground, Thalia was by my side, steadying me.

"I'm alright," I promised. "Just moved too fast."

She helped me gain my balance before stepping away. My vision slowly came back, and I felt stable enough to try another step.

"Are you sure?" she asked. "You could lie back down for a bit longer."

"No," I insisted. "The Warden will realize if I miss chores."

She nodded, realizing that wasn't a risk we could take. Instead, I needed to push through.

"Alright, then we start in the kitchen," Thalia said firmly.

She backed away, watching to see if I could keep myself upright. My knees wobbled, but I managed to steady myself and follow.

The walk to the kitchen felt like years before I made it. Nausea hit me every few seconds, and all of my energy was spent countering it. The moment the smell of food hit me, and I almost lost it.

At the sight of my face paling, Thalia was instantly by my side.

"You're drawing attention," I accused as she stepped in front of me.

I leaned against the doorway, breathing in and out as slowly as I could. The nausea resided, but my face was sweaty and my head ached.

The light pouring through the kitchen windows was enough to force my gaze down.

"I don't care," Thalia murmured.

I didn't have the capability to mull over her words. Her new interest in me was a puzzle I'd have to work through later. The only thing on my mind was making it through the day without the Warden realizing what I'd done.

Easier said than done.

"You should," I said, the words coming out exacerbated.

Thalia stepped back, looking me over.

"This isn't you," I hissed.

"I'm trying to help," she answered, eyes wide.

"You're making things worse," I spat, the truth stinging my tongue.

The harsh reality hit me. I couldn't accept any ounce of help from her, because the second I found my footing, I needed to destroy everything she stood for.

Thalia looked hit by my words, like they were an attack.

"You're about to collapse from the withdrawal. You can barely stand on your own," she said.

"And I'll figure it out," I countered.

She bit her bottom lip, and my gut twisted.

Stop caring.

I couldn't allow myself to feel anything more. Gratefulness was the only thing I could allow to wash over me. I held on to that and took a deep breath.

"I appreciate the help," I said, trying to calm her clear growing frustration that was starting to draw attention.

Attention we didn't need.

"But I need to figure this out myself. I don't know why you did it, but for both of our sake, things need to go back to how they were before."

The words came out more strained than I intended. Why was it so hard for me to push her away?

She was loyal to the Warden, I kept reminding myself.

She nodded, slowly coming to the same understanding.

"You're right," she admitted.

"I'm sorry, could you say that again?" I teased, gaining my balance and pausing beside her on my way to start the awaiting chores.

She rolled her eyes, and I knew things were falling back into place. Maybe in another life, Thalia could've been my friend, but here, she was my captor.

"You have work waiting for you, princess," she pointed out, and I wanted to savor the way she said the last word.

No longer did it feel like the insult that cut so deep. The way she spoke it felt like she saw right through me, saw everything we couldn't be, and understood.

The world was a cruel place, one I accepted a long time ago.

CHAPTER 23

THALIA

THE WARDEN CALLED me to his office. One of his most loyal personal guards fetched me while I was watching Nyla work in the garden. I didn't trust anyone to watch her after the stable, but I couldn't refuse the Warden.

Sylvan barely spoke. I recognized him by his ashen hair and blue eyes when he approached. When I arrived to the Market, he was already here. Most assumed he was one of the first, his loyalty to the Warden unmatched, but he never spoke.

The Warden told me he was from Zetron but born with the ability to manipulate fire. His mother was a non-manipulator and his father could manipulate the earth. It was an anomaly that he was born with the capability to control flames.

He was cast aside by his family, and now, he bore the scars of burns on his hands and legs to remember it all.

The Warden found him and took him in, the same as others. I didn't know whether the story was true or not. Sylvan never spoke enough to ask.

I gave a quick glance back at Nyla before leaving him with her.

Each day, she was starting to settle in more. It should've made me happy to see, but all I felt was dread. I'd been through the same process, broken until I gave in. If she continued, she'd never leave.

That thought should've uplifted my spirits, but it didn't, and I hated that. My loyalty to the Warden was unquestionable. Years had passed, and nothing had forced me to question my place at the Market.

Until her.

The Warden wanted her to bend to his will. She barely spoke of why, if she knew at all. I only understood pieces of the bigger picture. The Warden never trusted me with his full plans.

But there was always one.

That, I was sure of. The longer it went without it becoming apparent, the more worried I grew.

The more confused I grew even thinking about it, I knew I had to be going mad. The summer sun had to be getting to me.

I weaved through the estate to his office and knocked on door. I heard the muffled sound of his voice behind it, beckoning me in.

"You asked for me?" I asked, walking inside.

I wanted to get it over with and returned to watching over Nyla. She was my responsibility, and I hated being away for even a second. If something went wrong…

I told myself it was because of my duty, but I was starting to believe that reasoning less and less..

"I have an assignment for you," he stated.

He was reading in an armchair in the corner of the office, barely glancing up.

"And what would that be?" I asked.

My entire focus had been the princess, and he hadn't assigned me to anything in weeks. Even Lee and Gryo were growing restless. I wanted desperately to get back to my normal, but that also meant delegating Nyla to someone else, and I couldn't take that chance either.

"There's someone who owes me. I'm sending you to collect," he said.

"You can't send someone else? The princess–" I started to remind him.

"You're taking her with you," he interrupted.

I didn't want to play his game, but I didn't have a choice. "Why?"

"If she doesn't want her dragon tortured and or her Inum cut off, then she'll cooperate. She'll be of use to you," he explained.

I swallowed, trying to hide my emotions from my face, knowing Nyla was no longer taking the Inum he thought he was controlling her with. I didn't know how to balance the two sides I was torn between. I was loyal to the Warden, but I couldn't continue to perpetuate her use of it. Not after everything I had run from in my past. It would be betrayal to myself if I did.

That was it.

No more favors to the princess.

I was a loyal servant to the Warden. I couldn't continue down this path.

"Why does she need to come?" I pushed.

"It doesn't matter. What does matter is I need you to keep her controlled. We need her."

I was tired of the lies and hidden motives. I'd given years to the Warden with little in return.

"For what?" I demanded.

His brow raised at the tone of my voice. My hands drifted behind my back, clasping, and I averted my eyes.

"How much do you know of dragons?" he asked.

Beyond the basics, I couldn't say much. The beasts mainly resided in Abelon. Until recently, I hadn't so much as seen one in person.

"Little," I answered.

"They are bonded to their rider, similar to the way you are to your Pantherus," he explained. "A dragon won't take commands from just anyone. They know everything their rider feels. They can sense them even from a distance. It is almost impossible to tame one that already has a rider."

Almost.

I didn't miss the way he emphasized the word.

My stomach sank watching the eager look grow on his face.

"Not even if the rider were to die?" I asked, dreading the answer.

He shook his head.

"So you want to use her for what exactly? To force her to let you manipulate her dragon?"

"It's not that simple," he answered.

"She'll never do it," I snapped, not meaning for the words to spill out so harsh.

He paused, walking closer to me. His hand drifted to my

face and tipped my chin up. I cringed but refused to look away.

"She already did."

His brown eyes held mine, and I saw the pure hatred in them.

"You will listen to my orders and continue to break her. Keep her reliant on the Inum and watch her closely. It won't be until she is on the brink of giving in that we have truly accomplished anything."

He held up his other hand and called a flame to the tip of his finger. It danced there before he brought it closer to my face. His grip tightened on my chin, holding me in place so I could not move.

The fire kissed my skin and burned. I tried to pull away, but he held firm.

"Do not ever question me again, Thalia," he warned. "You have more freedom than anyone here, but that can all disappear."

<hr>

I walked to the stable after returning Nyla to her cell for the night. I still hadn't told her we'd be leaving. She still needed rest after the withdrawal, and I knew this might be her last peaceful night's sleep before a few days on the road.

The stable was quiet as I approached. The dipping sun sent most people back inside for the evening.

My hand reached out for the door and pulled it open with a slight creak. Inside, the Pantheruses shuffled in their stalls. Some let out small grumbles as I passed. I knew my own sat at the far end.

I heard shuffling ahead and paused. Dex appeared, closing a stall at the end behind him. His eyes widened as he saw me, and his hand clung to his chest.

"You startled me, Thalia," he said.

The sight of him filled me with more rage than I cared to admit. I knew he was the one who told the Warden about Thalia, the reason I was forced to withhold the Inum from her and torture her for days.

Weeks prior, it would have been everything I wanted, but now…

I paused.

Now, I didn't know what I wanted, only how I felt in the moment.

And that was pure anger.

"Shit," Dex muttered, seeing the fury growing across my features.

"You told me you'd keep quiet," I accused.

"The Warden already knew," he countered.

"No, he didn't," I said. "You confirmed what he suspected, but without that, he had nothing!"

Dex took a few steps back.

The nerves were written on his face. Seeing him panicking in my presence gave me a moment of satisfaction. There was little I asked for from those at the Market, and this felt like a direct betrayal.

"I–" he stuttered. "I didn't mean to–"

"To what? Give the Warden what he wanted, thinking it would help you?" I asked. "Or didn't mean to infuriate me because now you'll lose access to all the favors I've been dishing out over the years?"

The words fell out of my mouth before I could stop

them. It had nothing to do with Nyla; at this point, his actions felt like a stab in the back. I'd stood up for him countless times, defended him working in the stable all day when the Warden thought him to be useless. This…

This hurt.

"I'm hear to prepare Olia for travel I'll be taking the next few days," I said, walking toward him.

"Thalia, I'm sorry," he started.

I brushed by him, ignoring the words. My feet carried me to the end of the stables, where I found my Pantherus.

She moved immediately to the edge of the stall to let me run a hand along her short, smooth fur. The sleek black beast let out a small sound of appreciation. That praise alone was enough to make me forget about Dex and push past the anger dragging me down.

I couldn't let the Warden control my emotions. Everything, all the way down to winning over Dex, was a test and manipulation. He'd test my loyalty, see how I reacted. Him sending me on this trip so soon after was enough for me to realize he wanted me to explode at Dex.

If I did, it was the confirmation he needed to realize I was no longer the obedient second in command.

He was smart enough to suspect it, to see the signs. Like with Dex, he just needed the confirmation to act on it. Otherwise, the game wasn't as satisfying to him. Everything was a game; he always needed to be one move ahead. Killing me served no purpose to achieving that, and ridding the Market of me didn't either.

Many of those still at the Market were loyal to me. Just removing me without proof of betrayal to the Market risked others turning on him.

I knew that fact alone kept me alive.

On top of that, he still had the key to controlling my loyalty. I couldn't risk that either. It was why I continued to follow his orders and go through the motions. Anything to allow me to see the one thing I loved most.

I moved away from the stall and found a small satchel, shoving supplies to care for Olia inside. Once I finished, I set it aside to grab in the morning.

Dex joined me where I stood and tried to place a hand on my shoulder, but I shook it off.

"Do not ever touch me again," I warned, my tone deadly.

"Thalia, I truly am sorry," he whispered weakly. "We're all just trying to survive here."

"And you chose wrong to do so," I spoke before striding out of the stable.

CHAPTER 24
NYLA

THALIA CAME EARLY in the morning. She'd barely spoken to me since the incident, and I assumed she'd drop off food and leave until it was time for me to help around the Market.

"Come," she called. "We're leaving."

"What?" I said, following her out of the cell.

She handed a cheese pastry to me and continued walking. It wasn't until we were down on the ground floor, in the grand entry, that I caught up to her.

I finished the last bite of food and reached out to grab her arm.

Her body tensed at my touch, and she quickly pulled away.

"Where are we going?"I asked.

"I have to leave to do something for the Warden, and you're coming," she answered.

My stomach sank. I should've been full of excitement, but I wasn't. Everything had been off since my withdrawal and the incident. Was this finally it? The moment she'd kill me?

"I'm not going until you tell me where," I insisted, stopping in place.

"You don't have a choice," she said.

"Actually, I do," I said. "Either tell me or force me."

The ultimatum hung in the air between us. She sighed heavily.

"We're going to collect a debt," she said simply. "And the Warden ordered that you join me, so I can't leave you here, as much as I'd like to," she grumbled.

Those last words stung. For a second, I thought they felt forced. Maybe I was making it up, but it was like she didn't believe them. Maybe I was far too desperate for her approval.

I held her rich eyes for a moment before deciding she was telling the truth.

She led us outside, and I followed until I realized exactly where we were heading.

The stable was the last place I wanted to be when Thalia led me outside. I paused by the doors as she stepped inside. The last time I'd been here, my fire had lost control.

The memory still haunted me weeks later.

The nightmares of losing further control and hurting those around me plagued me. Without the Inum, I knew it would grow far worse.

"Are you coming?" Thalia asked, holding the door open.

"Yes," I answered, wiping a bead of sweat forming on my head away.

"Are you feeling faint?" she asked, her features turning to worry.

"No it's just—" I started, but I didn't have the words to describe it.

She paused, assessing me, and for a second, I felt like she could read through every thought I had. The door shut when she let go and moved toward me. She reached out her hand and took mine.

The warmth of her skin touching mine sent chills racing up my arm. She pulled me forward, guiding us both through the doors. The second we stepped inside, she gave my hand a firm squeeze and continued to lead me to the very last stall.

It was solely to keep me moving. I was a nuisance, a hindrance to her task, and this was the easiest solution.

There was no other explanation for why her hand remained firmly grasping my own.

The way my stomach flipped in reaction was confusing enough to distract me from the fears that had taken hold of me only minutes before.

She let me go to grab a satchel from the table at the end and handed it to me.

I sat on the back of the Pantherus for what felt like hours. We moved slow enough that I could keep my balance without clinging to Thalia. A few times, I almost lost it and wrapped my arms quickly around her, only to remove them just as fast. I could feel the way she tensed beneath my touch each time it happened.

I heard the disgust loud and clear.

The road was clear for most of the journey. We only

passed a few others from Zetron. I wasn't entirely confident where we were heading. The only thing I knew was it was the opposite direction from the capital.

"How much further?" I asked.

"If we keep this place, we'll be there around sundown," she answered.

Thalia barely spoke to me the entire ride. Since my incident in the stable, I felt she was avoiding me. Every day, she did the bare minimum—she brought me my food, let me out to help around the Market with chores and jobs, and then locked me back just as quickly.

Each time I tried to speak to her, she brushed it off. This felt no different.

My mind wandered back to the single night I thought would change everything. Thalia had been there, not allowing me to withdraw alone from the Inum. She'd been there when one else could pull me from it.

I hated the way that made my heart beat a bit faster. It was hopeless. That small spark in me that started to care knew it would only end in pain.

Thalia hated me.

"What?" Thalia asked.

"Huh?"

I'd been lost to my thoughts too long, her voice pulling me back.

"I can feel the way you tensed. You're trembling now."

My cheeks heated, and I was glad I was behind her so she couldn't see. I placed my hand on my thigh and found she was right. Inhaling for a few seconds and letting out a large exhale, I attempted to calm myself.

"Just growing anxious, wondering where you're taking me," I lied.

Even I didn't believe the words coming out of my mouth.

"Mhm," she muttered in front of me. Everything in my soul screamed for me to ask her the question that burned in the back of my mind. Multiple times, she helped me. When I first arrived at the Market, she promised revenge, and I was certain it would mean my death. I likely deserved it. I'd seen what the Warden's punishments looked like for weeks at the Market.

I swallowed hard and clenched my fist.

"Why did do you do it?" I asked.

"What?" she responded, and I saw her head move to glimpse back at me. Her brown eyes met mine for a second.

"Why did you come that night?" I asked.

The second the words fell from my lips, a knot formed in my stomach.

Maybe she'd wanted to see me suffer. Maybe she'd prayed to the goddesses for the withdrawal to take me. Or maybe I truly had dreamt it all.

"You needed someone," she said, as if it were obvious.

"You didn't have to come," I pointed out.

"I would never let someone fall to the Inum if I could help it," she breathed, her words distant.

My entire body tensed again. The scenery around us passed in a blur, and the only thing I could do was keep my eyes on Thalia. It took everything in me not to reach out to her. I could cross that line.

My captor, I reminded myself. Everything I was feeling

had to be a result of the Inum no longer dulling my senses. I hadn't allowed myself to feel in months.

A trick of my mind, desperate for someone to care.

That wasn't Thalia. She was loyal to the Warden.

It couldn't be her.

I reminded myself over and over until I felt a sickening feeling wash over me.

"The Warden ordered you to give me the Inum," I pushed, needing her to answer. She told me as much herself, but I needed to hear the words, to remind myself who she truly was.

"There are some things even the Warden cannot force me to do. My actions may cost me, but it was not a line I was willing to cross," she answered.

From the way she said it, I knew she was stuck, same as I was. Even after years at the Market, the Warden had her in a firm grasp.

"Sorry," I said.

It was the only thing I could think to say.

"So am I," she answered and went back to riding silently.

It wasn't long before we got to our destination, and the sun was dipping under the horizon. The sky grew dark above us, almost a bluish purple. I kept quiet as Thalia navigated the streets of the city we entered.

It was similar to the capital but smaller. There was no palace in sight, and the streets were filled with tiny apartments and stone houses.

There were still the familiar dirt and cobblestone roads, and the lively shops were filled with patrons, but I knew we were in an entirely new place.

We passed by a tavern, and I heard cheers from inside as people celebrated the night. I swallowed, wishing I could be one of them. The freedom was tempting.

Thalia gave me a chance once to escape, and I completely disregarded it. With Inum in my grasp at the time, it was far too tempting to stay.

Thanks to her, I no longer relied on the medicine that kept my senses dulled.

If I wanted, I could try to escape, but Thalia would never allow it. She was strong, and I still wasn't convinced my abilities were back to what they were before the war. I needed every ounce of strength I had if I was going to face her.

Somehow, I knew that wasn't a choice.

I'd grown to care for her, whether I wanted to admit it or not. A good part of me didn't want to hurt her.

The Pantherus walked through the streets, and people avoided us when they saw the beast approaching. I wasn't sure how Thalia knew where she was going, but she seemed to have her sights set on something.

CHAPTER 25
THALIA

THE CITY of Huile was smaller than Gralar but still one of the larger cities in Zetron.

Lush forests surrounded the city, but inside were bustling businesses, and many residents filling the streets.

Markets popped up on multiple roads, and people moved out of the way for my beast passing through. Olia's large presence drew attention, but most moved on after a curious glance.

The Warden had given me the name of a business and general location of where to find it. This wasn't my first trip to Huile, and I was confident I knew where I was going.

Nyla sat behind me, quietly taking in the city. I wanted to point out small details to her and share a bit of the kingdom I'd come to love, but since she'd stopped taking the Inum, we'd been stuck in a strange place.

The second she'd made the decision, I'd found a new respect for the princess, one I should've always had, but my rage blinded me.

Over the past weeks, I was coming to see the error in my

ways. The Warden couldn't be my solution forever, and Nyla opened my eyes to that, whether she realized it or not. Her withdrawal was the final straw.

If she could break free of what shackled her, maybe I could too.

I couldn't voice that to her, though.

There was so much I couldn't tell her, even though she deserved answers. I hadn't figured them out fully myself. The one thing I did know was she reminded me so much of myself. Seeing her find freedom from the Inum, I wanted a taste of that too.

Freedom from the Warden.

We turned onto a street I recognized, and I spotted a nearby post to tie off Olia. I guided the beast over to the shaded spot and tied her rope to the wooden pole.

It was more of a formality than actual precaution. She could easily leave if she wished, but she wouldn't, not without my command.

"We walk the rest of the way," I said, jumping down and holding out a hand to Nyla.

She took it and slid down.

I led us up the stone street and kept watch for the sign. The Warden gave me the name of the shop and not much else.

Nyla took in every detail of the city, dragging her feet as she walked. I tried to keep patient with her slowing the pace, but part of me was anxious to finish the job and get back.

The task was far too simple. The Warden never gave me minuscule tasks like this. It put me on edge.

The sign was painted black with white lettering, and I

spotted it from a few shops away as we neared the end of the street. The words *Sephi's Gems* was written across it.

A jewelry and precious stones shop wasn't uncommon in a city this size, but if they did business with the Warden, it was more than that. It was a business to cover for moving illegal items through the kingdom, a shop to sell fake gems while funneling the real ones to the Market, or even just an outpost for the Warden to use as he wanted.

I swallowed, hating not knowing which I would walk in to.

We walked up to the wooden front door, and pushed inside. A small bell chimed to signal our entrance. Nyla tensed behind me, taking in the shop.

We walked through it, finding everything from necklaces to gems to any accessory one could dream of.

The only thing it lacked was people.

The eerie quietness set off alarms in my head.

Nyla walked the length of the store, and I watched her fingers brush against necklaces as she examined a few. They swayed as she moved on from them. I pushed onward into the store, toward the back, where I could see a doorway.

A crash to my right froze me in my path, and I caught sight of Nyla scrambling to pick up a display of jewelry she knocked over. My lips pulled into a thin smile. For a princess, she looked entirely out of place in the shop. Her discomfort was obvious, and I held back a laugh, witnessing the princess who almost destroyed the world defeated by a simple jewelry shop.

"What?" Nyla asked, catching a glance in my direction.

I shook my head, starting toward the door again. My

path was quickly blocked by Nyla. Her hand rested on her hip, and she glared up at me.

"Why are you grinning like that?" she asked, assessing me.

I stared down at her, the feisty determination in her eyes tempting my smile to grow further. I hated the way she pulled such complicated feelings out of me. I tried to shove them back down.

She sighed and shook her head, glancing away.

"You're impossible," she groaned, starring past me.

"And you're far too stubborn," I reminded her, which made her gaze snap back up at me.

"I'm not. It was a simple question you refuse to answer," she argued.

The door behind her opened, cutting us off. Nyla moved beside me, waiting for my signal of what to do. I shifted closer, protective of her. It wasn't my first time collecting a debt, and they never went as easy as the warden described.

A petite woman rushed out from the back, a smile plastered to her face.

"Welcome in," she greeted. "Can I help you with something particular? A jade necklace, or perhaps ceremonial rings?"

She eyed me then Nyla with a mischievous look and raise of her brow.

I realized what she inferred after a second longer.

"We aren't—" I started.

"No, it's not like—" Nyla said at the same time.

"Don't be shy about it. I saw the way you two looked at each other," she laughed.

I glanced to Nyla and watched her cheeks turn a shade

warmer. The thought was beyond unreasonable. Nyla and I together could never happen. I didn't even look at her that way…

Or did I?

Did I not spend far too long getting lost in her rich brown eyes, or admiring the way she looked wearing the clothing that once belonged to me? Part of me loved the idea of her in my clothes. The tight tank tops clung to her far more perfectly than they did me. The linen pants always hugged her hips just right.

Stop.

I pushed all the thoughts from my head, knowing my own cheeks had to be bright red by that point.

"We are here on behalf of the Warden," I said, trying to bring my face back to neutral and refusing to meet Nyla's gaze I could now sense settled on me.

We followed the woman through the back door, her demeanor far too upbeat still. The second I stepped through the door, I realized it led to a set of stairs.

The darkness at the bottom felt uninviting, and I hesitated before Nyla almost slammed into my unmoving frame. She caught herself with her hand on my arm and kept us both from stumbling down after the woman.

"You okay?" she whispered.

"I'm fine. Just being cautious," I assured her.

My heart raced, hating whatever the Warden had walked us into.

The bottom of the steps only led to a small, empty stone hall with a metal door at the end. The woman unlocked it with a single swipe of her hand. That was when the voices hit us, multiple people concealed behind it.

She ushered us into the room, and my chest tightened. The only option was forward or to turn back up the stairs. I trusted in my own abilities to get me out of this, but Nyla's were unpredictable. Forced into a split second decision, I wasn't sure I could protect us both, not trapped behind the metal door.

The time to decide passed, and I slipped into the room with Nyla close beside me. She was far quieter than usual.

Her brown eyes took in the room, giving me a worried glance.

Coins filled tables, and three men hurried around the space, checking over them and sorting them. I knew exactly what I'd walked into the moment my eyes settled on their work.

They were using the shop as a cover for creating fake gold coin. It was near impossible to create counterfeit coins that would pass within the kingdom, but it wasn't *completely* undoable.

The men sorted through the product, deciding which passed and which would be too easily identified. They barely paid us any attention as we moved further into their space.

The Warden had multiple of these operations throughout the kingdom, but this was the first I'd ever seen one in person.

"Hal, the Warden sent them," the woman called out in a sing-song tone.

Her upbeat demeanor set me on edge. No one mentioned the Warden and stayed so positive.

One of the men, the largest of the three, glanced up. His brows pulled together, and he frowned when he saw exactly who was sent. I already felt the judgement radiating from him, which I despised.

"I don't have a delivery for him," the man grunted at us.

My fists clenched, my fingers digging in to the palms of my hands. Already, he wasn't making this easy. I couldn't imagine he'd just hand over whatever debt he owed.

"The Warden would like your debt collected," I stated, trying to keep my tone even and uninterested.

My face remained neutral, only my fists giving away my growing displeasure. Nyla tensed next to me but kept her face trained as well. She kept glancing in my direction, waiting for my order.

Sometimes, it was easy to forget she was my prisoner, not my equal. I no longer viewed her the same as the day I dragged her back to the Market. Guilt even crept in for damning her to this life.

The thoughts were distracting, and I couldn't lose focus. Instead, I let my nails sink further into my hands, the pain a refreshing pull back to reality.

"Tell the Warden he will receive that debt soon," he said and waved a hand to dismiss us.

Nyla muttered words of displeasure under her breath but made no move toward him.

"I won't be leaving without it, I'm afraid," I said, giving him a wicked grin.

He stood fully, backing away from the coin he'd been preoccupied with and shifting around to stalk toward us.

The other three in the room pretended to continue with working, but their hands barely moved, eyes shifting up to watch.

"You are no longer welcome here. Leave and take the message with you back to the Warden," he ordered.

He stood only feet away, staring down at me and waiting for my answer.

So the far more difficult way it would be, then.

I glanced to Nyla and gave a subtle nod before throwing out my arms and letting vines fly toward him.

She moved quickly in reaction to my attack, throwing her own flames toward the others. The woman ran, heading for the metal door and locking us in as she slipped away. At least that left one less person to deal with.

She likely ran the storefront and had little to do with what happened beneath beyond her knowledge of its existence. I didn't blame her for fleeing while she could. She didn't stand a chance.

The large man before me backed away before any of my attacks could hit him, the other two men placing themselves between us and him.

Nyla remained at my side, ready to fight through them.

The man was a coward, letting these men fight for him. I was surprised he didn't flee like the other woman. Instead, he watched, uninterested in dirtying his own hands but wanting to make sure the job was done right.

Frustration bubbled inside me.

I released a wave of vines in the direction of one man, pouring all the annoyance I held into the attack. The man tried to control them, but they moved too fast.

Nyla broke away from me pursuing the other man.

My body moved sideways to dodge a returning attack and quickly threw more right toward him. The inexperienced man made a misstep, trying to dodge far too slow. His large frame in the tight quarters didn't help.

My vines caught his wrist and latched on. He struggled against them, but with control over his arms, his own ability was rendered useless.

I let out a sigh of relief, watching my vines climb up to his neck. The first was easy, but I knew my actual target wouldn't be.

The vines constructed, cutting off his air. Within seconds, he dropped to the floor and lost consciousness.

I risked a glance to Nyla, and she fought continuously against the other man. His control over his abilities was far superior to the other man.

I couldn't waste time worrying.

There was one more target, and he was mine.

The second the man moved, I realized just why the Warden sent Nyla with me. Flames danced in his hands, and I realize I made a mistake in assuming he was from Zetron.

Abelonians were a rare sight in Zetron. Before the war, under their former king, they were not welcomed across the other kingdoms. After the war, their home was far too broken to leave just yet.

I swallowed hard, wishing he could've chose the easier route. I knew how this would end. The Warden sent me to a fair share of these meetings. It was always the greedy criminals who wanted more than what the Warden gave. Everyone wanted a slice of what he had.

I wanted to put myself as far from it as I could, but that was impossible.

The second he threw flames in our direction, Nyla

contained them, completely extinguishing them while turning away from her own opponent.

Each moment she used her hand to wield the same element set me on edge, remembering what happened in the stable. In these close quarters, if she lost control, we were all dead.

Had she tested her flames since? I doubted it, not after what the Warden did to Veros.

The man threw fire in my direction, but each time, they never made it to me. Nyla continued to stop them.

Self preservation, nothing more.

If she let me get injured or we failed to finish the task, there would be punishment awaiting us when we returned.

She continued to act as my shield as I tried to pin the other man down with my vines to protect her. It kept him distant from her, but I knew we couldn't continue on like this.

The shop had a completely earth-made floor at this level, but I was afraid to manipulate it and bring the entire structure down on us. My vines were the best option, but they were less effective with a fire manipulator in the mix.

He continued to burn through the vines that got too close to either man. The clashes of our elements drained us both, and I could see the way his forehead creased with a concerning look.

I just had to push through a bit longer while Nyla continued to act as a shield.

We pushed on, fighting back to back, protecting each other from attacks that came too close. The men did the same thing from opposite sides of the room.

I split off from Nyla, focusing on my target. She didn't

need instruction to know what to do. She parted from me to hold off the other man.

We each locked in on our separate battles. I threw everything I had at the man in front of me. I dodged each of his attacks, the flames narrowly missing me.

My own vines and branches grew around me and flew toward him. Branches as sharp as daggers narrowly missed stabbing him or were burned as they flew toward him.

I breathed hard, trying to catch my breath. This needed to end.

Before I could throw another attack, a loud thud behind me caught my attention. I saw the flash of worry in the man's eyes as he glanced beyond me. Quickly, I turned my head to catch sight of the other man slumping to the ground.

Nyla breathed heavily and wiped sweat from her brow.

The man in front of me grunted, and I turned back to attack him. I expected Nyla to join me, but she never came.

Instead, Nyla cried out, and I threw a quick attack toward the man before I turned, again distracted by the noise. The woman stood behind her, a dagger dripping with blood in her hands. Her face was lit with horror, stepping back as she turned back for the metal door to run again.

A non-manipulator, I guessed.

Nyla grabbed at her shoulder and hunched over in pain. The second she did, I knew exactly whose blood was on the dagger. It began to coat Nyla's hand and fingers.

Distracted, I almost forgot about the man across from me. A scream slipped from my mouth when intense heat slammed into my body.

I fell over from the force of it. Before I could lift myself back up, his heavy weight pinned me down.

The man sat on top of me, his fire close to my throat. I could feel the heat against my skin.

"No!" Nyla screamed out, her voice filled with fear.

She could've let me die, left and never returned to the Market. Why was she still there?

The man on top of me hesitated and entertained her for a second before redirecting his focus again. I tried to buck against the man, but he was twice my weight and strong.

Flames licked at my skin, and I cried out in pain as he brushed them against the side of my neck.

Nyla shouted again, still grasping at her injured shoulder, unable to help. Her fire had failed her, the control she once had no longer there.

I closed my eyes; whatever the goddesses had in fate for me was beyond my control. I always knew working for the Warden would get me killed. It was just a matter of how and when.

Nyla shouted again, but this time, I couldn't hear her. My mind was blank, envisioning what it would be like to just let go, to slip into the darkness, the one that chased me for years. My eyes stayed shut as I prepared for the final burn to claim me.

Every muscle in my body tensed, but I stopped fighting. It was useless; he would never move, and my energy was drained.

The moment felt like an eternity as I waited for the scorching agony.

But the pain never came.

Instead, I heard a grunt before the man shifted off me.

Opening my eyes frantically and glancing around, I tried to figure out what happened. One second, I was preparing to die, and the next, I felt nothing.

The moment I saw her, I almost thought I was already dead.

No longer did the hopeless princess stand before me. She was a goddess. Flames surrounded her, mixed with a light blue color, almost ethereal in appearance.

Blue fire danced at the end of her residual limb, and the man only a step away from me now stared in horror at the woman restraining him. Nyla moved impossibly fast. She held her limb controlling the flames near his face and used her hand to keep him in place.

To my surprise, he barely struggled. Somehow, though injured and exhausted, she found the strength to save me.

Her power was a sight to behold. I had never seen flames like it before. The blues and reds mixed in a balance, pulsing and bending to her will.

Part of me wondered if it was the same shock that held me in place, that kept him complicit.

The longer I stared, the more I realized I wasn't imagining it. The flames truly were the blue hues. Without touching them, somehow, I sensed they burned hotter than any other fire.

After a moment, the man seemed snap out of it. At the same time, I did as well. I saw the moment he shifted to attempt to break free from Nyla. Before he could, my vines flew straight toward him, wrapping around his lower body and holding him in place.

Nyla let go, allowing my vines to do their work, trailing up his body. She stepped back and watched. The vines constricted around his neck, cutting off his air. I barely had the energy to finish the job. The second he lost consciousness, I let go, breathing heavily.

He wasn't dead, but he'd be out for awhile.

Nyla let the blue flames trail away from her and toward the walls and minimal furniture. It all caught and burned, leaving us surrounded by her power. We had minutes before the entire place would be engulfed in the flames.

Nyla collapsed, the intense power disappearing. I didn't hesitate. I pulled Nyla from the ground and carried her out. There was little time to waste before they woke or the entire place burned, and I didn't wish to be there when either happened.

I carried her in my arms, close to my chest, out of the building. Her hand gripped the material of my shirt, and I knew she was dipping in and out of consciousness.

Olia still stood by the post where I left her. The second she spotted me, she shifted nervously, sensing the urgency in my approach.

I untied the beast and ordered her to kneel. With her back more at my level, I was able to slide Nyla up and climb on behind her.

I hated the sight of her draped limply over Olia, but I had no other options.

"Take us out of the city," I ordered the beast.

She moved quickly without running through the streets. People stayed far from her, and within minutes, she had us on the dirt path leading out of Huile.

I guided her in the direction of the Market and ordered her to continue. Sunset was approaching quickly, and I wanted far more space before I dared stop.

It wasn't for another hour before the darkness creeping down the sky forced us to set up camp for the night.

We pulled off the main path, and Olia found a spot in the forest where the trees were cleared enough to pitch a makeshift tent.

The beast knelt to let me off, and I carefully lifted Nyla off and set her down in a soft patch of grass.

She looked peaceful, but the red seeping into her shirt had me moving faster. She was losing blood, but I needed cover before I could help her.

I set up the tent and dragged her inside. Before I could tear her shirt away to assess the wound, she began to stir.

CHAPTER 26
NYLA

I WAS BACK in the sea of bodies, staring out into the city of Raden and all the destruction after the war. No one wandered the streets but me. The silence was what struck me the most. The usual busy, lively city was dead, not a single sound echoing through the landscape.

My feet moved slowly, and I knew I was brought back to this dream for a reason. It was where I'd met her.

Her powerful presence carried through the air, and although I couldn't see her, I knew she was close.

I walked through the streets, seeing the familiar shops and buildings. It was exactly as I remembered it after the war. Rubble filled the path before me, and I climbed over it, searching for the woman I knew was somewhere in the heart of Raden.

The further I walked, the stronger the immense power became.

The city center held a statue of my father, one I had grown to resent. In my usual strolls through the city before everything, I did everything to avoid it. Now, I was drawn toward it. The center of the city, the center of power, and where I knew I would find her.

I passed by a few destroyed buildings and recognized one that made me pause: the orphanage, the one my bother loved so much. My heart ached, even though I knew the dream was not real. I still felt the responsibility weighing on me for such a tragic sight. I had done this.

The orphanage was being rebuilt by my brother, but I had taken this from those children. The home they first came to know after the last war was torn from them during this one.

I forced myself to move forward, to forgive myself for the atrocities I had caused. I couldn't change the past, but I could push forward in the future to do better.

I walked through the rubble and stone and found myself entering the center of the city. A large square sat before me, clear of any buildings. The stone square had minimal rubble, and in the center sat the same statue I expected to be there.

I glanced up, and to my surprise, I found it had changed. No longer was my father standing tall in the center of his city; instead, his head had been broken clean off, and the statue stood completely decapitated.

My stomach turned at the horrifying stone sight. I hated my father, but the vision before me was also disturbing.

A noise startled me and pulled my attention behind me.

I turned to find the same woman from before approaching me. She was beautiful in all aspects of the word. Her long white hair flowed down her back, and she had markings all over her skin. Her blue eyes reminded me of Koraine's.

I opened my mouth, but she spoke before I could.

"You came back," she stated.

I nodded, unsure what more to say.

"You've made your choice then," she added.

"I have," I said.

I let my palm fill with fire. Instead of the normally vibrant red, it was a stunning blue and white. The fire burned hotter than my normal flames. It took concentration and more energy to control them, but they began to bend to my will.

The goddess smiled, pleased.

"My blessing runs through your veins," she said. "Strange, the way it has chosen to manifest within you."

She studied me, like she'd never seen something like this before. I wouldn't expect she had. The blessing of the moon goddess had been passed through Koraine's family for years. They kept the power in existence but never wielded it, not until Koraine. It always consumed them alive.

It almost consumed me. It drove me to the brink of insanity and tore apart the other power that existed within me until I learned to find peace with who I was.

The chaotic and destructive part of me would always be something I had to live with, but this was a new piece of me, one that would forge my future.

"She waits for you," the goddess stated with a soft smile.

"Who?" I asked, but the goddess just shook her head.

Before I could ask again, she vanished. The power I sensed before was gone, and I held my breath, waiting for her to return. She did not. For a few moments, I stood in silence, waiting, until finally, I felt the tug of being dragged back to reality.

The world came crashing down around me until all I knew was darkness.

CHAPTER 27

NYLA

I OPENED MY EYES, trying to blink away the blur. My shoulder ached, and I winced as someone touched it, sending more pain shooting through it.

"Sorry," Thalia whimpered. "I'm trying to close the wound."

Wound?

I tried to remember where I was or what happened. It came back in small flashes. The fight, Thalia being strangled, the intense power that coursed through me.

I tried to sit up, but gentle hands held me down.

"Don't move," Thalia ordered.

I groaned in protest. Her hands pulled at the sleeve of my shirt, trying to move it from covering my shoulder. My cheeks heated in embarrassment, knowing I couldn't help her or reach with my one hand.

She pulled away the fabric and exposed the wound. I couldn't tell if the wince came from me or her. Pain again seared my shoulder, and the look on Thalia's face said the wound was more extensive than she thought.

"We need to close it," she said.

My stomach turned, knowing what that meant.

She pulled a dagger out of her bag that sat nearby. Her eyes met mine, and the look of hesitation pulled me back into reality.

"I didn't start a fire yet—" she began.

"Let me see that," I said, holding out my hand slowly to prevent further pain.

She handed over the dagger, placing the hilt in my palm. I turned it over, looking at the blade and knowing in only moments, I was going to despise the small weapon.

My residual limb lit with flame, bright blue in color. The newfound power came far easier to me in the moment. My acceptance of what I had been become allowed me to access the full extent of it without losing control and incinerating us both.

Thalia's eyes widened.

"How—" she started.

"I'll explain later," I told her.

My hand moved and held the dagger in the flames. It turned a glowing red as the metal heated. I swallowed hard before handing the weapon back to Thalia. She froze, holding the hot metal and staring at my shoulder.

"You have to," I told her.

"I know," she said but still failed to move.

I reached back out to grab the dagger from her before the wound bled any more. She moved and pressed it to my skin without warning.

The metal touched me, and I almost lost consciousness immediately. I forced myself to stay upright and not give in, the worst of it slamming in to me.

The pain was blinding, and I couldn't stop the cry of pain that escaped my lips. I needed a distraction, anything to pull my mind away from the feeling of burning flesh. It plummeted me into the memories of my father's punishment, and my breath picked up in pace. I was losing control, and soon, I would slip into darkness.

I met Thalia's eyes and saw the panic and horror in them. She reached out, trying to grab my hand, but I could barely feel it. I needed more.

The mere touch of her skin was not enough to drive away the pain I felt. The desperation in her eyes hurt me, and I wished I could stop the agony coursing through me. I could see she wanted to help but didn't know how.

My eyes trailed down to her lips. They held on them for a moment, and I swore, the thought of them pulled me out of the spiral I was heading toward. The idea of them pressed to me, of being able to taste Thalia... I wondered how soft they would feel compared to the rough front she put up.

I looked back to her eyes and found her gaze dipped to my own lips before meeting my stare again. Her cheeks heated to a pink that filled them with an inviting warmth.

Before I could stop myself, I leaned in and kissed her.

The immediate shock of it left my mind in shambles. I couldn't think; I just let go and did it. The pain become a second thought.

Thalia froze at first, her entire body tensing but not pushing me away. Maybe I had misread the entire thing. The doubt crept in, and I pulled back, readying my apology. I was stopped before I could move away.

Her hand held the back of my head, stopping me from

pulling away too far. She was gentle but demanding. I opened my mouth to say something, anything, but nothing came out.

She leaned in to kiss me, and I let her. I begged for more, each kiss greedier than the last. The sting of my shoulder was receding, and I barely noticed the agony anymore with the adrenaline coursing through my body.

My hand reached out, tugging at her shirt. It was a test, me searching for permission. I tensed, readying myself for her to deny it, for the moment to end, but it never came. Instead, Thalia pulled off the shirt in one swift motion, exposing her chest and torso to me. Her skin was beautifully tanned, and I pulled back to take her in.

She was stunning, every inch of her.

I wanted to reach out and touch her, but I hesitated. She spotted my nervous glance, and her hand reached out for mine, pulling it in and guiding it along her muscular abdomen. I leaned back in to kiss her again, letting my hand run up her body.

It brushed along the edge of her breast, and my stomach turned with nerves, still not believing what was happening. Without overthinking it, I let my hand cup her breast. Her soft skin was a welcomed distraction, and my core became slick as my finger brushed over her hardened nipple.

Thalia explored me just as desperately, her hands trailing up my body, moving the tan shirt I wore away. She pulled back and looked to me for confirmation.

I gave a firm nod, afraid if I opened my mouth, I'd ruin the moment or wake up from some dream.

Every inch of me felt like it was on fire. Was I seriously doing this?

Thalia was trapped me, brought me to the Market—how could my body crave someone like that?

The second I thought it, I knew it wasn't true. Thalia was more than just the Warden's weapon. She fought for everyone under his control, more fierce and beautiful than anyone I'd ever encountered. I'd been at the Market long enough to watch the way she looked after the others there. She was their protector.

Part of me wished she looked at me like that.

I knew, after this night, everything would be over. This was one single moment away from the Market, a night to give in to our desires and never speak of it again, a way to distract myself from the pain, the agony I knew Thalia wanted to drive away.

For weeks, I felt the tension building between us, and I ached to be closer to Thalia. Even after my head cleared of the drugs, she remained magnetic, and this was the only way to give in to the desires and never speak of it again.

I blamed it on spending every moment with her. It was impossible for our bodies not to crave each other. There was nothing more than that.

Thalia had to feel the same. She told me herself she hated me. I couldn't let this be more than that. Otherwise, I did not believe even the medicine would be something I could use to numb the pain.

Thalia's hands moved up my body and pulled my shirt over my head and off.

I sat exposed in front of her, on display for her to take in. My cheeks warmed as her eyes drank me in hungrily.

I could tell she wanted me as much as I wanted her.

She crawled closer in the tent and used one hand to tip

me back. The soft blanket set up on the ground caught me, and she climbed over me, her warm eyes staring down.

I moved to grab her waistband, but she caught me, stopping me.

The twinge of pain hit me in the chest, and for a moment, I thought maybe I misread it all.

"Wait," she said.

Before I could answer, she moved, lowering her head down to my abdomen. Her lips pressed against my skin, and I felt like little fires exploded everywhere they touched. She kissed me until she reached my chest.

Her hands found my breasts, her thumb trailing over my hardened nipples.

My back arched at her touch, craving more of her. I hated that the second the sun rose, this would be over. A small reprieve from the Market we created after a long, grueling day, nothing more. I repeated it over and over, almost believing it.

She dipped her head down, and her mouth closed around my nipple. I again arched my back and let out a slight moan mixed with a wince. My shoulder ached from the movement and took me by surprise.

Thalia pulled back immediately, concern in her gaze.

"I'm okay," I promised.

Her eyes trailed from my chest to my shoulder, where I knew the wound was still red and angry after cauterizing it.

"It's too soon," she said, and disappointment slammed into me.

I didn't want her to stop. The second she did, this fantasy we were in ended. But I knew she was right. Any movement or pushing myself too soon risked making the injury worse or infection. If my shoulder didn't heal fast, it set me back from everything I came to the Market for. The entire reason I had stopped taking the Inum was to prevent that.

"Thalia—" I said, letting myself reach up to her face.

My hand cupped her cheek, but she turned away, her eyes leaving mine. The regret was there; I saw it, and it slammed into me, more painful than the stab wound on my shoulder.

I pulled my hand away quickly, as if it had been burned just by touching her. She sat up and moved off me, all while avoiding my eyes. The shame written in her expression killed me.

My heart shattered into pieces, and I felt like all the air had been sucked out of my lungs.

"Thalia, I'm sorry," I started, hating the words.

I knew I couldn't bear the thought of her returning to ignoring me. Even if this was only one night, I never expected to see her regret it so deeply so soon.

The only way I came to survive my withdrawal was her. Every day, I looked forward to her little remarks and teasing jabs. I knew we would never be anything more than captor and prisoner, but I still let myself feel it all, because that was how I pushed through.

Seeing her with everyone at the Market, the way she motivated them and kept them all pushing forward, made me want to claw my way back and fight for what I knew was right. A piece of me enjoyed spending my days in her presence. I even came to crave each teasing moment we shared.

She was the only thing giving me hope. She was the one who told me to live, and the second I did, my heart broke.

If I lost that all now, I didn't know if I could finish what I set out to do, if I could ever pick up the pieces forming in front of me.

I needed her, but I couldn't say that.

"I shouldn't have done that," she whispered.

The pain returned to my shoulder and spread across my chest, constricting me in its grasp. I wanted to reach out to her, to drive the look of sadness on her face away.

"Thalia, please look at me," I begged.

She turned, and I saw the tears filling the rims of her eyes. It was the first time I was really able to take her in after the fight. Her eyes were heavy and filled with guilt. She looked exhausted and defeated.

I couldn't bear to see her suffer anymore.

I held out my hand to her, and she looked at it with hesitation.

"Come rest," I said.

"Princess…" she warned.

"It's just rest," I promised. "We can go back to ignoring each other tomorrow if that is what you wish, but after everything today, we both deserve rest. It's going to get cold soon now that the sun set and took all the warmth with it. This is the best way to stay warm and not wake from the chill."

She paused, but soon after, she took my hand and moved toward me. We settled down on the soft blanket. I let her nestle in closely for warmth. Careful not to anger my injury further, I slid back slowly and pressed my body against hers.

Arms wrapped around me and held me tight. I tried not to let myself give in to the hope it stirred inside me. It was one single time, and this was one single night. There would be no more than this moment.

———

I tossed and turned, unable to fall asleep.

The strong arms that held me before remained unmoved. I tried to keep myself still, for her sake, but it was impossible. My shoulder ached, and with the adrenaline gone, the pain returned. Lying on my should wasn't helping. No matter how I angled myself, it still hurt. This stab wound was becoming a pain in my ass.

Fucking daggers.

I hissed under my breath as I moved a bit too quickly, and pain shot down my arm.

The arms around me tensed at my wince of pain, and I realized Thalia was not as asleep as I originally thought her to be.

I rolled over, and my eyes met Thalia's, realizing she was awake too.

"I'm sorry I woke you," I said softly.

"You didn't. I've been awake."

Somehow, that hurt even more to know. Was her mind racing like mine? She searched my features, and I knew she was trying to make sense of everything the same way I was.

"This can't continue—" she started, and something took hold of me, panic perhaps.

"No," I stopped her. "Don't say that."

All night, I had tried to convince myself this was it. This was all I got, and then we would move on. But with her, that was impossible.

It should have been one night away from the Market, an escape from reality. Until she started to say those words, I fully believed that too.

For once, I tried not to overthink it and just let my emotions guide me. I denied myself everything I wanted, needed, far too long, and I made a guess that Thalia had too. And I knew exactly who was to blame…

"What does he have over you?" I demanded, knowing the Warden was the one thing holding her back from everything she wanted.

I watched as she swallowed, her eyes holding mine. For a moment, I thought she may just get up and leave, run away from this all before I could see the truth.

"Thalia," I said her name, a small plea.

Silence carried through the air, her eyes pleading with me to let up. I held them firm, refusing to back down. If she kept dragging me on the Warden's errands, I deserved answers.

"My sister," she answered.

My stomach sank, and I felt my breathing speed up. Never once had I heard her mention a sister. She wasn't anyone I'd come to know at the Market.

"What do you mean?" The words tumbled out of my mouth.

"When I came to the Market, I was seeking refuge for myself and my sister. I needed protection from powerful people."

I listened carefully to every word, afraid to miss a single one.

"We never knew our father; he wasn't around. My mother was good at times, but the second she started taking

Inum, she became a new person. She was absent; half the time, she didn't realize we existed. The more she craved and needed it, the less she cared for us."

My heart stung, realizing how much pain I'd caused Thalia. She'd watched me choose to take the same drug that pulled her mother from her, and she still chose to help me break free of it.

Devastation washed over me, and feelings I knew I could not acknowledge plagued me. The Market had to end, no matter Thalia's reasoning. I tried to hold on to that thought but failed, letting a war break out in my mind.

"You couldn't have known," Thalia said, reading my every emotion. I hated that she could do that.

"My mother angered the wrong people. She owed a very powerful man in the city. When it became very clear to him that she had no money or means to pay for all of the drugs she'd happily taken from him, the only thing she had was us. So, he demanded my sister and I as payment. We would work for him to pay her debt."

My breath caught in my throat. I wanted to move closer, to embrace Thalia, but I couldn't move.

"My sister and I managed to escape, and for a bit, he hunted us. We needed somewhere to go to protect us. I was young, and I couldn't keep us both safe. I'd heard of the Market, I knew the Warden took in those who needed help, gave them protection in exchange for working for him. I was far too young to realize the extent of what he was actually doing. All I knew was I needed to keep her safe. I came here, knocking on his door, looking for an answer to my problems, and he gave me one. He'd protect her so long as I worked for him."

Her eyes drifted down.

"He has held that over me since the day I arrived. He keeps her elsewhere. I have no idea where, and I can only see her every once in a while. The more work I do, the more satisfied he is, and he allows me to visit. The second I make a mistake, he uses her against me, threatens her and takes away my privileges of seeing her. It's been months since I've been able to visit. My mistake with you cost me."

I started to open my mouth, but no words felt right.

"You didn't know," Thalia said.

"You have every right to hate me," I answered, finally understanding where all her anger came from.

"No, I don't," she said. "I let you go, I made a choice, and now, I face those consequences. I blamed you at first, but I know I have only myself to blame. You saved my life today, and I owe you for that," she answered.

"No, you don't," I assured her. "You saved mine from the Inum."

She gave me soft smile.

"I'll never be able to repay that debt," I added.

"There is no debt," she answered. "I've seen the way it destroys lives, and never once did I wish that for you, no matter how much I thought I hated you."

She paused, her brows pulling in, the way I noticed they often did when she was in thought.

"Why did you choose to stop?"

I sucked in a breath, knowing this question might come.

"I couldn't bear to see the way you looked at me every time I took it, the way you were disgusted with me," I admitted. "No matter how much I thought you hated me, my heart ached every time I saw the look of disappointment on your face."

"Why did it matter?" she asked.

My heart picked up speed. I wanted to run, to push Thalia away the way I had everyone else.

But I couldn't keep running.

Not now.

Not from her.

"Because no matter how much I fought it, I care what you think. I care about you."

She froze at my words.

Anxiety took over, convincing me she'd leave. I'd poured my soul out to her, and now she could crush it in an instant.

"The second I saw you in Lipal, I knew you'd be impossible to get rid of," she started. "But never once did I think I would fall as hard as I have for the woman I thought I hated most."

The words sank in, and I let myself feel every last one of them. She searched my gaze for any hint of a return of the same feeling. I gave her a soft smile and positioned myself to lean in and kiss her lightly. She let me.

Her lips were soft, and the kiss was less frantic than before.

I pulled away and looked over her beautiful features.

"So again, I am insufferably right," I pointed out.

She rolled her eyes.

"Just this once," she said before helping me get comfortable again, curled up with her.

I let myself drift off to sleep, held safely in her arms.

The next morning, the travel back felt easier. No longer did the weight of being the Warden's prisoner weigh me down.

My arms were wrapped comfortably around Thalia as we sat on the back of the Pantherus.

Overhead, birds flew and chattered. Their sounds were almost lulling.

"I wish we head these in Abelon," I commented.

"You don't?" Thalia asked.

"No," I admitted. "I think the only creatures flying around in Abelon are dragons and ember butterflies."

"Butterflies? she asked.

"You don't know what that is?"

She shook her head.

"I'll take you to see them some day," I said without thinking.

She tensed. My arms felt the entire shift the second the words left my lips.

"To Abelon?" she asked slowly.

"Once I finally rid this world of the Warden, we'll be free to go wherever."

She remained silent, and for a second, I thought I'd ruined everything by running my mouth.

"Perhaps change is what Araya and I need."

Araya?

"Is that your sister?" I asked.

She hadn't spoken her name to me before, and now I felt ashamed I hadn't asked.

"It is," Thalia confirmed.

"I'm sorry, I should've asked before," I started.

"Don't apologize. I'm sharing now because I want you to know I trust you and your plan."

"My plan?" I asked, tilting my head.

"You have a plan to kill the Warden and end the Market. That's why you're here, isn't it?" she asked, turning her head slightly to view me.

"Well, yes, but my only plan so far has been to find a way to kill him. I haven't figured out a weakness to do so," I admitted.

"You're saying you have no plan?" Thalia asked and raised a brow.

"Absolutely none," I confirmed.

She let out a deep sigh, and I thought she might just leave me there on the side of the path. Instead, she did something unexpected. Thalia began to laugh. Not just a small chuckle—a complete deep belly laugh.

"What?" I asked.

"You really are surprising, princess," she answered through her chuckles.

Hours passed on Olia, and we continued at a steady pace.

I was becoming used to the bumpy ride on the back of Olia. It was nothing worse than being in the sky on the back of Veros. There was just far less trust between this beast and me, but I trusted Thalia.

I soaked in the warmth of the summer sun beating down on my skin. The heat was never something I thought I'd miss about Abelon until I'd been locked in that metal cell. Each day of sun and the outdoors was a privilege.

The sting of the warmth on my shoulders made me feel alive. For the first time in days, I no longer felt like I'd collapse at any given moment. The headaches that plagued me had receded. I couldn't pinpoint how much of it was the withdrawal coming to an end and how much was the newfound power within me.

I recalled how sick Koraine had described others with power. Was that what I had been heading toward?

The goddess wasn't very clear on what this all meant, but somehow, I imagined this was the first she'd encountered this problem in her existence.

A fire manipulator with power from the moon coursing through her veins was unprecedented.

Olia took a small leap over a fallen tree across her path. The bouncing jostled me, and I winced, my shoulder aching as I tensed.

"Are you alright?" Thalia asked, concern lacing her voice.

Olia steadied, walking at a slow pace again. My residual limb reached up to where my shoulder hurt and gently touched the spot to assess.

I hissed in pain; even the slight touch sent a burning sensation through me. Immediately, nausea slammed into me, and my eyes slammed shut to will it away.

The second they did, the memories hit me. The burning agony as my father burned my hand. My cries for help and begging him to stop. It turned me cold, emotionless. I became his weapon he forged through pain.

I hated that version of myself.

It was the immense agony I'd hidden from with the Inum.

"I'm fine," I managed through clenched teeth.

Thalia heard the tenseness in my voice and turned around on the beast. She straddled the feline with her back to the road ahead.

"Thalia—" I started.

"Don't start," she scolded. "Let me help."

"But—" I stopped and nodded past her to the path she was now ignoring.

"Olia is fine. She knows exactly how to get home. They are clever little creatures."

I gave a soft laugh, knowing the same could be said for Veros. A twinge of pain stabbed my heart, missing the beast.

"Sorry," Thalia said softly, her fingers hovering over my shoulder.

She glanced to me for permission, and I nodded. The touch was a welcomed distraction from the pain of missing my dragon.

She pulled back the sleeve of my shirt to look at the gash. It was closed up, and the cauterization had stopped any bleeding, but the skin around it was still inflamed.

Her finger brushed a particularly nasty spot, and I winced. Immediately, her eyes shot to mine.

"It's alright," I assured her.

She dropped her hand and instead took my own in it.

"We'll be back soon," she promised. "And I'll take you to the healer as soon as we are."

"I'm really alright," I insisted. "This will heal in a few days, and then it will just be a scar."

She tensed at that. Her face shifted into guilt, and I hated watching the pain she carried from what happened.

"It wasn't your fault," I told her.

"I never should've brought you," she said.

That stung even more than the wound on my shoulder. Was she regretting everything now?

The pain of realization replaced much of the guilt at what her words had insinuated.

"No, princess," she said. "Do not for a second think I wouldn't give anything to be back in that tent."

I swallowed hard at her insistence.

"I just hate seeing you hurt. No matter how hard I've tried not to care, or tried to enjoy your pain these past months, I cannot bring myself to. I hate it. It kills me inside to see you suffer."

"I'd do it again if it meant protecting you," I whispered.

"I know, and that's what terrifies me," she admitted.

I searched her eyes and gave her hand a gentle squeeze. Everything we'd both been pushing down was rushing to the surface. These feelings were so new and unexplored, and neither of us knew how to navigate them.

"I don't regret it," I insisted. "And this scar will always be a reminder of what saving you brought me."

"And what would that be?" Thalia asked and raised a brow.

"A chance to live," I said. "A chance to finally make something of my life that I want."

Thalia leaned in before the last word was fully out. Her lips pressed softly to mine. The kiss was gentle and savoring, and I hated that I had to let go of it the moment we stepped foot in the Market again.

CHAPTER 28
THALIA

WE APPROACHED THE MARKET, and the second we were close enough, the gates parted for us. I led Olia inside and toward the stable. Before I got to them, I allowed Nyla to hop off. I knew she wasn't ready to see Dex again or accept what had happened there before.

I didn't blame her.

The barn was humid from the hot summer, and I walked Olia to her stall. I refilled her water and found some of the food I knew Dex gave to the beasts, putting some of it in her stall. The beast let out a low sound of approval.

I made sure to lock the stall, and she stalked over to the door to watch me leave. Her head hung over the side, and I reached up to give her an adoring stroke before I went.

After returning Olia to the stable, I found Nyla standing in front of the door, staring in.

Her long, dark hair hung down her back, and her shoulder sagged inward from the pain of the stab wound. I needed to get her seen by the healer soon.

I knew the Warden would hate it, but I would push for it anyway.

She was no use to him broken.

She startled when I stood next to her, and her brows pulled together.

"Do you hear that?" she asked, worry in her tone.

I listened close, stopping in my tracks. At first, there was only silence, but then I heard what she meant. A distant cry carried through the air.

I rushed toward the door, praying Nyla would follow. The sound hit me full force the second I pulled back the wooden door.

Hysterical sobs came from down the hall, and I followed them. I risked a glance over my shoulder to see Nyla rushing in behind me.

My heart raced, unsure what had happened. I had been gone and left these people without someone to protect them. It was my one role, and I couldn't bear it if someone was hurt without me there...

We stepped into the large room where many hung out when they were not working. The cries came from the corner, where a small crowd formed around someone. I could hear the cry was female, and my heart sank at the agony I heard behind it.

Nyla didn't wait for my confirmation and instead pushed forward, trying to break through the crowd. I followed, struggling to make it by the concerned people.

I made it past them, bursting through into the center.

Nyla had already found the person and knelt next to them.

"He burned it," Xora said, her eyes brimming with tears.

"Burned what?" I asked.

Nyla stood deathly still beside me. I could feel her muscles tense, her body leaning slightly against me.

"My home."

———————

Almost an hour later, and Nyla still sobbed into my arms as I tried to calm her down. The shaking of her entire body slowed, and I could hear her trying to grasp for words.

"Take it easy," I said. "There's no rush."

Xora stood on the other side of the cell, watching with silent tears streaming down her face. She barely met my eyes, her gaze distant.

I knew she had family still living. She hadn't run from a loveless home. When Xora arrived, I'd overseen her processing myself. She'd come with her twin brother, looking for opportunity to help her struggling family.

Her gaze dropped to the floor, the tears coming faster.

Her only surviving family now was him.

The Warden kept him the same as my sister, to control her and keep her in line. Her brother was strong and muscular, powerful, a risk to the Warden if he kept him for labor but the perfect key to controlling Xora.

"He used Veros," Nyla finally said, snapping me from my thoughts.

She pulled away, the devastation on her face slamming into me. I tried not to let my own feelings show on my face. It took everything in me not to fall apart with her.

"What?" I asked.

"The Warden," she choked out. "He used my dragon, Veros, to burn that village. He forced me to command her to listen to him. I never should have—"

"This isn't your fault, Nyla," Xora spoke shakily, surprising me.

"Your family is gone because of me," Nyla said, meeting her gaze.

"My family is gone because of that bastard," she growled.

"He tortured her until I said yes. I couldn't let her endure that. I was selfish. I should've let us both die to save them. There will be others. He won't stop there," Nyla went on.

I grabbed her hand, trying to stop the spiral I saw coming.

"Nyla you can't blame yourself," I said. "Most would've done the same thing."

Xora nodded.

"If it wasn't through you, he would've found another way," she added.

Nyla glanced back to her, brows furrowing.

"Wait, how are you here?" she started, glancing between us both.

"I let her come," I said softly.

Nyla frowned and tilted her head.

"I've been sharing information with her about you," Xora admitted before I could explain.

The princess' frown deepened, and she slowly pulled back from me.

"Wait—" I started.

"Don't blame her," Xora said. "She was only looking out for everyone here, the same as you looked after your dragon."

I could see Xora brace for Nyla to yell at her. Guilt filled me, knowing I was the force that drove a wedge between them.

I didn't regret doing it, I needed the information, but I never wanted it to come to this.

"I understand," Nyla said, and her muscles relaxed next to me.

Xora's eyes widened.

"Who does he have that he holds over you?" she asked.

Xora shifted uncomfortably, her arms crossing to cover her exposed midsection.

Clever.

I never expected Nyla to put it all together so quickly. I told her about my sister, never realizing she'd link everything together.

"My brother," Xora said quietly.

"I'm sorry," Nyla said and glanced down.

She never talked about her own brother, but I could tell from the sadness filling her eyes she missed him.

Nyla's features softened a little as her muscles relaxed, and a shiver ran down my spine when her side pressed back against me.

"I would've done the same," she admitted with a tense smile.

"This is why he wanted you to go with me," I said, realizing now what the Warden's move was the entire time. "So that you weren't here to object or change your mind."

Nyla's eyes widened, knowing I was right. I wanted to be

sick, my own blindness helped him carry out what he wanted. I never should have agreed.

Silence hung in the air for a minute, everyone catching their breath as the crying slowly died out. When Nyla wiped away the last tear, she looked back at me.

"What now?" she asked, but I wasn't the one to answer.

"Now, we kill him," Xora stated.

It took all night discussing back and forth before we settled on something that resembled a plan. Even then, we had near nothing to start with.

The Warden kept everything that mattered a secret only he knew. As his second for years, there were many privileges I had, but he had to keep power over me as well. The single key that controlled us all was unfortunately how he kept me in line.

The only person who didn't have someone locked away somewhere else was Nyla. Her dragon was chained beneath the Market, but at least we knew where she was.

It was a start.

"If it's anywhere, it's in that study of his," Xora insisted.

"Do you really think he's foolish enough to leave that sitting around?" I asked.

It felt like a hopeless task. The only person who knew the location of the others was the Warden, and that information lived inside his head.

"He's careful," Nyla started. "But also he's calculated, and if only he knows the location, that could be a large misstep for him."

My brows pulled together.

"How?" I inquired.

"Think about it," she pointed out. "He has loyal guards who stay wherever it is he holds them, correct? And what happens if he needs to replace them quickly? Or if something were to happen to the Warden? How would he pass along the information to his successor? This place is his life's work. He wouldn't let go of it that easily," she pointed out. "I'm willing to believe he has information stashed somewhere so someone could pick right up where he left off if something did happen."

"He doesn't have a successor," I countered.

"He does," Nyla insisted. "What about Sylvan? He's different from the others. He solely answers to the Warden and barely interacts with anyone else."

I thought it over.

"You're right," I said, my hand running through my hair. I pushed it back from my face. "He's been here far longer than me and only answers to the Warden."

"I doubt he's joining our cause," Xora scoffed.

Nyla laughed, and it brought a moment of warmth to see them forming some level of friendship.

"Stay far from him," I warned.

The pair nodded before diving back into conversation. They continued to discuss ideas and timing. My mind wandered, and I barely heard their words after some time.

The destruction of the home I'd come to know would be only days or weeks away. I should feel sadness, but all I felt was relief. The weight of the Warden's demands sat on me far too long. There was nothing more I wanted in the world than to see my sister.

"The next auction," I heard Nyla say and tried to refocus.

"It will be in a few weeks," I said, coming into the conversation late.

"We can use it as our opportunity. I watched the guards during the last one, and they are spread far thinner throughout the estate. Most of them are moved to the auction room when it happens," Nyla said. "One of us can check the Warden's office while he's occupied, and the other can find a way out of this place for when the time comes."

"Why not the front gate?" Xora asked.

"We'll need a plan in case things go wrong, a way to escape and take as many as we can with us before the Warden can stop us," I answered, and Nyla nodded to confirm my line of thought.

"I can handle that," Nyla said.

"How can I help?" Xora asked.

"Thalia will handle figuring out where he is keeping everyone. You need to prepare the others. Spread the word to anyone we can trust, anyone who hates the Warden enough to join when this all begins," Nyla said.

"And if they tell the Warden?"

"That's a risk we have to take," I said.

We needed every last willing person to fight.

CHAPTER 29
NYLA

Thalia and Xora left, and I was once again alone in the metal cell. It took awhile to convince Thalia I didn't need a healer. Already, my shoulder looked less red, and pain medicine would do me no good.

I would never forget the look of horrified guilt on Thalia's face when she had to lock me in. She wanted to take me with her, but we agreed it would draw too much attention.

I laid in the cot, staring up at the ceiling. It was the horrid grey metal that matched the walls and floors. Nothing about it was particularly interesting, but I let my mind wander and imagined it was.

I pictured what it would be like with splashes of color, deep reads that reminded me of Abelon, swirling patterns spread across the boring grey.

It's why I didn't notice when the metal door clicked open.

"Finding this cell to your liking?" the deep voice asked, startling me into sitting up.

The Warden stood by the door, and I could barely see out as the metal slid shut behind him. His eyes studied me, a predator waiting for its prey to make a mistake.

I tried not to flinch.

"Relax. I'm not here to hurt you," he said.

"You already have," I growled.

"So you heard," he mused. His lips pulled into a thin smile.

I wanted to use my new abilities to burn him where he stood, but without knowing where he held the rest of the people captive, I couldn't. We needed him, and I hated that. I tried to keep my face neutral and not give in to the emotion he was trying to pull from me. That was the game.

"Come," he ordered.

When I didn't move at first, he scowled. I slipped off the cot and stood, moving slowly toward him. I didn't want to obey, but he left me no choice. He knocked on the metal wall three times, and it clicked and slid open.

I followed the Warden down hall to the main steps of the Market, which descended to the grand entry. I still wore my night dress Thalia had lent me, and a shiver ran down my spine—not only from being out of my cot, but the feeling the Warden wrung from me.

I crossed my arms, trying to cover my exposed chest.

He continued to the front door, where he finally paused to check if I was following. His eyes wandered to my bare feet, and I felt self conscious. There was little I could do to prepare for this, dragged out of bed with no notice.

He didn't say anything and instead opened the door and ushered me out.

Outside, my mouth dropped when I spotted the beast in front of me. Veros stood in the front of the estate.

Her dark eyes met mine, and I saw the desperate plea. It broke me to see her suffer.

The dragon had been through enough while I was gone, and now the Warden paraded his victory in front of me.

"What do you want?" I growled. "Wasn't using her to burn a city enough?"

"So you heard?" he mused.

I didn't speak and continued to glare daggers at him.

He adjusted the collar of his black shirt. His entire outfit, and most of the clothing he wore daily, always consisted mainly of black.

Odd, considering he hated the fire kingdom he came from. Black was not a color of Zetron.

"We're going for a ride," he said and walked toward Veros.

The beast looked to me for confirmation, and I gave her a nod, unsure what the Warden could want and needing to find out. If it could help me put an end to everything, I had to follow.

I climbed onto Veros and directed the beast to take off. The Warden sat close behind me, keeping himself upright without grabbing hold of me.

"Where are we going?" I demanded.

The beast needed direction, and I had none to give. We aimed north, and my hair blew behind me as the wind slammed into me. This high above the kingdom was the first time I felt free in a while.

"Continue in this direction. I'll tell you when to land," he said.

My stomach sank. Was this finally it? The moment he found way to get rid of me and never have to deal with the consequences.

I wanted to turn back, but it was far too late.

Veros sensed my discomfort and let out a sound of frustration. I used my hand to stroke along the base of her neck to comfort her. The beast settled, and I let out a breath I'd sucked in.

A while later, the Warden finally signaled to land. The closer we got to the ground, the more the anxiety in my chest grew. I saw where he was taking me, and I wanted to be sick.

We landed, and I slid down the side of Veros and almost collapsed with grief. The small town around me was nothing but ash and rubble.

The scene reminded me of my own home after the war but far worse. Not a single survivor remained. Homes were obliterated, and ash littered the ground around me. I recognized the destruction a dragon could bring. It was why we tamed them, assigned riders who bonded with them.

Without control, they held the power to destroy kingdoms.

This was only the beginning.

The Warden smiled cruelly beside me. I grasped at my chest, hit with overwhelming grief for people I hadn't even known. I signed their death sentence.

"Why did you bring me here?" I rasped out.

"Because this is what happens when you fall out of line. This is what I am capable of. If you step even a hair out of line, this is the fate that awaits everyone you love."

My breathing sped up, and my heart pounded in my

chest. This was the consequence if we continued with our plan. We couldn't fail, or this is what awaited everyone. I heard the threat.

How the Warden sensed something was coming, I didn't know, but I knew this was our one warning. Stop what we were planning, or he would burn everything we ever loved.

I swallowed hard.

The choice was impossible, but one we had to make.

"The Inum may not have been enough to persuade you," he started, "but I imagine that brother of yours is someone you care about."

I clenched my fist. I wanted to command Veros to burn him where he stood, but I knew we still needed him. Without him, we risked never finding Thalia's sister. I hated the power he held over us.

"Calm, princess," he said. "I won't hurt him…yet."

"If you lay a single hand on him…" I growled.

My beast stepped closer to me and let out a low grumble. I could feel the heat radiating from her, ready to attack whatever I felt threatened by. I needed to get a grip on my emotions. A dead Warden was of no use to me.

"Escape is impossible. Let go of the idea, or you will only end up hurting more. You've already taken Xora's family from her. Do you really want me to burn Enri's next…or Thalia's?"

The threat slammed into me. He knew her name. He had targeted her family for a reason. I was responsible for what happened. I felt it in my core. Every single death was on me.

I shook my head.

Our plan had to move forward, but it could not fail. If the Warden survived, the terror would never end.

"Let's go," he said, returning to the beast and climbing on.

Veros bent to let me on, and I commanded her to fly back to the Market. She knew the way without my direction.

The cool air was enough to keep me focused and awake. My entire body ached with exhaustion, the pain in my shoulder still prevalent. I tried not to show it, afraid the Warden would use it against me.

The second we landed, I slid off Veros and moved toward the entry to the Market. I needed sleep and to be far from the man who held power over me. Guards rushed toward the dragon and secured her. They led her to the back of the building, and I winced watching her disappear.

The Warden's hand grasped my shoulder as he moved me forward and inside. I flinched at his touch but was thankful it wasn't my injured shoulder. Part of me suspected he knew and did it on purpose.

The way I favored one side and moved slower with the arm injured was a clear tell.

Thalia appeared at the top of the staircase when we stepped inside. The Warden beckoned her down, and her eyes held mine. Her brows pulled together, the only indication of worry on her face.

She greeted the Warden, and I barely heard the words exchanged after.

I needed to sit down, to let myself feel the grief filling every inch of me.

Thalia brushed past the Warden, and he stalked off. Her face looked grim, and I let her guide me back to my cell.

I collapsed into her arms the second the door closed. Thalia managed to carry me over to the cot. Her strong arms maneuvered me, and she climbed in behind me. She pulled the blanket up over us both, and I turned to look at her.

"You don't need to stay," I said, a tear slipping down my cheek.

"I won't leave you like this," she said.

"What happened?" she whispered.

"He took me to Xora's home," I admitted.

"Nyla—" she started, her eyes widening.

Her body moved closer to mine, and her hand found my hip beneath the blanket. The touch was a steadying force.

"I never should've let this happen," I said.

"He never should've taken you there," she countered. "He never should've killed all those people. That isn't your burden to carry."

"But it is," I insisted.

My hand squeezed tightly, my nails digging in to my palm.

"I know it feels that way now, but you had nothing to do with this. This isn't all on you," she said.

The words were desperate, but I struggled to hear them, to really hear and take them in.

"He told me if I step out of line, this is what awaits everyone I have ever cared about," I said.

Fear laced each word. I missed my family, and I wanted to see them again, but now, I risked their lives with this.

"He knows?" Thalia asked.

"He suspects," I answered.

She bit her bottom lip, lost to thought. I watched as it all raced through her mind.

This started out as a simple mission: kill everyone working at the Market and burn it to the ground. That was the only thought that raced through my mind when I arrived. That was, until I realized how many innocent lives lived there. So many had been forced into labor for the Warden with the threat of violence lingering over the ones they loved. "We can't fail," she finally said.

CHAPTER 30
THALIA

Four weeks passed, and the auction day came before we knew it. I tried to limit my conversations with Xora, and Nyla still spent most days with me observing her. At night, we met in her cell, where prying eyes could not see us.

The estate bustled with people coming from across the kingdoms. It had been weeks since the last auction, but this one was set to be smaller. The Warden set it to clear out some of the cells beneath the Market.

I wandered through the crowded entryway, trying to make my way toward the stairs.

Before I could make it very far, a hand on my shoulder stopped me. Dex stepped around me and stood in my path.

"She won't be in the stable this time," I said and sighed, already annoyed with the event.

"That's not why I'm here," he said, frowning.

The last auction was when Nyla lost control of her flames, and I assumed he wanted to prevent a repeat of it all. His concerned look had me pausing to listen.

"Then what?"

I didn't have time for this. I needed to get to the office, fast. The auction wouldn't last forever, and the second it was done, the Warden would return to the office where he locked himself in every day.

"There's been whispers," Dex started, eyeing me carefully.

My heart stopped. The plan was supposed to spread to those we could trust, and Dex certainly was not one of those.

"I don't know what you mean," I answered, even-toned.

"I know what you're planning," he said more directly.

"Whatever you think—"

"I want to help," he said.

My jaw dropped, brows raised. I hadn't expected his answer, but I knew I still couldn't trust him. He already broke that trust once before. Turning over Nyla had cost her far more than he even knew, but I was there to see the fallout.

"I know," he said, his head hanging. "You don't trust me, and I don't blame you. All I wanted to say was the stable is yours when the time comes."

Was he how the Warden knew? He'd confronted Nyla and inferred he knew what was coming. Someone could have told him, or the Warden sensed it. He always had a good sense of when things were happening. Either way, I couldn't say more to Dex.

"I have to go," I said to excuse myself.

He nodded solemnly and walked off into the crowd. The stables would be helpful if it came to fleeing. All the beasts had riders who I expected would join our cause, aside from a few. Using them to help people run from the Market if things went wrong would be an advantage. I prayed to the goddesses that Dex was being truthful.

It would all unfold in the near future.

The plan was simple.

I had limited time to search the Warden's office while the auction took place. The Warden has already ordered Nyla stay in her cell, and I had to make sure she didn't cause issues. It worked perfectly in our favor.

I slipped Nyla out of her cell the second the auction began. We hurried down the halls, careful to avoid any straggling attendees. They were mostly quiet, void of any workers. Everyone, as expected, was attending the auction.

My stomach sank at the prospect of more innocent people having to be sold off. If we could end this all, it would never happen again.

"Wait here," I told Nyla when passing by my room.

"What? No, I want to come with you and keep an eye out," she argued.

"No. Absolutely not," I said firmly, stopping.

She looked up and placed a hand on her hip. It was almost comical when she tried to look so serious and stern with me. I was taller than her, and her small frame was not stopping me from going where I needed.

"You aren't serious," she argued.

"Completely serious," I said.

My hand reached for her face and brushed a strand away from it. I gently cupped her chin and tipped it up further to have a better view. She tried to keep a frown plastered to her face, but I could see her struggling not to melt at my touch.

"I don't want you alone. What if someone comes back or the Warden needs to go to his office?" she argued.

"Then I don't want you there if I am caught. I can find an excuse for being there. You cannot," I pointed out.

She frowned deeper and her brows furrowed. I had won the argument.

"Fine," she said. "But I don't like it."

"I know, princess," I said with a gentle smile. "I never expected you would."

She broke her frown and gave me a weak smile. Her hand moved from her hip to my waist, and she stepped closer. Our bodies pressed against each other, and for a second, her touch made me forget where I needed to be.

Everything with her was a haze.

I leaned in and pressed a gentle kiss to her lips.

"I'll be back, princess, and when I am, we will finish this," I promised and watched her cheeks warm.

I turned, and she slipped into my room before I made it far down the hall. The Warden's office wasn't far, and I made it in only minutes to the door. I knocked before pushing it open after hearing no response.

Xora would be outside by then, and Nyla was hidden safely in my room, yet my heart still pounded, fearing for their safety over my own.

I moved through his office, looking for anything that might help. I knew he had to keep some record of my sister's location in there. It couldn't just be all in his head.

The journey was long enough that he drugged us. If he had to risk traveling with someone incapacitated, I knew he needed multiple options, a new plan for if something went wrong.

He'd keep that somewhere with the rest of his life's work. I knew him well enough to know everything of importance was held in his office.

It was his entire life's work, stacks of papers piled high with new business ventures or opportunities. There were letters to him from across the four kingdoms—his loyal servants checking in or others begging to be let in.

I cringed, spotting one on top asking for his consideration on another shipment of people from the air kingdom.

I tried to put everything back where I found it when I was done. He would realize if even the smallest of items was out of place.

A sinking feeling spread inside me, realizing I may not find what I came for after checking most of his drawers and shelves.

A tall set of drawers on the opposite side of the room was my last option. I pulled the first few open and found nothing of interest—some old papers, a set of knives, and a drawer shoved with everything you could ever need for traveling outside of the Market.

The last drawer on the bottom remained, and I pulled it open, finding a bunch of schematics, drawings of the new Market layout. I almost closed the drawer of junk until something caught my eye.

A parchment with the entire building drawn up, but I did not recognize part of it. I brought it over to the Warden's desk, laying it out flat. The Market was shown, but there was also a separate space built beneath it for cells.

That wasn't unusual, except that this parchment depicted a second space beneath *that* that shouldn't exist.

I followed the drawing, realizing where the staircase

leading to it was, and I my heart dropped. It was a space connected to the Warden's room, and I knew exactly what that meant.

All this time, he'd lied to us, made us believe he kept them elsewhere.

It fit.

The Warden would never give up control. Having them close by meant they never could escape. He could take each one of them away in an instant, and he held that over our heads.

My chest ached knowing how close they'd all been all along.

Others had to know. There had to be someone guarding them, someone taking care of them, feeding them. I knew there were those loyal to the Warden without anything hanging over their heads. They made their decisions long ago and stuck by him, his most trusted guards.

I was his second in command, and never once had he truly trusted me.

My heart raced, and I knew I had to take the information back to Nyla.

People spilled into the hall, and chatter echoed in the air. I knew the auction had ended, and I had slipped out of the Warden's office just in time. Wealthy men and women passed, ones who would leave early the next day.

I returned to my room and slipped through the door, careful not to open it fully. With many walking through the halls, I couldn't risk a view outside. I slipped inside and found Nyla where I left her, sitting on my bed.

The way she had her legs pulled into her, her head

tilted, looking to me with such hope, I couldn't help the little leap my heart did.

I wanted to pin her back into the bed and explore every inch of her. It took everything in me to resist. I knew there wasn't time to waste.

We'd have all the time in the world the moment we ended the Market.

A smug grin grew on Nyla's face, and I knew she knew exactly what I was thinking.

"Don't look at me like that," I told her.

"Why not?" she protested.

"If you continue, I won't be able to hold back."

"Maybe I don't want you to," she said.

She moved off the bed and walked toward me. She reached out and pulled me closer. I could feel the way her chest rapidly rose and fell, pressed up to me.

I leaned down and brought a gentle hand to her face. I brushed hair away from her eyes and gave a sad smile.

"I found something," I told her.

That was enough to snap her out of it. She stepped back, only a little, enough to give me room to speak.

"I know where they are," I answered.

"Where?" she asked, her eyes filled with hope again.

"Beneath us," I answered.

CHAPTER 31

NYLA

I PACED BACK to Thalia's bed. I tucked my legs back into my chest, and I watched her walk the length of her room deep in thought.

The family members being held were beneath the Market. Never once had I thought they'd be so close. There were cells beneath the building, but this was different. A whole separate room, holding people for years.

Thalia rambled on about all the details she'd seen. The staircase entrance was on the third floor of the Market, a space only the Warden had access to. It was fitting but also an extreme upset in our plan.

We needed to kill the Warden and destroy the Market, but not before making sure everyone in that room escaped first. I wanted to burn the building to the ground, but I would not do so with innocents inside.

"Thalia," I said, her rambling growing more jumbled.

She kept going, out of breath, words catching on each other.

"She was just so close. So close, and I never realized," she said.

"Thalia," I said more forcefully, and she paused. "Come here."

I motioned for her to join me in the bed. She ran a hand through her hair before moving toward me. I watched her approach slowly, and the bed sank a bit as she sat beside me, her deep brown eyes staring into mine.

My one hand reached to her face, and my thumb stroked her cheek.

"We will save them," I promised. "I will do everything I can to get her back. We will not leave here without them."

The promise meant any escape we planned if things went wrong was now useless.

Her hand moved slowly, and I didn't pull away as she reached out to my shoulder. The strap of the tan tank top she lent me fell, exposing my skin on my shoulder fully. Her fingers brushed lightly against it.

The wound had mostly healed there, turning more into a nasty scar, a reminder of what I'd given to protect her and the new person I'd become.

My body ached for her, the tips of her fingers trailing up my neck. She stopped when her thumb brushed against my cheek, and the rest of her hand cupped my head.

Without hesitation, she pulled me in, her lips crashing to mine. I inhaled the sweet smell of vanilla and kissed her back with equal desperation.

This wasn't a dream. This was real.

No matter how many times I played that night over in my head, thinking I imagined it, there was no denying it.

Thalia chose this. She chose me.

Everything in me urged me to take everything she offered. I wanted more. She needed a distraction, and I could be that for her, an escape from the cruel reality we faced.

I pulled back, and her forehead pressed against mine.

"We won't be stuck here forever," I said. "When that day comes, I want everything."

Her thumb brushed gently against my cheek.

"It's all yours to take," she whispered.

She dipped back in and pressed a gentle kiss to my lips. It grew more desperate by the second. I wanted to taste every inch of her. My mouth wandered and moved to her neck. I sucked and nipped at the skin there, and she let out soft, breathy moans. Each one made my core warm further.

She pulled back, and the warm smile on her face brought me sweet relief. Everything she'd been through and sacrificed, she deserved a moment of peace, distraction. If I could be that for her, then that was all I needed.

My eyes dipped to her shirt, and I cursed under my breath, seeing the perfect outline of her breasts. Her nipples hardened, and I could see them through her shirt.

My cheeks reddened, realizing I was staring far too long. She let out a soft chuckle and moved in again to kiss me.

"I love the way you get flustered," she whispered between kisses.

I scoffed.

"I do not get flustered," I countered.

"Oh, really?" she asked, pulling back.

She pulled the shirt off, exposing her bare chest to me. Her tan skin and perky nipples caught my attention. Her breasts were perfect, and I wanted to dip my mouth and nip and kiss at them.

Again, my face heated at the thought.

She smiled, satisfaction written all over her face.

"See?" she said.

"It's not my fault you insist on teasing me," I argued and moved closer to her.

Our lips crashed together again, and my hand found her breast, playing and massaging at it. She moaned into my kiss, and I felt how desperately she wanted more.

I moved myself into her lap, straddling her, determined to give her everything she wanted.

CHAPTER 32

THALIA

Nyla sat in my lap, my hands cupping her ass. The fabric of the skirt she wore was too much. I needed it gone.

I moved one hand to her waistband and let my fingers hover at it. The brown skirt fit her perfectly, hugging her hips, outlining the shape of her.

My gaze pulled up to hers, half expecting she might stop me, that this had all been some dream.

Instead, she nodded, encouraging me on.

"Are you sure, princess?" I asked.

The night in the tent was one thing. It was a single night away from everyone and everything. Our own little paradise. But this was real.

Whatever choice we made now, we couldn't run from.

"Thalia, if you don't tear this skirt off me and let your fingers get to work, I will be forced to go take care of myself," she warned in a low tone.

Absolutely not.

I pulled possessively on the waistband, I hated the sound of anyone but me pleasing her right now. I needed to feel her, to explore her body. In this moment, she was mine. A distraction from what I learned, but more importantly, the thing I had been missing this whole time.

"Don't threaten me," I warned.

"Then stop hesitating," she countered. "I promise I'm sure about this."

She leaned her head forward, our foreheads touching.

"The question is, are you sure?" she whispered.

I dipped in and kissed her, tugging her forward by the waistband. Her hips moved, grinding against me. The friction was enough to make me feral.

"I've never been more sure in my life."

I lost control.

Her nipples peaked beneath the tank top she wore, and I pulled the fabric up and over her head in a single motion. It had taken everything in me not to rip the thing off her before when the strap fell. She was beautiful in every way.

The pad of my thumb grazed over one nipple and then the other. The way they tightened against my touch warmed my core. I leaned in, kissing her, tasting the sweetness of her lips and craving more before I had even finished.

Her tongue slipped past my lips, groaning in approval at the movement of my hand across her chest. I let it trail back down to her waistband. She nipped my lip, and I flinched at the surprising tinge of pain.

"If I don't taste you soon, I'm going to lose all my sanity," I warned.

She let out a soft chuckle that warmed my core. It was a sound I could listen to forever.

My fingers pulled at her waistband, and she rose from sitting on me to allow me to tug it down. I pulled the material off quickly, finding only her undergarments separating us now.

Even through my linen pants, I could feel the friction when she sat back down and ground against me.

I let out a moan, one that was hungry and greedy. She smirked down at me, wrapping her arms over my shoulders.

"I thought I was insufferable," she teased.

"You are many things," I said and leaned closer. "But that's not one. I think I like beautiful or irresistible more."

She dropped her head, but before she could kiss me, I moved to the side and whispered to her.

"Or, goddesses damned, sweet and delicious," I said softly.

I pulled back to watch her cheeks heat.

"You can't possibly know that," she countered.

"I do know, but I'll happily confirm it if you'd like."

I watched her features for the invitation, the one that said this was more than just a dream or trick of my mind. Part of me worried she would pull back.

She moved off me, and I started to feel like that might be the case until she crawled onto the bed, lying down.

"Perhaps just to be completely sure," she suggested, propped up on her elbows, watching me.

I moved quickly and slid off the bed to kneel beside it. My hands reached for her thighs and pulled her to the edge of the bed. She let out a delighted yelp.

"Unless you want the Warden at that door, you'll have to find a way to keep quiet while I do this."

"Impossible," she protested.

I dipped my head forward and kissed the inside of her thighs. They trembled beneath my touch with anticipation.

My mouth moved higher up her leg, deliberate kisses trailing every inch of her. Her breath caught, and I knew I approached a sensitive portion of her.

Nyla's fist gripped the sheets, and my hand moved her undergarments down her legs. I let my mouth slowly taste her center. My tongue explored, licked at her wet pussy, now entirely mine for the taking.

She let out a loud moan.

"Princess," I warned in a low tone.

The sound pulled another moan from her.

"Fuck," I cursed.

Her hips rolled as my tongue moved in circles at her clit, and she begged for more just with one movement. She tasted sweet as I suspected, but there was more to it. Divine was the only way I could describe it. Made for me.

I let my tongue dip inside her, and her back arched in response.

"Thalia," she begged.

My mouth continued to work, wringing every moan I could from her, each one a sound that begged me to go further. My strokes of my tongue began slow, but increased in pace as I went. I let a finger slip inside of her.

The second it did, she let out a gasp. I moved quickly, keeping my finger pumping in and out, but I stood and climbed above her. I dipped my head down and kissed her, letting her taste what her flavor on my tongue.

"Princess, you need to keep quiet," I whispered.

Her eyes met mine, dark with heat.

"Fine," she growled, trying to clench her teeth and quiet another moan as I moved back down.

My mouth moved to her clit and sucked. She squirmed

beneath me, but I held her in place with my free hand, my other one still hard at work. I nipped at the bundle of nerves lightly with my teeth, and the mix of pain and pleasure was enough for her to let out a whimper.

"More," she begged.

Each motion of my fingers her body tightened around me. Her muscles tensed, and I knew she was close. Her hips rocked against my mouth, and I almost lost my own composure, a slight moan slipping past my lips.

"Finish for me, princess," I commanded and pumped my fingers into her a bit quicker.

I let them curl inside her and felt the way her entire body shuddered at the movement. The sweet taste on my lips drove me to the brink of insanity. I would never be satiated.

I needed more, and she hadn't even finished. She was mine, and I wasn't about to give this up.

She shattered, legs trembling and head tipped back. I continued to let my fingers slide in and out of her as she finished her orgasm.

I watched her chest rise and fall quickly, her breath speeding up. The moan that escaped her was low, and she tried to hold it back but couldn't.

Goddeses, I loved that sound.

"Good girl," I praised.

"Come here," she ordered, and I moved up in the bed next to her.

Her hand lightly touched my face from beside me. She stared into my eyes, a pleased smile on her lips. I wanted to remember every detail of her, of this moment.

She turned onto her back, and stared up to the ceiling.

Her hand moved to behind her head, and she let out a sigh of relied.

"I think I'm falling for you," she admitted without warning.

I turned onto my back and slid my hands above my head as well. My lips pulled into a smile, mulling over the words.

"I think I might be falling for you, princess," I answered.

She chuckled softly before going silent. The silence hung in the air between us for a minute before she found the courage to speak again.

"I used to imagine what it would be like to be wanted–not for my title or abilities, but just for me," she admitted. "And now, I think I have that..."

Her voice trailed off.

"But?" I asked.

"But I am terrified," she admitted. "Terrified of losing you, terrified you will realize I am a mistake, and terrified we will fail at all of this."

My heart clenched at the words. I knew exactly what she meant and hated that she felt similar fears to myself.

"I'm scared too," I admitted.

"You? Scared?" she scoffed.

"I am," I insisted. "This is all so new for me, and I'm scared I will do something wrong, something that makes you realize how damaged I am. I have done terrible things, and I'm terrified you won't like the person I really am."

"More terrible than the destruction of the four king-doms?" she asked.

"No," I admitted.

"Then there is nothing you could possibly tell me that would scare me away," she promised.

I turned toward her and met her gaze. She rested on her side, watching me for my answer.

"I don't deserve you," I said.

"You do," she said. "We deserve each other. We deserve happiness. We deserve to live."

She threw the words back at me that I had once said to her. I had begged her to choose life, and she was. Life with me.

"Goddesses, I hope we don't get ourselves killed," I murmured.

"Not even the afterlife could keep me away," she laughed and kissed me.

CHAPTER 33

NYLA

A WEEK AFTER THE AUCTION, the Warden called everyone to gather in front of the Market. My stomach dropped with the announcement. Thalia led us outside, and I spotted the tall pole that indicated I was right.

Thalia and I made our way into the crowd to watch.

This time, I recognized the man tied to the pole. Enri had a horrified look on his face, and fear filled his eyes.

The Warden stalked slowly toward the crowd.

My friend, the person who had convinced me to give grace to Thalia. The one who had first shown me kindness at the Market and didn't treat me like I was terrifying.

I tried to step forward, but Thalia grabbed my hand. I hated this. I couldn't watch another burn helplessly while I stood by.

The Warden's palms ignited without notice. I looked frantically between Thalia and Xora, who had followed us. Both gave me slight shakes of their heads. They knew what I was thinking. I shouldn't interfere. It would only make things worse. But at what point did I finally stand up to him?

If it had to be someday, why not now?

We had to attack eventually, and saving Enri from the pain I knew far too well felt like the best way to do so.

The fire flew from the Warden's hand to the floor, racing toward Enri. I watched his entire body tense and teeth clench. I moved forward a step, but Thalia tried to pull me back.

I had to decide.

This was it.

She tugged me back, and I let her. My body relaxed, making my final choice. I turned to Thalia and gave her a sad smile.

"I'm sorry, but it has to end," I said and moved, breaking free of her grip.

I stepped up and redirected the flames toward the Warden. He easily stopped them, locking eyes with me. We stood in a standstill for a minute before someone moved. Water flew toward the Warden, and he dodged before moving forward toward the Market.

Others began throwing attacks, and guards moved in to stop them. Before I knew what was happening, the fighting picked up.

I threw my fire in the Warden's direction, but he easily tamed it. The Warden stalked off, past the others, without once being slowed by the attacks thrown his way.

Chaos broke out around us. People pushed to get toward the Warden, but his loyal guards surrounded him. Others targeted the guards, using their abilities to drive them away.

It was now or never. I gave the signal without realizing it. This was the revolution.

I pushed forward without thinking and trailed after the

Warden. This could be the one chance I got. Others joined in, and I heard Xora call out, directing them. Elements flew around me, but I didn't care.

My eyes locked on the Warden, and I didn't let go.

I chased after him as he stalked inside. He moved swiftly, and I fought to keep up. By the time I caught him, he slipped inside his office. Its window faced the front, a perfect vantage point to keep an eye on the battle outside.

He stared out the glass and barely acknowledged me as I slipped inside.

"Your reign is over," I stated, my fist clenched.

"Is it?" he asked.

I let blue flames form in my hand and at the end of my limb. Ready to use them, I held my arms in position, ready to go on the offensive.

He turned and raised a brow.

"How interesting," he mused. "I have to admit, I didn't expect this."

He nodded to my flames.

"I imagine the power that woman from the water kingdom used to save you had something to do with this," he guessed, barely phased by my newfound power.

"How–" I started.

"I have people everywhere. Even during the war, I had people there."

That filled me with even more anger. When did it end? When was enough enough?

I threw a flame in his direction, unable to contain my anger any further. He controlled it easily. So my new power did have limitations. I hadn't known whether it could be manipulated the way normal fire could.

"Hmmm," he mused.

"Enough," I demanded.

I threw another and another, which he easily blocked.

The Warden moved quickly through the space and closed the distance between us. His hand shot forward for me, and I tried to block it. This close, my flames were useless. His hand wrapped around my neck, and I fought against his grasp.

I couldn't fail this quickly.

My body writhed, trying to loosen his grip, and I kicked out at him. Flames formed in my palm, just enough to be an annoyance, and I pressed it quickly to his arm. He hissed and dropped me.

I choked, coughing and trying to get my breath back. My hand moved up to my neck to rub away the soreness.

"You don't see it, do you?" he murmured.

"See what?" I asked.

He moved again toward me and reached out, tipping my chin up and looking over my features.

"You look so much like her," he answered.

"Who?" I asked, my stomach sinking.

There was only one person I'd ever thought I resembled, but she was dead. The Warden had lived in the fire kingdom, I was confident of it. Had he been there when she was alive and ruling?

"Your mother," he answered.

My entire body tensed; my breathing stopped. Even the mention of her was enough to bring back painful memories, ones I wished my father never tainted.

"How do you know that?" I asked.

The Market had been going on for years, an empire

built from nothing before anyone knew what was happening.

A picture could have made it to the earth kingdom, or perhaps on one of my mother's visits, he'd seen her. It wasn't impossible.

He took a step back, holding out his arms. A smile grew across his face that made my stomach turn.

"Come, niece," he beckoned.

My world came crashing down around me.

Everything I'd known, or thought I knew, was a lie. My mother's family, her surviving sibling, stood in front of me.

I wanted to refuse, to push back. Another trick of his to control me. But the second he said it, I knew he was telling the truth.

The eyes, the piercing rich brown color, was the same. The face shape and familiarity, I could never place it until now.

"No," I whispered, staying in place.

How could he do this? Betray my mother like this?

I swallowed bile back down my throat.

"I know you can see it, child," he stated.

"Why?" I spoke.

"Do you know what he did to your grandparents when your mother married him?" he asked, deflecting.

"He cut them off from her," I answered, only knowing the little my mother ever dared to speak of her family.

"We were a wealthier family from another part of Abelon," the Warden started. "When the king first came to my parents, stating he'd like to ask for their daughter's hand in marriage, they were overjoyed. Who wouldn't want that for their child?"

He dropped his arms and paced through the office.

"I never knew where she was from, or I would have looked for you," I stated.

It was the truth. If I'd known they were out there, I would've found them when she died.

He shook his head.

"I was gone by then," he answered "At first, your father was kind. He would bring your mother presents and take her on adventures she could only dream of. It wasn't long before we saw her less and less. He stopped allowing her to visit. Then, one day, he showed up and demanded the land my parents had. A strategic port by the sea he could use for his army."

The Warden pointed to a spot on a map that hung on the far wall. I knew the place. It was a vital port during the war my mother died in.

"When they refused, he had them executed. Our dragons we'd been gifted were slaughtered. Your mother never knew. I fled before I met the same fate. It was years before you were even born."

A year slipped down my cheek, grieving the family I never knew. He'd killed them too.

"I'm sorry," I whispered. "Why all of this?" I asked, my arms raising in question.

"When I fled, I knew I couldn't stay in Abelon. It was only a matter of time before the king found me and finished what he started."

"So you chose Zetron," I guessed.

"Your mother loved it here. Every time she visited, she wrote to me about it before your father stopped even that."

My heart felt like it'd been torn from my chest.

"I don't understand," I said. "Why put me through all of this if you loved her so much?"

His eyes settled on me, narrowing and pinning me like knives.

"Because you knew," he answered. "You and your brother knew what he did to her. And yet, you stayed all of those years. You remained obedient servants to him. You were ready to ruin the kingdoms for him," he accused.

"I didn't know," I started, shaking my head. "I didn't believe it, didn't want to."

"But you both figured it out," he said. "It didn't take much for me to know, for others to realize he used her as a pawn. You both turned a blind eye. You were as bad as he was. When I saw you both here, I knew I had an opportunity. The revenge I sought on your father had walked right up to my doorstep."

I shook my head, refusing to believe it. He'd planned to sell Bellamy to the highest bidder and let them torture him to get back at our father.

"Until you ruined that as well," he said. "Now, he's dead, and my sister still hasn't found justice."

I swallowed hard, realizing he was beyond reasoning.

"So now what?" I asked. "After all of this, will you just kill me?"

He let out a deep laugh and stopped to assess me. "So long as you are alive, your dragon will obey me."

"What do you want? To burn down the rest of the earth kingdom?"

"No," he said, walking closer. I could feel the heat radiating from him with each step. "I want to kill your brother and take back what should have been my sister's."

My breath caught in my throat, and my vision turned blurry. The blood rushing in my ears made it hard to hear even the sound of my own thoughts.

"You can't," I pleaded. "It's not what she would've wanted. She loved us."

"I have no doubt she loved you. Her heart was bigger than anyone I knew. But I also loved her more than anything, and you all took her from me. If not for you two, she would've left him when she realized what a monster he was."

"No," I said. "She never would've left her people."

"We will never know because of your father," he pointed out.

My heart sank, shattering into a million pieces. After almost a year without him, he still managed to haunt us. He took everything from us.

The Warden grabbed my arm and tugged me back to the map hanging on the wall. His free hand grabbed my chain, forcing me to look at it.

"This city was only a test to see how loyal she really was." He pointed at a spot in the earth kingdom that I knew was where he took Veros to burn the city.

"She won't burn down her own kingdom," I said. "And you said you wouldn't hurt him."

"Oh, but she will," he answered. "Because you told her to listen to my every command. I promised not to hurt him if you obeyed, but look at what you began."

My fist clenched, and I pulled back as he motioned toward the window.

"Fortunately, I don't need her to burn the kingdom. I intend to rule it. I just need her to kill your brother."

Without thinking, I swung my hand, letting it catch fire as I did. The blue flames came inches from the Warden's face as he moved faster and dodged my attempts.

He caught my wrist, and I struggled to pull it away from him. His nails sank into my skin, and the flames disappeared.

"I only need you alive. I don't not need you in perfect condition," he warned. "Cooperate, and this will be far less painful."

His hand lit with fire, and the intense heat burned the skin of my wrist. I snatched the arm back, and he let me. I tucked it in to my chest, afraid to look at the angry red skin.

"I leave today," he stated. "You will stay here and remain out of trouble, or I will have Sylvan burn your other hand too."

I swallowed hard, remembering the agony of losing my hand. The memory had me nodding, frozen with shock and fear.

"But first, I need to handle something," he said before stalking to the door and slipping out of it.

It locked behind him, but I was too stunned to follow. If I couldn't stop him, I prayed to Mavalu that Thalia could.

I collapsed to the floor, the realization of everything hitting me like a ton of stones. My chest ached, and I grieved for my mother and her family. I hated what my father turned the Warden into. Even dead, he still haunted me.

My hand held the residual limb where he took my hand. I couldn't bear the memory. It was enough to send me into a deep spiral. I forced myself to breathe and tried to prevent the growing panic.

I had to pull myself together.

My vision turned fuzzy, and blood rushed to my ears. I grasped at my chest, the constricting feeling growing worse.

A noise behind me grabbed my attention, but I didn't have the ability to look. The panic sank in deeper. Bellamy was in danger, and it was my fault. The Warden threatened to take my other hand, plummeting me right back into the agony, mentally and physically, I was in when my father took mine. It crippled me, left me unable to move.

Weak.

I had all this power handed to me, and I couldn't even bring myself to use it to stop him. Shame spread through me, and I nearly fell over completely when a hand touched my shoulder.

"Are you alright?" Xora asked, glancing down at me.

Her voice pulled me back, and I looked up to see her worried features. She held her hand out to help me. I froze for a moment, still stuck in the feeling of hopelessness.

I knew the Warden was already moving to find Thalia. That was the one thought I latched on to as I took Xora's hand. I had to push forward for her. I couldn't let this weakness stop me, not when Thalia was somewhere fighting for everyone else.

Xora helped me to my feet, and my senses started to come back.

"Thalia…" I said.

"We'll find her," Xora assured me.

We rushed out of the office and down the hall. Fighting broke out on the bottom level, and I spotted multiple people I recognized in the entryway. We joined them, pushing past loyal guards who tried to stop us.

"She's in there," someone said to Xora, nodding down a hallway.

We raced in that direction, knowing it would lead us to Thalia. I had to find her, to warn her, but my stomach sank when we made it to the end of the hall without her. A small room opened before us, three large men standing inside. By the looks on their faces, I knew they wouldn't help. I also knew from the door locked behind them that I was far too late.

The Warden had already found her.

"Move," I demanded.

Xora stood firmly behind me. We both moved quickly, my flames and her vines flying toward them. She manipulated a nearby metal bust and tried to contain one of the men, but he dodged the attack.

I fought with everything in me. There wasn't much more I could do to help Thalia, but I could give her this.

His loyal guards fought brutally, though some had surrendered before the fight even began, not willing to be on the wrong—the losing—side.

Others were too far gone to save.

Three men fought before us, all earth manipulators. At least I had an advantage there. My blue flames would burn through anything they sent in my direction.

Thalia was just beyond the door in front of me, but I tried not to think about the battle she'd be locked in.

The three men attacked, and I moved swiftly, throwing blue flame in their direction. The power coursed through me, and I barely could keep it from exploding out of me. It was a balance, trying to tame the different flames warring within me while manipulating them. That was who I'd become. The past still lived with me, but I was forging a new, stronger future.

Xora fought hard beside me, the first I had ever seen of her power.

CHAPTER 34

THALIA

I walked through the Market, searching for my target and encouraging others to flee. The fight outside continued, and the Warden's loyal guards tried to contain who they could. I was proud of the others for standing up.

Xora led them, fearlessly guiding them to fight and those who couldn't to flee.

Some still remained inside, many trapped in cells beneath.

I wandered into the largest room of the Market, where many gathered on other days. Today, though, it was empty. I walked the length of it slowly, the eerie silence setting me on edge.

I took in my surroundings and tried to listen for the sound of anyone approaching, anyone who could be a threat. Instead, I just found silence.

Nyla had ran off after the Warden determined to kill him. I didn't have time to react or keep up. When I followed and entered the Market, they were gone. This was one of the few rooms I had checked.

A sound behind me startled me, and I turned to find my target had found me first.

The Warden closed the wooden door he came through and locked it, trapping us both inside.

"Where is she?" I growled, realizing Nyla wasn't with him and fearing the worst.

"Occupied," he stated.

Not dead. That was a start, but I didn't love the sound of *occupied*. As soon as I killed him, I needed to find her.

"Thalia," he stated. "Will you truly hurt me? Would you do that to her?" he asked, and for the first time, I didn't know if he meant Nyla or Araya. Both had become ways to control my heart.

"This has to end," I stated.

Before I could move, flame spread across the room, fast and deadly. They outlined the length of the room and threatened to close in on me. I had to act fast.

My vines flew across the room.

Each earth manipulator preferred a different part of the land, which became our strength. My favorite was vines, but I favored manipulating other plants and branches. I was also one of the few who could control metal.

I spotted a metal bust nearby and manipulated it to break apart. Tiny, sharp daggers formed and pointed toward the Warden. He burned through the vines I sent, but I was quick-thinking. I sent the metal flying in his direction.

He narrowly dodged but did not emerge unscathed. Blood dripped down his cheek, a small cut appearing. One of the daggers caught him, just barely. It was a start.

We continued on, and I tried to catch glimpses of Nyla holding her own against the few guards who continued to stand with the Warden. They were too far gone to save. If they continued to stay by his side through this, they deserved whatever fate he met.

It was hard to catch if she was alright. Her shoulder had completely healed, but I knew it still bothered her when she worked in the Market. Fighting was far worse on the body.

The Warden came at me hard with flames. They filled the room with heat, and I could feel the sweat dripping from my face.

The intensity of the heat only added to the sheer exhaustion building the longer I fought.

My vines aimed to pin him down, but he continued to dodge them, burning through them the second they got close.

This was the first time I'd seen the true extent of his power.

It was a magnificent showing, and if it were not my life on the line, I would've found myself impressed. Instead, I found myself fighting tooth and nail to live.

Araya's face was all I continued to picture, forcing myself to push on. If I didn't have it in me to win, I needed to find it for her. She deserved a life outside of captivity, to be a kid and know the world.

A single tear streaked down my face as I threw another attack in his direction. My arms burned as I moved them in fluid motions to manipulate the Earth to my will.

The Warden barely appeared strained. His perfect movements and attacks continued without effort.

Far more experienced than me, he had the advantage.

I rolled to the side, narrowly missing another stream of fire.

The attacks came in waves, volleys back and forth of earth and fire.

The faster I ended things, the better, but I still hadn't found a weakness.

I struggled to find any metal since I sent my daggers flying, far too shattered and melted now from the Warden ruining them.

The Warden sent a spiraling tower of flames in my direction. His hands moved in an elegant manner, conducting the path of the terrifying attack.

There was nowhere to run. The room contained me, and I didn't have time to dodge.

I threw up a wall of stone, breaking through the thin tiled floor. It blocked the majority of the fire from slamming into me. Rock shattered around me, and as a last defense, I threw my arms up. Little fragments tore through my skin.

I hissed in pain.

I lifted my head to find the Warden's gaze on me, a grin on his face. The sight was terrifying.

I wiped sweat from my brow and felt as blood from my arms smeared across my forehead. I cursed under my breath.

I focused my attention on the back on the Earth. The ground beneath the tile helped me sense the Warden's movement. It wasn't much, but it was enough to give me a chance to dodge his attacks.

The Warden didn't hesitate to attack again. He moved his arms until he manipulated a ring of fire around himself, a barrier to stop my vines and keep me away.

Whips of fire lashed from it, threatening to hit me.

"Are you ready to give up and go back to being the obedient little bitch you once were?" he cursed.

"I will leave here only when you are dead," I spat back.

Another stream of fire barreled toward me, and I rolled to the side, avoiding it. When I stood again, I slammed my foot into the floor, causing the Earth to shake. A large crack tore through the room, headed straight for The Warden.

I let my self catch my breath while he regained his balance.

The split in the floor tore through his ring, but as fast as it tore apart, it was back together again.

My hands moved to manipulate vibes across the space. They climbed up the walls and over the ceiling. If they burned across the floor, there had to be other ways to reach him.

The Warden raised his hands, and fire sprang to life. The ring grew into a floor-to-ceiling wall, encasing him. The vines on the ceiling stopped in their path, burned by the wall of flame.

I growled my frustration.

The wall dropped, and before I was ready, an orb of fire broke through and slammed into my chest. The searing pain turned my vision white. I forced myself to stand back up, ignoring the agony from the burn.

As I steadied myself, I spotted something out of the corner of my eye.

On a nearby shelf sat two metal vases. An idea formed in my head.

The Warden was fast.

But I was faster.

My hands moved at impossible speeds, manipulating the

metal vases and aiming them straight toward his hands. Before his flames could fully form, the metal wrapped around his hands, trapping the heat.

He let out a yell of agony and dropped to the floor, weighed down by the metal.

The second his knee hit the ground, my vines snaked along the floor and wrapped up his legs. Before he could move and fight, they covered his body and dragged him down.

"You wouldn't kill me," he said, choking beneath the pressure I put against his throat. "I gave you everything."

"No," I said. "You took everything."

"Your mother was a nobody," he said. "You needed purpose, safety. I gave you both. I kept your sister safe all these years."

For a moment, I almost believed him. He was right, he gave us a home and protected her. That didn't mean he hadn't made our lives just as miserable.

"You threatened her," I noted. "You kept her from me."

"You needed motivation, a reason to keep fighting," he argued.

He was correct about that. It was the only thing I cared about, the people I loved. I'd give my life to protect them.

"I will always fight for my family," I pushed back. "But you are no longer that. You never were."

His eyes widened, and I leaned back, letting my vines take over, pinning his body. Flames ignited in his palms as he tried to burn them away, but he couldn't work fast enough. My vines wrapped around his throat, quick and deadly. They looped around his neck and tightened until he could no longer breathe.

A sinking feeling grew inside me, and I couldn't watch what came back, no matter what he'd put me through.

I stood and stepped back. For one last second, I watched the Warden as he struggled against my power and then turned. I walked out of the room, knowing my vines would handle the rest. I would feel it when they did. I felt everything the Earth did.

Only mere moments after I left the room, I called my vines back to me, no longer feeling the struggle against them. It was done, and I never wanted to look back.

I found Nyla, chest heaving, in the hall outside the room, three men collapsed in front of her.

"You took them out yourself?" I asked.

She shook her head.

"Xora helped, but I sent her to start freeing people," she answered.

I nodded. That was our cue to move and free the others as well.

"Let's go," I said.

"Wait," she said as I brushed by her. "Is he—"

I nodded firmly.

She didn't pry further. Instead, she took my hand and followed me. We ran through the Market, heading for the third floor. My legs were exhausted, but I pushed on anyway.

I led Nyla up the stairs to the third floor and into the large space the Warden kept for himself. Her eyes widened as she stepped inside.

"Where—"

"I don't know where it will be," I admitted. "Spread out?"

She nodded firmly and moved around the space. I checked the area where his large bed sat and even the bathing chambers. Nyla took the library space and the secondary study. Neither of us found what we needed.

I walked the length of the room multiple times before crying out in frustration.

"We'll find it," Nyla assured me.

"And if we don't?" I asked. "I just killed the one person who could've told us."

Reality sank in, and the death of the Warden weighed heavily on me. I didn't regret it—he deserved it—but I couldn't help but fear I might have ruined our only chance at saving all the people he held captive. How long could they go with him gone?

"Have you ever been up here?" Nyla asked, walking toward me.

I nodded.

"Few times," I admitted.

"Did anything ever seem out of place? Or was there anything particular he gravitated toward?"

I glanced around, nothing standing out to me. My memory of the few times I had been in the room was hazy. Most of the times were years before. The most recent had been....

"The tapestry," I said slowly.

"What?" Nyla asked, following my gaze behind her.

The tapestry that hung on the wall, floor to ceiling, was what he had shown me the last time I was there.

"He told me it depicted power. Having control was the key to power."

Nyla walked over to the tapestry before I could, grasping

the material and pulling hard. The artwork fell to the ground, and behind it, I almost didn't believe what I saw. A door sat hidden, simple and metal.

I quickly moved my arms and unlocked it, allowing the door to open. Nyla gave me a quick glance, and I nodded before we both headed inside.

We made our way down to the secondary basement, where I knew the Warden kept everyone he held over each of us. At the bottom of the stairs, a man moved in my way–I recognized him.

"Move," I commanded.

"No," Sylvan said. "You have no business being here."

"Your leader is dead," I said, and for a second, I thought he flinched.

His neutral look remained on his face, but I could tell I hit a nerve. He still didn't budge.

"I'm not going to ask again," I said.

I heard footsteps behind me and didn't have to look to know Nyla had followed. Her presence was a comfort and gave me the strength to stand a bit taller and hold my ground.

I called on my vines and let them snake down the stairs toward him. His hands lit with fire and illuminated his face.

The stairs were far too narrow to effectively fight in. Nyla pushed forward as a shield to protect me.

The flames came fast and all consuming. The staircase filled with fire, which Nyla tamed and protected me from. Regardless, the heat reached me, and I winced at the intensity.

She threw an attack back, which only forced him to move one step inward. I tried to let my vines trail along the ground toward him, but he burnt them as they approached.

"I'm only asking one more time," I warned. "Let us pass!"

He didn't answer, instead throwing another volley of flames in our direction. Nyla stopped them and pushed forward, quickly throwing attacks of blue flame his way. He stepped back, forced to by her.

It gave us the chance to move off the stairs and into the narrow hall.

My vines tried to push through his defenses again but with no success. They burned the second his fire touched them. I couldn't use the earth around us this far beneath the Market, afraid it could impact the people beyond him.

I called on both vines and sharp branches to send in his direction. He dodged and burned through them. Nyla mainly acted as a defensive shield. We alternated attacking and her absorbing his flames to protect us both.

Flames barreled in a line toward us, and Nyla parted them, sending them twining up the wall to extinguish. I took the opportunity and sent my vines crawling along the ground toward him. Nyla sent blue fire through the air toward his chest. He redirected her friend to my vines and burned them.

It was too late, though.

He hadn't notice the other vines I sent, the ones climbing slowly across the ceiling toward him. They dropped down quickly and grabbed his neck. The second his hands flew up to burn them away, the vines spread. They pulled his arms to his sides and took hold of him.

My vines worked their way up his body and snaked

around his neck. I manipulated them to tighten until I watched his last breath escape and his face turn bluish. I let go of my control only once his body went limp and he collapsed.

The second he hit the ground, a shaky breath escaped him, but he did not wake. I wouldn't kill him, but he wouldn't follow us.

CHAPTER 35

NYLA

SYLVAN FELL TO THE GROUND, alive but unconscious.

We had little time to move before he'd wake, and then he'd be a bigger problem. Part of me wondered why Thalia stopped her vines. Why had she risked him waking and stopping us over killing him?

I knew the answer in my heart.

Thalia felt everything for these people. She protected them from the Warden and the cruel world around us. That didn't end with those who had been loyal to the Warden. Many still deserved another chance. This gave him the chance to escape and start fresh, even if we burned the place to the ground.

We walked past his limp body and down a narrow hall.

A metal door at the end separated us from the room we'd been searching for. Thalia hesitated before raising her hands, and in a swift movement, she unlocked the door.

It slid open, and the room on the other side was for too dark to see from the hall. We stepped forward, and I called fire to the palm of my hand to help light the space. As I stepped inside, my eyes adjusted to the darkness, and I sucked in a breath, looking around.

Dozens of people stared at us, cowering in the corners of the room. I spotted a small off shoot to the room that I assumed was a waste room. Beyond that, there was a table with a pile of food, enough for a week. It was all food that would last a few days.

My heart sunk, seeing the conditions they lived in. It had to be days before the Warden even checked on them.

We walked into the center of the room. It was long, and the entire space was made of dark stone. Even the ceiling was stone. A chill ran down my spine, the space cold and damp. People huddled together, elders holding children tightly. They'd formed their own family while trapped.

I wished the Warden had been given a slower and far more painful death than the mercy Thalia gave him after seeing this.

"Have you seen my sister?" Thalia asked, worry in her voice, but each person stared blankly back.

She should have been there. This was where the Warden held her. He'd taken Thalia many times, but that all ended after I escaped the Market. Guilt washed over me the further we pushed in without seeing her.

I held my breath, turning in a circle and trying to look for anyone who could be young enough to be her sibling.

Thalia's panic emanated from her, and I reached out to hold her arm. I tried to ground her before she completely lost control.

"Thalia?" a small voice called out, and a girl came running from the furthest end of the room.

She looked exactly like Thalia, just younger and far smaller.

"Araya?" Thalia called back.

The young girl threw herself at Thalia, and she caught her just in time. The look of pure joy on her face as she embraced her was enough to know this was the right decision. I would've sacrificed my life to give Thalia this type of happiness any day.

I never wanted it to be torn from her again.

"You're free to leave," I called out across the space. "Find your loved ones and get far from here!"

Most stared blankly at me. Many still cowered in the corners, terrified. Whatever the Warden had done to them was enough for them not to trust anyone. I didn't blame them.

"She's telling the truth," Thalia called out. "Most of you know me. You've seen me here before to see my sister. The Warden is dead. You are free to live your lives."

Some began to stand, watching us skeptically. We didn't have time for this all. We needed them to get out quickly before anyone else tried to stop us or Sylvan woke.

"Please!" I shouted. "Go while you can."

It might have been the desperation in my voice or the fear that someone worse may come along, but many began to stand and hurry for the door. Dozens of people fled, and Thalia turned to join them. I didn't wait to see if everyone else followed. Instead, I turned to follow her.

Many murmurs of thanks broke out across the crowd as people passed us. The hall was filled completely as they poured out of the room. The stairs felt impossibly steep, and before we climbed them, I noticed Sylvan was gone.

At least he had chosen something right for once.

He fled before we could come back for him, and I prayed I would never see him again.

We raced back through the Market, heading for the ground floor again.

We found Xora and Enri in the entry on the ground floor of the Market. Xora watched as people poured down the steps, searching the crowd for her brother. I didn't get a chance to wait and see if she found him.

Thalia tugged me through the crowd toward the door to the cells below. I knew where we were going, and my heart pounded with anticipation. Our feet flew down the steps, and Thalia kept Araya close.

The young girl clung to her sister's side, quiet and afraid.

My heart ached for each of them. All they knew for years was that one room the Warden kept them in. I was amazed at how many fought and survived the conditions. There was no sunlight or privacy, just a large stone room where they had all been kept.

We made our way through the maze of cells. Some had been emptied, and many had others working to get them open. I tried to look for the girl I had seen that one day, but I didn't find her. I could only hope she already escaped and was not a victim of the last auction. The thought made my stomach sink.

"Nyla," a small voice called out.

I glanced behind me and found the girl waving to me while the woman with her worked at the lock of a cell. I'd run right past her and hadn't realized it. A sigh of relief escaped from me.

"You came back," she shouted.

"I did," I answered.

"Thank you," she called back.

I nodded and turned to follow Thalia and Araya. A few more turns, and we were at the door I had been to months before. Thalia unlocked it and took her sister's hand.

"How are we going to get the beast out?" I asked, following her through the metal door.

It wasn't like there was a way we could squeeze Veros up the stairs.

"There's another way," she answered.

Thalia raced to release Veros from the shackles that held her. I couldn't help but stay close to the dragon. My hand reached out for her cheek, and she nuzzled into my touch.

Once the final metal shackle fell to the ground with a clang, Veros stood fully in the space. She was small enough to fit standing, but there was no room for her to extend her wings. They remained tucked at her side.

Thalia moved her hands, and the wall opposite us slid open. It was made of metal, and she easily manipulated it. On the other side, a wide tunnel led away from the holding room.

I followed Thalia's lead, my dragon hurrying down the tunnel. It was short, and before long, it opened to a spot further behind the Market's property.

"This is how they brought her in," Thalia said, and I remembered the day I arrived. They'd led her behind the building while I was hysterical.

I looked back at the Market, knowing I could never step inside again, the memories painful.

"Get everyone out," I ordered.

"What?" she asked, taking her little sister's hand and leading her away.

"Make sure everyone is out," I said.

"What are you going to do?" she asked, raising a brow.

"End this, once and for all."

I didn't take time to wait for her answer. Instead, I climbed on the back of Veros, commanding her to take off.

I caught a glimpse of Thalia sprinting off to gather everyone inside and bring them out. Her sister waited outside, moving toward the front of the building to meet Thalia when she returned.

I knew it would take her a little bit to find them all.

Veros took off, rising into the sky. I waited for what felt like forever until I finally saw people pouring outside. They filed out one by one. I recognized a few. My stomach sank realizing just how many people had been trapped. Seeing them gathered in a single space was enough to bring bile to anyone's throat.

Many on the ground looked concerned toward the sky, but they had nothing to worry about. None of them were my target.

I let Veros coast through the sky, waiting to see the one person that mattered most.

I spotted Xora running out from the building, a man of similar age following her. His brown hair matched hers, and even from Veros' back, I could tell they shared many more similar features.

The key the Warden held over her. A brother.

My heart hurt, missing my own brother, but I was over-joyed to see my friend back with her only surviving family.

Finally, after a while, Thalia reappeared beneath me, and I noticed the crowd had grown tenfold.

We dove back toward the building, the flight down pushing my hair out of my face as we got closer to the Market.

I looked for Thalia and caught her eye when I was finally close enough. She gave me a firm nod, and I knew everyone was accounted for.

She spent years learning everyone from the day they arrived. She was their protector. If she gave me the confirmation, I trusted her.

Only feet away from the Market's rooftop, I hesitated, taking a deep breath. I had to end it there.

"Burn it," I said.

Veros let out a deep growl before her flames barreled from her lungs toward the building.

CHAPTER 36
THALIA

I watched in delight and devastation as the Market burned to the ground.

It only took Nyla minutes to have the entire building covered in flames. My stomach sank watching pieces of wood fall from the sides. The flames consumed everything in their path. I'd been living there for years, and even though we'd only been at this location for months, the Market had been my home for longer than that.

My sister grabbed my hand and squeezed, watching with me. Others around us comforted each other, letting out tears of joy and fear.

Without the Market, many had nowhere to go. I wouldn't let them suffer.

I was their protector, and that didn't end just because the building and the Warden were gone. I wouldn't abandon my people.

The dragon's shadow passed over my head, and I glanced up to find the beast descending. I couldn't see her, but I knew Nyla was directing the dragon.

They landed close by, Veros kneeling to allow Nyla off. She rushed over to me, stopping only feet away. Her dark brown eyes searched mine for any hint of what was running through my mind.

We'd been caught in our own bubble until now. Whatever decision I made would change everything, and the same for her. If either of us wanted to walk away, this was it. Her eyes seemed to offer me that escape.

I held her gaze, afraid to move. The bubble we were in was gone, and I wanted it to stay that way. Without the Market, it was only a matter of time before Nyla would return to her kingdom. Would that be without me?

I tried to brush the thought aside, afraid to ruin the one good thing I had created.

My sister dropped my hand.

I took a single step forward, deciding my answer. Nyla didn't wait and closed the distance, throwing her arms around me, and squeezing tightly.

In that moment, I knew it wasn't the end. All those spoken promises and hopes for us suddenly felt like they could be a reality.

She pulled back only a little, her arm still wrapped around my neck.

"I'm sorry," she said.

"For what?"

"For burning it," she answered, her eyes snapping away from mine.

"You had to, "I said. This place can't be allowed to stand any longer."

My hand found her chin and tipped her gaze back to mine.

"What will they all do?" she asked, looking around at the many people staring helplessly at the burning building.

"I'll find them somewhere," I said softly.

Her eyes lifted back to mine.

"We will find them somewhere," she said, a new promise.

My hand cupped her face, holding it firmly before my lips crashed into hers. Her lips were soft, and I wanted to hold her forever, but I knew we didn't have long before we needed to leave.

I pulled back.

"We will. Together," I promised.

"Together," she breathed and pressed her forehead against mine.

CHAPTER 37

NYLA

Veros flew overhead, stretching her wings before we made it back to Abelon. I could feel the genuine delight seeping from her. It emanated to me, filling me with happiness and excitement to return home.

I knew Bellamy would be waiting at the docks the moment our ship was back. He was expecting us, and I knew he'd never allow it to be anyone else who greeted us first.

The breeze rolling across the waves blew my hair out of my face, and I took a deep breath in. The salty smell and fresh air cleared my mind, and after months of torture, I finally felt at peace.

Everyone from the Market found their new purpose and homes. Thalia and I had made sure of it.

We were the last ones to start our newest chapter.

"The last time I saw your brother, he was being sold for auction," Thalia said, walking up beside me.

"I doubt he'll remember," I said and shrugged.

"Nyla," Thalia said with a pointed look.

"Okay, I'm sure he's forgiven all of that by now," I answered. "And besides, if he hasn't, he has me to deal with."

She leaned in, pressing a kiss to my head. I wouldn't admit it, but I soaked up every time she did it, secretly adoring it.

We stayed at the edge of the ship for awhile, taking in the view and watching for land. It would be before nightfall that we reached Abelon. The nerves were starting to hit, and my hand gripped the edge of the railing tightly.

Thalia's hand covered mine, giving a reassuring squeeze.

Without her, I wasn't confident I would have ever returned to Abelon, too many painful memories buried there. I didn't need to tell her that. The look she gave me told me she knew.

"Thank you," I whispered.

"We're in this together now," she answered.

Veros dove back toward the ship, and I moved closer into Thalia's side. Her arm moved to wrap around me and hold me tucked to her. The dragon soared over our heads, and I caught the contagious smile that spread across Thalia's lips.

The small ship continued to sail at a steady pace, the crew working hard to keep it on track. Eventually, Veros landed as we grew closer to land, wanting to rest before returning to the mountains she craved.

"Can I join?" a quiet voice behind us asked.

I turned to find Araya standing behind us, hands clasped behind her back. Her untamed curls fell in her face, and the sun above highlighted the freckles on her cheeks.

"Of course," I answered, stepping aside to make room for the younger girl.

She settled between us, just tall enough to peer over the ship railing. I winced, knowing the Warden was at partially fault for her small stature. The conditions we found the children and loved ones in was heartbreaking. My stomach sank just thinking about it.

"When will we be there?" she asked Thalia in a sing-song voice.

"Soon, my love," she promised, the way a mother would to their child.

Her own mother had abandoned them. She'd been left to raise Araya herself. The girl knew nothing more than the years they spent at the Market. Thalia had broken down and explained everything on one of the many nights following the ordeal. We'd felt empty the moment everything caught up to us. Everything we had in us, we poured into helping everyone else find their way.

Now, this was our chance to finally start over and heal.

Together.

I felt his presence before I saw him, waiting for me at the docks.

Veros flew overhead and passed by cheering people. She headed straight toward the mountains, and already, I could see other dragons rising into the sky to meet her. She'd been away from home, missing her own family too.

I waved the moment I spotted them, standing side-by-side. Bellamy had his arm wrapped around her middle, holding her close. Koraine beamed, a large smile on her face. For the first time in a while, a genuine smile grew across my lips at the thought of being home in Abelon.

I could never make up for everything I'd done in the war, but I would continue to live a life worthy of a second chance.

One with Thalia beside me.

Her sister ran to the edge of the ship brimming with excitement. I watched as Thalia smiled, watching her sister's happiness.

Everything inside me felt warm, surrounded by the people I cared most about.

The moment the ship docked, Bellamy didn't wait for me and boarded. Koraine trailed closely behind him.

I immediately ran to him, embracing him.

"I would've sent an army for you had you not come back," he said.

"I know," I said. "But I had it handled."

"Did you?"

"Yes, well, Thalia had it handled," I admitted.

I moved for him to see the woman I brought back with me. She moved forward slowly, as if she were afraid to approach my brother. I almost forgot, for her, it wasn't just my brother. He was the King of Abelon.

She bowed her head.

"No need," Bellamy stated.

She could barely register before Bellamy moved, embracing her. I watched as her eyes widened with surprise.

"Thank you for taking care of her," he said.

"Always," she promised, looking beyond him to me.

A promise not only to the king, but me as well.

He pulled back and gave me a knowing look that made my cheeks warm.

Thalia and I trailed behind Bellamy and Koraine as we made our way off the ship toward the palace. Horses waited for us, but I requested to walk. I was excited to show Thalia every bit of Abelon.

Her sister followed closely behind us, pausing at each exciting thing.

"I suppose I could get used to this," Thalia commented.

"I hope you do, because I'm never letting you out of my sight again," I answered.

Araya stopped again, this time at the door of a bakery. I could smell the pastries baking, Abelon returning to some semblance of normal.

Thalia grabbed my hand, pulling me in. Her hand slipped to the small of my back, and a shiver ran up my spine at her touch. Her rich brown eyes looked down at me, and I held her gaze.

My lips crashed to hers before I could think clearly. My hand moved up to her cheek and held her face firmly, afraid to let go. I wanted to stay that way forever.

She pulled back, her cheeks warming, realizing there were eyes on us. Her sister still watched through the bakery door as those inside hustled around, but my brother and Koraine had paused ahead, smiling at us. There wasn't a single ounce of regret inside me.

I prayed to the goddesses not a day would pass when I had to go without this and thanked Aeris for the eternal moorlands that led me to the person who gave me life once more.

The End

WHAT'S NEXT

The Final Book of The Elemental Arrangement

Caspian and Asena coming early 2026

ACKNOWLEDGMENTS

This is such an amazing moment to be able to conclude Nyla's story and still be extending the world of The Elemental Arrangement. There are many people I need to thank, who without, this book would not exist.

To my husband, thank you for believing in me and my stories even when I doubted myself.

To my sisters, thank you for showing up to every little event, and constantly sharing my stories. I am so thankful for your love and support.

To Biz, I have said it once and will say it again, this would and series would not be here without you.

To my parents, thank you for always shouting about my books, reading and listening to them, and never doubting my crazy plans for them.

To my PA Mikala, for believing in my writing and championing these stories for me. There is not a single day that passes where I am not amazed by your creativity.

To my editor Alexa, thank you for believing in me, and pushing me to be the best I can be. I have grown so much in this career because of you. Thank you for the endless love and support.

To my readers, thank you for your support of these characters and never once giving up on them!

The Elemental Arrangement Series

Aftermath

ABOUT THE AUTHOR

MK Ahearn grew up in Massachusetts as one of three sisters. She now lives in Maryland with her husband, son, and their four cats. She received her bachelor of arts in international relations and a master of professional studies in homeland security. When not writing or studying she can be found planning her next travel adventure.